Worthless

J. Grayland

*Mum & Dad You're everywhere, but here.
That's why your story lives in our hearts.*

Prologue

Castle Hill, Sydney, Australia

Tilting my head up, I feel the warmth of the sun on my face. I have to squint my eyes, the glare of the sun strong against the darkness of my sunglasses. It's such a beautiful day, warm with a slight breeze, scented by the frangipani trees surrounding the small old cemetery. A beautiful day to celebrate the life of a beautiful woman. I find myself distracted by the muffled sounds of voices talking; some voices belong to faces I know while others are nameless or unrecognizable to me. I know they are here to say goodbye and get closure by releasing their thoughts through words of appreciation for knowing her, but I tune out their words as I focus on the blueness of the clear sky and the rustling of the trees in the breeze. Feeling a gentle squeeze from a hand clutching mine, I am brought back to reality and look down into the watery eyes of Molly, my baby sister. Right now, with her dark hair framing the fine bones of her face and her big blue eyes, it stabs me sharply in the middle of my chest just how much she is like our mum.

Her eyes speak a thousand silent words, so full of pain and regret that I wish I could take away from her. Standing beside her, and gripping her other hand, is her husband, Caleb. I give her hand a gentle squeeze of reassurance. Molly's eyes turn from mine, drawing my attention to the last of the people slowly walking past the open grave and dropping single red roses into it. Giving her a supportive smile, understanding what we need to do, I move towards the open hole in the ground. Still holding onto her hand tightly and trying to give her some kind of emotional support, I drop my own rose and watch as it falls down onto the polished dark wood of the coffin. With that, I feel the bubble of pain that has been sitting deep in my chest for the last week burst open and release the deep ache of relief, causing me to catch my breath. Relief that the wonderful woman we are laying to rest today is finally at peace; relief that she is now free of her pain; relief that finally, after all of her fighting to live, she is finally at peace and exactly where she wanted to be - with our Dad, at last.

Later that afternoon, as people gather to offer their condolences and comfort each other by sharing fond memories, while sipping tea and nibbling on finger foods, Molly and I sit on the old comfortable sofa in mum's home which now feels like an empty shell without the sound of her chatter and musical laughter filtering through it. Molly's husband, Caleb, carries a tray full of empty cups and glasses to the kitchen, giving us some space to just sit and breathe. Sinking into the comfy cushions, Molly flops back and leans her head against my shoulder, bringing a huge photo album filled with years of memories with her. It feels like a perfect moment to share those memories with her right now. The pile of albums sitting on the table in front of us is nothing compared to the ones stacked in the spare room upstairs; our parents always had a camera at hand.

Looking through the endless pages filled with photos of our life when we were all together, we laugh at the craziness of parents who spent most of their time with two small kids living a nomadic life in an old school bus Dad had worked on endlessly, converting it into a livable traveling home.

"Look," I say, pointing to a photo showing a side image of the bus. "It's the BBB." I smile.

"Yep, the famous Big Brown Bus. Why the hell did Dad paint it that awful brown color?"

"Because it was the cheapest house paint and he had plenty of it in the garage." I chuckle.

"A kid asked me one day if I liked traveling around in a turd." Molly laughs.

"Great times," I say.

"They sure were." She sighs, leaning into me.

And they were. Most of our childhood was spent traveling around Australia in that bus, living the hippy lifestyle as we moved from town to town while my parents earned money working on local farms picking fruit and vegetables. Both Molly and I grew up being home schooled by our mum on the road and it was a wonderful life, full of perfect childhood memories of a close family.

Our nomadic life came to an end when I was old enough to start high school and Dad announced that it was time for us to settle down so Molly and I could finish our education in a stable environment. And that's what we did. My Dad took a job working at a local farm and my mother became a teacher's aid at the local school. I could never figure out how they seemed to make such a smooth transition from one lifestyle to another, two totally different ways of living, but they did. Dad told me, some years later, that it didn't matter where we lived, as long as he had my mum, Molly and I, he would always be happy.

"I can't believe she's gone." Molly sighs. "I know."

"I wish..." she starts to say. When I look down into her watery eyes, I can see guilty turmoil starting to brew in them. Placing the album down on the coffee table, I put my arm around her shoulders, pulling her closer into me.

"Don't do that. She wanted you to be happy and you gave her that by living your life with Caleb."

"Yes, on the other side of the world. Why didn't she tell me how bad the cancer was, Jaxon? Why didn't she let me come home to look after her?"

"Because she wanted to go in her own way, knowing that her children were happy. I guess she wanted us to remember her healthy and vibrant, like she was at your wedding, not as the weak shell of a woman she became. She was happy, Molly, she was ready, and she wanted to be with Dad."

"I know. I just wish I would have been here sooner. The last time I talked to her, I sensed something wasn't right when the last thing she said was, you know I love you, right? Normally she'd just say, bye love, before hanging up."

"She knew what she was doing. She didn't want you to see her like she was, she wanted you to remember her at her best." "And what about you?" Molly says.

Breathing out a defeated sigh, I scrub a hand through my hair. "I didn't pick up on anything. She always seemed fine, always smiling and happy. When I questioned her about her weight loss, she said she was trying a new grain-free diet," I say with frustration about how I hadn't noticed that my own mother had started withering away from a body full of an aggressive cancer that was spreading fast. Molly placed her hand on my arm.

"You're not to blame, Jaxon."

"And neither are you. By the time I found out the full extent of her cancer, she was almost gone, Molly, and I promise I called you straight away."

"I know."

"I have no idea how or when she was diagnosed, or even how long she'd been dealing with it. Why did she have to be so bloody secretive?" I whisper to myself.

"Because that was her. She spent her whole life protecting us, right up until she took her last breath. I'm just glad we were both here with her at the end. I mean, I wish we could have had longer, but the way she looked on the night she passed...," she pauses and lets out a sigh. "She looked so "

"Peaceful," I finish for her. It sounds so weird, but the look on our mum's face when she passed was one of relief; she looked so serene and tranquil as we held her.

"Yes, peaceful, and now she's with Dad," Molly says, leaning her head against my shoulder as we just sit in silent remembrance of a lifetime full of wonderful memories. No words are needed, just the silent emotional support we are drawing from each other.

That night, I lay on the couch trying to get my six-foot-three frame into a comfortable position, which at this point seems to be on my back with my feet hanging over the arm, and I'm kind of regretting agreeing to spend the night here when I could be at home, spread out in my own man-size bed, but I could see how upset Molly was at the thought of me leaving and returning in the morning. I can understand how she's feeling, even though I thought we'd managed to cut through some of the darkness of the day by sharing a pizza, a cold beer, and some hilarious stories from when we were kids, but when it started getting late and I stood to leave, she started to get teary and anxious. So, here I am, stretched out on my mum's comfortable to sit on, but too small to sleep on, couch, gazing up into the rhythmic spinning and ticking of the ceiling fan.

As I lay here, my mind drifts back to our conversation earlier tonight. Molly and Caleb are leaving on Friday to go back to the States, so it only gives us a few days to go through the personal things in the house before they leave. Then, after they leave, I'll clear out the place and put it on the market. I could see the concern on Molly's face throughout the conversation, and I know she's worried about leaving everything to me, but honestly, for me, the only hard part is the personal things. Once that's taken care of, the house can go. My mum had only been living here for a few years, so I have no memories or emotional attachment to the place. She sold our childhood home after Dad died because there were just too many memories for her to live there without him, then she purchased this smaller two-bedroom brick home. It was the perfect size for her. As long as she had a spare room for when Molly and Caleb visited, she was happy.

Molly met Caleb while she was travelling around the States on a working visa and had started work at the local hospital in Durandale California. He was a detective at the local police station there. They met, fell in love, and eventually she moved to the US and they got married - which brings me to the next conversation we had tonight. Molly wants me to go and stay with them for a while, so much so, that for at least two hours tonight she'd given me her best hard-sell lines. Now, they would have put a car salesman to shame; the words spilling from her mouth with such speed, with barely a second to breathe, at one point I thought she was going to choke.

If there's one thing I do know about my sister, it's that she's as stubborn as hell and when she sinks her teeth into an idea, she won't give in. I was trying to reassure her by reminding her that I have a job and a home of my own, and that I am the older brother here and quite capable of looking after myself. In fact, it's something I have been doing quite well at for many years now. Smiling and seemingly shrugging off anything I had to say, like at this point it didn't matter, she countered every argument I made right back at me, saying how I needed a break and a change of scenery, and how, because I was a firefighter and Caleb had plenty of connections, he could get me a job at their local fire station. Blah, blah, blah, and that's all I remembered as I sat back, sipped on my beer, and told her that I would think about it. When she went quiet, I knew she was satisfied, for now.

Looking up, I continue to watch the turning of the blades of the fan above me, waiting for its hypnotic effect to help me fall asleep when suddenly, a cool breeze drifts across my face, carrying with it the familiar scent of a perfume I know so well. Turning my face into the couch, it gets stronger. I smile at the memory of my mum, always warm and loving, with the sweet smell of night jasmine she loved so much. With a deep sigh of emotional exhaustion, I close my eyes and fall asleep to the metronome-like ticking of the fan.

Chapter One

Seven months later

Jaxon

As I continue to fidget and move around in my seat in an attempt to get comfortable, I finally give up, push the ear buds into my ears and try to concentrate on the movie playing on the small screen in front of me, extending my legs as much as possible. For once, my little sister had been right when she said I should upgrade to a business class seat for the leg room since it's a very long flight. Now I wish I would have, because we are only ten hours into this twenty-three-hour flight and I am so looking forward to the next stopover so I can get up and walk around. Instead of listening, my inner alpha male voice had convinced me that I was tough and if I could run into a burning building, I could certainly handle sitting in a seat and watching a movie while enjoying an ice-cold beer. Yeah, right. In actuality, my six-foot-three frame is now folded into what feels like a baby car seat, with a bunch of old movies and documentaries on the life span of honey bees, and a glass of foul-tasting beer because that's all they had.

On top of that, the guy sitting next me is almost as tall and obviously hasn't even heard of the word deodorant, because all I can smell is a combination of his body odor and the roasted peanuts that he keeps throwing into his mouth, only stopping now and then for a break so he can shove his finger so far up his left nostril that I'm sure he's digging for diamonds. Pushing the ear buds back into my ears, I turn away from his mining expedition and try to concentrate on the next documentary that's started. Although this one is a little more stimulating than the last one, I find myself thinking about the conversations I've had with Molly over the last few months, and how, out of everything that she'd managed to convince me was a good idea, the one thing that I should have to listened to her about was to upgrade to a larger seat. I chuckle to myself as I think about just how far my little sister will go to get me to spend some time with her. She has no scruples and it had started about two weeks after she and Caleb returned to the US after the funeral.

First came the calls to discuss how I was doing and how much she missed me, which quickly turned into what I call the sales pitch about how great Durandale and its weather is, how it would do me good to travel and take a break. Oh, and the cherry on top... how she'd met so many stunning single women lately. Now, this went on for a couple of months until the house was sold, then she went in for the kill and pulled the old 'You're breaking my heart, Jaxon. I miss you so much,' the 'Caleb has friends at the fire station and he talked to them about you coming over on a working visa and working there for a while,' and finally 'You know, Caleb and I are thinking of starting a family soon and our baby will need their uncle close by.' And so, before I knew what was happening, I had applied for a working visa, applied for a position at the Durandale Fire Department, resigned from my job, rented out my own apartment, and put everything into storage. Now, I was about ten hours away from hugging and strangling Molly at the same time.

So, I have no fucking idea what I am doing or where my life is heading. At thirty-two years of age I have no plans and no direction, yet it feels good. No, I'm not going to share that part with Molly, because I don't want her to do any more of a victory dance than she is already doing. Nope, I'll just keep that to myself. Although I do have to admit that even though she did all the pushing for me to come and spend some time with her and Caleb, for the first time in a long time I can feel an excitement brewing inside my chest for this adventure and the break from a life that was starting to become stagnate and repetitive with the same routine every day and every week, down to the sharing of a beer at the local pub after a long week with the guys from the station where we would decompress, relax, and share the week's stories of lives lost and saved, a way of self-therapy, all washed down with a cold beer.

"Can I get you something to drink, sir?" a female voice breaks into my thoughts. Opening my eyes, I see a pretty dark-haired stewardess smiling at me.

"That would be nice. Scotch, no ice, please," I say with a pleasant smile that's interrupted by a loud snort coming from my sleeping seat companion.

"Better make that a double," I breath out and she grins, shaking her head as she walks away, returning shortly with my drink. A drink that goes down smoothly enough to lull me into a sleep so deep that the next time I wake I can smell fresh coffee brewing and hear the rumble of food trolleys moving around.

A few hours later, the 'fasten your seatbelts light' pings on, followed by the captain's voice announcing that we are slowly making a decent and would be landing at San Jose International airport with an arrival time of 11am and that the weather was sunny and clear.

Then he thanked the passengers for flying with the airline and hoped we'd enjoyed our flight.

Pulling my backpack from the over-head locker as people start to leave the plane, I swear I feel almost every bone in my body creak in their fight to snap back into place. Standing to my full height, my muscles hurt like a bitch, but all I want to do is get off this plane and walk it off. At this point, I couldn't care less if I have to stand in line for five hours to get through customs; in fact, I'm looking forward to it. Seems I spoke too soon though, because it does in fact take me almost two hours to get through customs and find my luggage before I can get out into the arrival lounge. Scanning the crowd of people, it doesn't take me long to see Molly's beautiful smiling face, accompanied by a delighted squeal of excitement as she runs towards me throwing her arms around neck. As I drop my bag onto the floor, I stoop down to pull her in for a much-needed embrace.

"I am so glad you're here."

"Me too. The length of that flight is a killer," I state, placing a kiss against her cheek.

"So, let me look at you," she says, pulling back from me, her eyes scanning over me.

"It hasn't been that long."

"Seven months is a bloody long time," she replies, placing her hands on her hips and giving me a stern look.

"Not only do you look like mum, now you sound like her, too," I say with a shake of my head.

"Do I? Look like mum?" she asks.

"Absolutely," I say, hoping like hell that I haven't said something that's going to upset her, because that would not be a good way to start off what was going to be a long stay with her and Caleb.

"Cool." She smiles with great relief. "Come on, I can't wait for you to see the town."

Walking out to where she's parked, I cringe a little when she starts to make her way towards a yellow Honda Civic, a tiny toy car, which causes me to groan in anticipation of yet another size problem. I lag behind her as she walks towards it and stops at the passenger side door of the little tinker toy car, then turns and looks at me. "What are you doing?" she asks with a grin. "Not that one," she says, now smiling from ear to ear. "But I thought..." I say, gesturing to the Honda.

"You thought wrong. It's this one," she says, pressing the fob on her car keys, making the lights blink on a white SUV parked in front of the Honda, and causing me to let out a breath of air in relief as I grab my case and wheel it to the back.

"One thing you need to learn about living here is that everything is big in America." She chuckles as I toss my bags into the back and we get in.

"Thank you," I say, looking to the sky as I stretch out my legs in luxurious comfort.

"You're welcome," she says as we pull out and onto the freeway. "The jet lag will hit you later. It takes about a day to get your bearings, but you'll be fine."

"I'm just glad to be on the ground." "I told you to go business class."

"I know, I know."

"What was that?" she asks, putting her hand to her face and cupping her ear. "Molly, you were so right, I should have listened to you?"

"Yep, not going to happen. I was perfectly comfortable, it was just long," I say, trying to keep a straight face. "Uh, huh." She smiles knowingly.

"No, really, I had loads of room."

"You keep telling yourself that, mate." She said with a grin.

The drive from the airport wasn't as long as I thought it would be, and in this tank-sized car, I could stretch out and watch as we moved from the cityscape to the flat wide-open spaces of lush green land. We talk and laugh on the way while Molly points out things of interest and common sites until we start to see some houses dotted here and there which eventually turn into the town of Durandale. We pass the hospital where she works and the town firehouse, then pull into the driveway of the biggest house I think I've ever seen.

"Holy shit, Molly, this place is huge," I say, staring at the white ranch-style house.

"I know," she breathes out. "It's a family home." "What?"

"It's been in Caleb's family for a few generations. His great grand-parents built it. It was surrounded by quite a lot of land that got sold off over the years as the town grew, but they kept the house and passed it down."

"Wow, that's amazing," I say, looking over the front of the house. "It is, and there's more." She smiles as we both get out of the SUV.

"Come on, grab your bags and I'll give you the tour."

Walking up the steps to the massive double wooden doors, Molly slips a key into the lock then pauses, giving me a serious look. "Be prepared."

"For?"

"George."

"George?" Is all I manage to get out before the door swings open and I suddenly hear the sound of frantic scraping and tapping on the wooden floor, followed by a big black furry monster with a long pink tongue and drool hanging from its mouth, as it slides around the corner of the entrance hallway and bounds towards us.

"George, stop!" Molly shouts, holding up a hand to try and convince this huge beast of an animal to calm down. He ignores her completely, and the next minute I have two paws thrust against my chest and the slobbering, excited dog has pushed me against the door frame.

"George, get down," Molly tells the mutt as she pushes her hand into the fur of his neck, trying to grab at his collar.

"This is George?" I ask.

"Yes, the big oaf. He's got a heart of gold and no boundaries when it comes to smothering people with his love."

"Hey, buddy," I say, giving him a scratch behind his ears. "You have really grown since the last picture I saw of you." With his tail wagging so hard that his big body is shaking and I can feel it through his paws, I gently take hold of them and bend down, placing them on the floor, then give him some more attention until he calms.

"Great guard dog you have." I chuckle. "I know, he'd lick them to death."

"He would, but at least he's big enough to scare the crap out of someone. What the hell have you been feeding him?"

"You can blame Caleb, that's his job," she says, closing the front door once I pull my luggage inside. "Now, come on. I have a cold beer with your name on it waiting in the refrigerator." She smiles, looping her arm through mine and leading me down the hall. "Now you're talking."

Chapter Two

Jaxon

After a tour of the house, which is amazing and around ten times bigger than my apartment back home, we head into the kitchen. Molly hands me a cold beer and motions for me to follow her over to the big wall of sliding glass doors that open onto a patio surrounding a swimming pool.

"This place has it all."

"That's nothing. Come with me," she says and we walk around the pool to another large white building that I presume is used for storage. When she opens the door and we walk in, I am taken aback by the small apartment inside. It has a living area, a small compact kitchen, and two other doors leading off the living area.

It's neatly furnished, with the smell of fresh paint in the air. "This is yours while you're here."

"What?"

"I wanted you to stay with us, but I know how independent you are, so Caleb and I renovated this," she says, holding a hand out and gesturing to the place.

"Molly, I didn't expect..."

"Yes, I know, but like I said, I wanted you to stay with us and this way you have your own place. There's even a side gate for you to come and go as you please, and I get to keep you close as well." She smiles at me and I instantly see the joy that spreads across her face. I also see a tiny amount of trepidation in her eyes that I quickly put at ease.

"Thank you, it's great." "You like it?" She beams.

"I do," I say and leave the conversation there. I don't want to tell her that I had planned to rent while I was here, on account of not wanting to get in the way of an almost newly-married couple, but with the look in her face right now I find myself unable to upset my sister on the subject.

After the beer, I grab my things and take them into the apartment and unpack, then go back to the main house where Molly is cutting up vegetables at the kitchen counter.

"Do you need a hand?"

"No, but help yourself to another beer," she says, turning slightly to point at the fridge.

"I'll grab one later, I might need it to help me sleep tonight. What time does Caleb get home?"

"Usually around five, but he was going to try and get away a little earlier today. He's off tomorrow, so he's going to show you around town."

"He doesn't have to do that. I'm sure I can check out the place without getting lost."

"Believe me, he doesn't need much of an excuse to take the day off. Besides, I'm on shift tomorrow, so it's nice to know that you won't be alone."

"You know I've been on my own for some time now, right?" I ask her with a raised brow.

"I know. I also know how hard it is when you come to a new country. You kind of feel displaced for a while."

"I think you need to stop worrying so much. After all, I was visiting different countries while you were still swapping school lunches with your friends."

"Please, spare me the I'm the big brother act and let me smoother you just a little," she says, holding up her thumb and finger, showing me a small space.

"Hmmm, starting work next week is looking pretty good at this point."

"Oh, that reminds me, we'll be having a barbeque on Saturday afternoon and some of the guys from the station will be coming." "Really?" I sigh.

"What? It will be good for you to meet some of them. Besides, Caleb grew up with most of them and this is a small town, so we see each other all the time."

"You're making me feel like it's my first day at school."

"Well, it is, kind of." And when she throws that smile at me once again, I am reminded of just how big her heart really is, and instantly crumble.

"You know, we do have a dishwasher for that, right?" Molly says and I look up at her as I wipe the last bit of pasta sauce from my plate with a piece of garlic bread and pop it into my mouth with a hum.

"What can I say? I miss your spaghetti sauce," I say, grabbing my beer and washing down all of that meaty goodness.

"Good, want some more? There's plenty."

"No, I am full," I say, leaning back against my chair and patting my satisfied stomach.

"You definitely know when to stop in this house." Caleb chuckles. "What can I say? I like to see my man well fed," Molly says, standing and starting to clear the dishes from the table. "Here, let me help," I say, standing.

"It's alright. Why don't you and Caleb take your beers outside? I got this."

"You sure?"

"Yep, go on," she says with a shooing motion to us both. Once outside, we sit at the outdoor table.

"She's really excited that you're here," Caleb says.

"You think?" I chuckle, taking a pull of my beer.

"It's all she's talked about since we came back after the funeral."

"I'm glad it wasn't just me that was getting it then."

"You know what she's like once she gets an idea in that head of hers. There is no stopping her." He smiles proudly.

"I know. Look, while we're on the subject, I really appreciate all the work you both did on the apartment, but I feel like I'm intruding a little."

"Nah, it's all good. Seems stupid looking for a place to rent while you're here, when we have plenty of space. Besides, when you leave, I have plans for that place," Caleb says, pointing to the small white guest house.

"A man cave, huh?"

"A nice bar and pool table would look so good in there. Great place to invite my buddies around to on the weekends." Caleb leans back into his chair with a dreamy look on his face.

"Sounds good, mate. As long as I won't be getting in your way." "Not at all and what makes Molly happy, makes me happy," he says, a warm smile spreading across his mouth. "Did she tell you about the barbeque Saturday?"

"She did," I say with a slight grimace.

"Don't sweat it. We usually get together at someone's house at least every second weekend, so it seemed to be a good idea for it to be here this weekend so you can meet up with some of the guys from the station."

"Yes, she said you grew up with most of them."

"Yeah, well, it's a small town and a pretty close community, so keep that in mind if you start chasing the ladies. You'd be surprised at just how fast gossip travels in this place," he says with a pointed finger.

"Thanks for the heads up, mate," I say, lifting my bottle of beer in a salute before continuing. "So, speaking of which, what is the female situation like around here?" I say, grinning.

"You will have no problems there," Molly answers as she walks out onto the patio, slipping into Caleb's lap as he wraps his arms around her.

"You've got to say that, you're my sister and biased."

"Are you friggin kidding me? Have you looked at yourself lately?" she asks, waving a hand towards me. "You're tall, muscled, and you have this Chris Hemsworth thing going on with the messy dark blonde hair, trimmed beard, and blue eyes. Not to mention the accent. They are going to be crawling all over you."

"Now you're just trying to feed my ego," I preen, puffing out my chest a little.

"Did it work?" she asks coyly. "Maybe, just a little."

"I think he and Miller are going to get on like a house on fire," Caleb says, looking at Molly, who is nodding her head with noticeable excitement.

"Who?"

"Jacob Miller, he's a firefighter down at the station. You'll meet him Saturday."

"Is Lucas coming too?" Molly asks Caleb.

"Yeah, but Bennet can't. He's taking Everly and Luke camping for the weekend," he says before turning his attention back to me.

"I grew up with these guys. Lucas is a cop, Bennet works as a rescue pilot, and…"

"Jacob is the fireman," I finish for him. "Talented family."

"The Miller family are pretty well-known in Durandale. Their Dad was police chief until he retired some years back. Great family."

"Sounds like it," I say, finishing off the rest of my beer and standing to stretch the kinks from my back.

"You look exhausted," Molly says, standing too.

"I was doing alright, but I think it just hit me," I say with a yawn.

"Go, get some sleep," she says, reaching up and placing a kiss on my cheek. "We'll see you in the morning."

"Night guys," I say and make my way back to the guest house. I had planned on taking a shower before getting into bed, but as soon as I see the bed, my brain crashes and all I have the energy to do is pull off my jeans and T-shirt and slide under the covers. As soon as my head hits the pillow, it's lights out for me.

Prying my eyes open to a stream of bright sunlight slipping through a small gap in the blinds at the window, I groan with a thick, painful throbbing in my head that feels like I have the mother of all hangovers going on. Slowly pulling back the sheets and pulling myself into a sitting position on the side of the bed, I scrub both hands through my hair with a wince and snatch my phone off the side table to check the time. The phone shows that it's just after seven in the morning. It also shows a message from Molly. Clicking on it, I read, 'Come on in for breakfast when you wake up.' Dropping the phone onto the bed, I manage to pull myself up and walk straight into the shower in the hope of drowning myself under the hot water. I have to admit, I did actually come close to it, but I knew if I didn't get out, Molly would come looking for me.

Dressed in a pair of loose-fitting shorts and a tank, I make my way around the pool to the sliding glass doors that lead into the kitchen. I can see her sitting at the breakfast bar, head down, reading something while sipping from a mug that I am desperately hoping is hot coffee. She looks up when I open the door and step in.

"Good morning." She beams. "Hey," I answer groggily.

"Wow, you look like shit. What can I get you?"

"Coffee and drugs, please"

Standing and grabbing another mug, she fills it with some coffee from a carafe then reaches into a drawer, pulling out a box of Tylenol and slides them both towards me.

"That jet lag is a bitch," she sighs in pity.

"You're not kidding," I groan, taking two of the pills with a mouthful of coffee.

"Don't worry. Give it a couple of hours and you'll start feeling human again."

"I thought you had to work today?"

"Not until nine, so I thought I'd make you and Caleb some breakfast before I leave."

"No, really Molly, there's no need."

"Hey, I want to. Besides, live it up while you can, because I can guarantee you that it will not last forever."

After breakfast, Molly left for work, leaving Caleb and I to wash the dishes and tidy up the kitchen. After the Tylenol and a belly full of food, my head was feeling much better. My feet actually feel like they are planted firmly on the floor instead of on the deck of a small boat on the ocean, which made my day of touring the town of Durandale a lot more pleasurable. Taking the SUV, we drove almost around the perimeter of the town then made our way inwards.

It's a beautiful, picturesque place, what I would call back home a nice little country town; not too big, but big enough to have a good size police and fire station. I think I'm more shocked by the size of the hospital where Molly works; it's pretty big. Caleb explained that because Durandale sits almost smack bang in the middle of the state, the hospital had been built to cater to the other surrounding towns.

When Caleb pulls into a bar, I look at him with a raised brow. "I don't know; I'm not even here a day and you have me at a pub."

"It's not a pub, it's a bar. Finnegans," he says, pointing up at the wooden sign declaring its name proudly. "Local hang out for some of the guys, so I'm sure you'll be spending some time here. Might as well give you a sample." He grins, opening his door and getting out.

Following him through the wooden-framed glass doors, the smell of alcohol hits my nose like an enticing aroma and my mouth waters at the thought of a cold beer. Taking up a couple of stools at the bar, a burly barman smiles at us.

"Hey, Caleb," he greets us. "Hey, Dan."

"A little early for you, isn't it?" he questions with a grin.

"Just showing the brother-in-law around," Caleb says, flicking his thumb towards me. "Dan, this is Molly's brother, Jaxon. He just arrived from Australia."

"Hey, man." He smiles, reaching over the bar to shake my hand. "Nice to meet you, Dan."

"Jaxon's joining station 13 for a while," Caleb says.

"Then I guess I'll be seeing you in here a lot, seeing you'll be working with Miller and Cooper."

"Yeah, Caleb said this is the local hangout."

"I like to think I'm a little more exclusive than a local hangout. I do try to cater for the more refined patrons, and some of the officers do like to hang out at McGregor's as well." He chuckles. "So, what can I get you boys?"

"Just a couple of beers, please," Caleb says. Dan reaches down in front of him and pulls out two frosty looking bottles, flips the lids off and places them on the bar in front of us.

"These are on me," Dan says.

"Thanks. Cheers," I say, lifting my beer, first to him, then to my mouth.

"Yeah, well, I figure you'll be spending plenty of money here, so I might as well start you off with a free one." He grins.

"And what makes you so sure I'll be spending all of my money here?" I eye him suspiciously.

"Because Australians love their beer." He winks and walks away.

Now, don't get me wrong, I do like a beer. I mean, come on, I'm an Aussie for fuck's sake, but I also know my limits and my limits are pretty big. It takes a lot for me to get inebriated unless I hit the whiskey, which is why I try to avoid that evil, addictive amber liquid. Taking a look around the place, it's pretty cozy; not too busy. There are a few people sitting around with drinks in hand as they look up at a flat screen TV on the back wall, watching a basketball game with interest.

After serving a customer, Dan wanders back over to us, wiping his hands on a bar towel before tossing it over his shoulder. "So, you going to be staying for a while then?" he asks, leaning his hands on the bar.

"Well, at least until my work visa runs out, or I piss Caleb off and he kicks me out."

"Hah! Your sister would kill me," he says, taking a pull from his bottle.

Spinning on my stool, I take in the place. It's mostly done out in dark woods and brass rails, with booths along the large front window that looks out onto the street, then some round tables and chairs that seem to fit around a small dance floor. There's a small stage in the far corner, so I'm guessing this place has some kind of live entertainment as well. It's comfortable, in a rustic kind of way, and definitely has a homely atmosphere about it, so I can understand why people come here to relax after their shift. It has that relaxing, comfortable feeling about it. After a beer, or two, we head back to the house, where I make use of the beautiful cool water of the swimming pool. It feels so good to stretch out my muscles with a few laps of the pool, before going back into the apartment and lazing on the couch, where I easily fall asleep.

Chapter Three

Jaxon

Saturday was a great day. Not only because I had finally recovered from the bloody jet lag that kept causing me to doze off every couple of hours, but also because, on top of it being a beautiful clear warm day, the air was full of the opulent smell of steak and burgers cooking, which I would have to say is one of the best smells known to the human nose. People are swimming in the pool, while others just sit on the side with their feet dangling in the cool water while trying to avoid getting wet by the excited splashing from kids playing in the pool. I was introduced to Molly and Caleb's friends as they entered the house- all mostly couples; some married, some not - with a couple of singles tossed into the mix. I was happy to see that Molly hadn't decided to do some matchmaking by inviting her single friends along to introduce to her single brother.

So, I admit, in the beginning, I was a little bit apprehensive about this meet and greet my sister had organized, but it turned out to be a great day. *"Reminder to self - do not let on to my sister that she was right, once again."*

Currently, around fifteen of their friends and their children, are spread out around the pool and barbeque, where Caleb is cooking up a storm while chatting and enjoying a beer with a couple of guys he works with. Some others, including myself, go back for seconds from the large table that is set with an amazing spread of mouth-watering food. I've met two of the famous Miller brothers, including their wives and kids, and the Miller parents. The 'Chief,' as I've learned he still likes to be called, and his wife, Betty, are both wonderful people. Filling up my plate, I take it, with a carefully balanced bread roll on top, and my beer in the other hand to the table where Jacob and his wife, Ruby, are sitting and slide myself in beside them.

"You feeling a little hungry, Jaxon?" Jacob smirks, eyeing my plate.

"Starving, mate. The jet lag put me off my food for a couple of days, so I'm making up for lost time," I say, taking a huge bite of my burger with a dramatized moan and roll of my eyes.

"Load up on the carbs, boy, you'll be needing them for your first day at the station tomorrow." He winks.

"I know, my first twelve-hour shift as a newbie. Ah, I remember it well."

"I'm sure it won't be that bad. You're forgetting you're a newbie to the station, not to the job, the guys always have respect for a seasoned firefighter. Speaking of which, how're you getting to the station?"

"Caleb said I could borrow his truck until I get some wheels."

"I can pick you up, if you want; show you around the place, introduce you to the other guys."

"That sounds good. Thanks."

"No problem," Jacob says, taking a mouthful of his beer with one hand as he tenderly rubs at Ruby's noticeable baby bump.

"So, when is the baby due?" I say, looking at Ruby.

"Well, I know it's hard to believe, but another good five months." She sighs.

"Wow, looks like it's going to be a big one, then," I say, smiling and nodding at her belly.

"What would you expect when the baby-daddy is as big as this oaf?" she asks with a playful smack to Jacobs's chest.

"You love my size. Don't even try to deny it." He grins at her.

The seductive look Jacob gives his pregnant wife causes me to cough and choke on a mouthful of burger. "Jesus, Jacob, too much information, mate."

"Now, that's just something you'll have to get used to." Ruby laughs.

When my alarm goes off at six am the next morning, it's still dark outside. Pulling myself up and out of bed, I shower, dress, and enjoy a mug of hot coffee before heading out to the curb to meet Jacob who's already sitting in his truck. Opening the door, I ask, "Am I late?"

"Nope, I'm early. Hop in."

Sliding into the passenger seat, I close the door and pull my seat belt on as he starts the engine. Pulling away from the curb with a slight spin of the wheels, I look at him and I can see a tightness around his mouth. "Rough night?"

"Something like that," he says, keeping his eyes on the road, and I say no more. I don't need to. As a firefighter, I know exactly what it's like to carry some memories that will never leave you, no matter what you do. Unfortunately, with the unusual and often irregular sleeping hours, those memories tend to seep into your mind while you sleep. They do get less frequent as time moves on, but you're never free of some of the horrific things that you see in this job. Occasionally, I get a restless night of scattered dreams, just to remind me they're still there.

Pulling up at the station, it looks pretty quiet; all lit up with the engines parked in the bays. "Looks quiet," I remark.

"Yeah, nothing much usually happens overnight," Jacob says, pulling the truck into a parking spot and putting it into park. I give him a questioning look. "I usually have the scanner on at home - bad habit," he says with a regretful look. I give him a knowing nod and file a mental note to pick one up for myself this week.

Walking into the station and past the trucks, I take in the familiar sights and smells. Leather and charcoal, the smell of the polish on the fire engines keeping them pristine, making sure the color red glows with the bright pride of the firemen who ride in it and rely on it to be their lifesaver in times of need. Taking in a deep breath, my mouth suddenly waters at another familiar smell...bacon cooking.

"That'll be Cooper cooking breakfast," Jacob says, pointing to the stairs that lead up to the top level of the station house. "Come on," he says with a lift of his chin.

Once through the heavy door at the top of the stairs, Jacob swipes a card across the key pad on the wall and the door clicks open. I follow him down a long hallway that opens out onto a large open area that has a long desk in one corner with several computers and a printer on it. The rest of the room has a couple of comfy looking couches surrounding a large flat screen TV on the wall, and in the middle of the room is a large table and chairs which separates the lounge area from the kitchen where two men dressed in uniforms and aprons stand in front of a large stove, cooking and elbowing each other.

"Sorry to disturb you ladies, but we're starving here," Jacob says, causing the two men to turn quickly with slightly shocked looks on their faces which turn into wide grins when they see us standing there. "Fuck, Jacob, you scared the shit out of me," the taller, older looking guy, who I presume is Cooper, huffs out before turning back to the pan on the stove.

"What? Scared we might have caught you and Ethan grabbing at each other's asses?" Jacob chuckles, and I can't hold back a smirk as the shorter, younger guy grins.

"Yeah, talk about bad timing," he says.

"Shut the fuck up, Ethan. Don't give him an inch?" Cooper says, smacking the younger guy, who I now know is Ethan, across the back of his head, causing it to jerk forward.

"I bet you give Ethan more than an inch." Jacob laughs.

"See?" Cooper says, pointing at Ethan with a spatula.

"Come on, you walked right into that one." Jacob laughs, shaking his head.

"And look who's talking? Who's the arm candy?" Cooper says, wiping his hands on a towel and tilting his head in my direction. "This is Jaxon Cane, our new recruit."

"A probie?" Ethan asks.

"Nope, not a probie, but he is a newbie. Jaxon is a well-seasoned professional," Jacob says.

Stepping forward, Cooper holds out his hand, which I take with a firm shake, introducing himself, followed by Ethan.

"So, where did you transfer from?" Ethan asks.

"Sydney, Australia. I'm actually here on a working visa."

"Jaxon is Caleb Adams' brother in-law, he's Molly's brother," Jacob says and I watch as the expressions on their faces change in recognition. "Shit. You're Doctor Adams's brother?" Cooper says.

"Yep, that would be me."

"Hey, sorry to hear about your mom, man. My wife is a friend of your sister's, and I know she had a hard time there for a while," he says with an apologetic shake of his head.

"Thanks, I appreciate that."

There's a slight awkward pause in the air for a moment, until thankfully it's broken by Jacob's voice as he claps his hands then rubs them together eagerly. "Okay, well, let's eat. Then I can show Jaxon around the place before the Captain gets in," he says, sitting down at the table.

After demolishing a plate full of bacon, eggs, and pancakes, along with two cups of coffee so strong it could remove paint from the walls, Jacob takes me around the station. It's a good size, and looks like it's been recently refurbished with a new looking extension at the back to house gym equipment for the guys.

"There's usually at least four guys here overnight, with the rest of us on call, just in case we're needed, which thankfully is very rare," Jacob says as we walk into a room with a line of lockers against the wall, housing turnouts and helmets. When we stop beside one, I look up at the name that reads CANE in bold letters, and has boots, coat, pants, and a uniform hanging inside it.

"This one is yours. Everything should fit if you didn't lie about your measurements on the application form." Jacob grins. "But if there's any problem, just let me know and we'll get it fixed up."

"It all looks great, and thanks for all your help. I really appreciate it," I tell him.

"Not a problem, and you can show your appreciation at the end of the week with a few beers."

"You got it."

By the time I'd changed into my uniform, organized my locker the way I wanted it, and walked back out into the lounge area, an older man, sporting a head full of short-cropped grey hair and a face filled with deep lines that spoke of years of experience and respect, was sitting at the table with a folder in front of him. Standing when he saw me, he smiled, extending a hand for me to shake.

"Jaxon Cane, I'm Captain Wilson," he says with a firm grip of my hand, which I'm not surprised by as he's a fit-looking guy.

"Great to meet you, sir," I say, taking a seat across from him when he motions for me to do so.

"Just Cap is fine, son. So, I take it Miller has given you the tour?"

"Yes, he did. This place is amazing, more modern than I expected."

"Well, that's all thanks to the community which we're lucky to have here in Durandale; always pulling together in strength to get things done."

"I noticed the place looked like it had been refurbished."

"More like gutted." He chuckles. "The fire station and the hospital both got a make-over after a lot of fundraising," he states with pride.

"The hospital too?" I question.

"Yes, the hospital was extended quite a bit actually. I mean, don't get me wrong, it was a great hospital, it just needed to grow with the population so it could handle the demands of the area. It also means that we don't have to keep sending high risk cases over to Belville Hospital now and patients have a much better outlook."

"Sounds like a very supportive community," I say, impressed.

"It is, but I'm sure you'll get to learn that yourself. Now, we just have some paperwork to get through, then we'll get you on a truck and see how you handle the left-hand drive before we add you to the rosters." he says with a playful smile and I give him a nod. I knew that driving on the left-hand side was going to be something I'd need to get used to, but thankfully in the week that I'd been here I've taken Molly's car out quite a bit and it wasn't as bad as I'd expected. Well, once I'd stopped hugging the curb so closely, anyway. After showing my Captain that I was at least passable on the driving, I officially became a member of the Durandale fire station.

Chapter Four

Jaxon

"Man, I can't believe you've been here almost a month and haven't hooked up with anyone yet," Ethan says as we sit in Finnegans Bar with a beer on a Saturday night. The place is starting to fill up, which might have something to do with the live band playing tonight. Settling into life in Durandale has so far been a breeze. I've been made welcome from the beginning and once again Molly had been right; coming here was the change I'd needed and hadn't even realized it.

"How do you know I haven't?" I ask, taking a pull of my beer and giving him a wink.

"Because we spend a lot of time together and I am very observant. I mean, it's not as if you haven't had a wide variety of choices since you've been here, considering all the home-baked goods, fluttering eyelashes, and cleavages that keep turning up at the station throughout the week." He grins.

"Aww, are you jealous?" I say, making a kissing sound at him.

"Fuck off." He quips.

"Honestly, mate, I'm not really interested in the fake, high maintenance types. Don't get me wrong, they've all been stunning to look at, they're just too complicated for me, and it's not really what I'm looking for."

"I hear you," he says, bringing his beer to his lips and draining the rest of it, then signaling to the waitress for two more. "You still need to get laid though."

"I'm sure I won't implode," I reassure him.

"I would." He smirks.

"It's called control, Ethan."

"Fuck that shit," he says, just as the waitress returns, placing two beers on the table. Ethan pushes some bills into her apron pocket with a wink and she gives him a sultry smile, then turns and walks back towards the bar.

"See, now that's how I know I won't be imploding tonight. In fact, I'm pretty sure I will be exploding with her," he says, pointing at the confident sway of the pretty waitress as she walks to serve another table.

"I'm pretty sure she was interested in the cash tip you gave her, not the tip in your pants that you want to give her."

"Nah, that's Suzy. We hook up regularly. It's good, no strings attached, which is what you need," he says, pointing the neck of his bottle at me.

"You concentrate on your own sex life, mate. I am quite capable of looking after mine."

"Okay, just don't say I didn't try and help you when you look down at your dried-up balls one morning."

"Believe me, I won't."

Leaving Finnegans later that night, I say goodnight as Ethan and his waitress friend head for his pick-up. He gives me a warning to be prepared for a rough week ahead, as there was some bad weather heading in. I kind of take his warning with a grain of salt because, let's face it, a lot of what comes out of Ethan's mouth is pretty useless dribble. However, waking up on Monday morning to what sounds like a hurricane outside, then stepping out of the apartment into monsoon- like weather, I do believe I might have just changed my mind about his useless dribble.

Needless to say, it was all hands on deck. It was a week of never-ending drenching rain. From fallen trees to car accidents caused by the ridiculous amount of rain, the power went out several times this week, but was thankfully restored just as quickly. As soon as we'd get back from one call, the alarm called us out again and my skin was starting to wrinkle up like a prune from not even having enough time to change into a dry set of clothes between call outs. So, after a full week, and a call that involved a small dog being trapped deep in a water drain, we actually managed to get in a hot shower, some clean clothes, and had almost finished a steaming bowl of chili with freshly baked bread that Cooper's wife had brought over earlier in the day, when the station alarm sounded again. At least this time when we faced the wet weather, I was dry, warm, and my belly was almost full.

It's dark, but the rain has slowed to almost a spit, when we arrive at an accident site where a small Ford Focus has slid off the road and down into a ditch, flipping onto its roof. Thankfully, the young guy in it was wearing a seatbelt, and although he was now hanging precariously upside down, at least he appeared to be unharmed. Pushing the crow bar into the side of the door, I try to pry it open, but the sucker is jammed tight from the impact.

"What do you need, Cane?" Ethan calls out. "Need the Jaws, Ethan. This thing won't budge."

"On my way."

Within a few minutes, we have the door pulled open and I crawl in beside the young guy. "I'm Jaxon, do you have any pain anywhere?" I ask, running my hands gently over his legs and arms while scanning him for any signs of pain, bleeding, or distress.

"No man, I'm okay, but I think I might have twisted my ankle," he says. Shining my torch down towards where the accelerator is, I can see that his foot seems to be behind the peddle.

"Can you move it at all?"

"I tried, but it's stuck."

"Okay, I'm just going to see if I can loosen it enough to get your foot out. Let me know if anything causes too much pain," I tell him. As I slide my hand down under his leg, I get the distinct smell of fuel moving through the car, just as I hear Ethan yell out to one of the guys.

"We need some foam down here, I smell gas."

When the young guy who's trapped hears Ethan's words, his breathing starts to increase and he looks at me wide eyed. "There's gas?

Is this thing going to explode? We're gonna die, aren't we?" he stammers out.

"Not tonight, mate. I plan on getting you out of here so I can get back to my bowl of chili. You just concentrate on taking nice slow breaths in and out for me, okay?"

When he gives me an apprehensive nod, I slide my hand down and grab hold of the accelerator pad, pulling it upwards just enough to move his foot. "Okay, now I'm going to release your belt and Ethan and I are going to carefully move you onto a back board," I say as Ethan passes me a neck brace to slide around the guy's neck. Pushing the release on the seatbelt, I prepared to catch him as he dropped as carefully as possible, but there was no click. I try again, giving it a hard pull this time which does nothing. So, pulling the knife from my back pocket, I start to cut through the belt when there's a blinding sharp flash of white light.

"Fuck!" I curse out, dropping the knife as Ethan yells out.

"We got flames. Get a move on, Cane." The slight edge of urgency in Ethan's voice tells me that something under the hood of this car is brewing. Realizing I can't get a strong enough grip on the small pocket knife with my gloves on, I slip one off and reach down, scooping up the knife and gliding the blade across the webbing of the belt, which instantly releases the guy into the arms waiting for him. They just managed to pull him out and onto a back board when a roar of heat blazes up from under the hood of the car. Spears of fire push through the broken windscreen, searing painfully across the top of my ungloved hand resting on the steering wheel as I pull myself free of the broken metal. The painful strike against my naked skin causes me to gasp and grab my hand before making my way up to the fire truck and grabbing a bottle of water to douse it with.

"What happened?" Cooper yells, making his way over to me. "It's nothing, just the fire giving me a little bite," I say, continuing to pour water over the now reddened skin.

"Give me a look," he says, taking my hand, his eyes examining it like only a fireman can. "That's more than a bite, Jaxon. This will need medical treatment," he says, flipping open a door on the truck and pulling out a barrier dressing and wrapping it around my hand. I give him a nod, because my experience tells me that this burn is going to hurt like a bitch later and will definitely need a medical dressing.

As soon as we walk through the doors at Durandale General, I look up into the worried eyes of Molly. Looking at Cooper, I give him a narrowed look that says, 'You called my sister, dude, really?' All I get from him is a shrug.

Shaking my head, I look back to Molly. "Its fine."

"I'll be the judge of that. Come on, let's get you into a room so I can take a look," she says, walking away. Once in a room, she starts to pull on gloves. "Sit," she commands, pointing to the bed

"It's a small burn, Molly. Besides, you're a pediatrician."

"And I have dealt with a lot of burns." She scowls.

"But isn't there some protocol about treating a family member?"

"Look, most of the doctors here are snowed under, so if you don't want to sit around and wait for hours to be seen by someone else, I suggest that you shut up and give me your hand." Sighing in defeat, because I am a smart man and know when not to push my luck with her, I let her take the dressing off. The sting of the material peeling off causes me to take a sharp intake of breath. Looking down, the small patch of redness has now turned into an angry, swollen bubble of skin. "A small burn, right," she grumbles under her breath as she turns and starts opening cupboards, pulling out dressings and bottles of fluid. Filling up a bowl of cool water and adding something from another bottle to the water, she places my hand into it. "It looks like a second-degree burn," she says, pulling a phone from her pocket. "I'm going to call someone up here from the ER to confer on the right treatment," she says, putting her phone to her ear and walking out of the room, only to return thirty seconds later.

"So, what do you think, Doc?" I ask with a grin.

"I think you're going to have some pain, but not too much scarring, and as long as it doesn't get infected, I think you'll live," she says, giving me a forced smile.

"I'm fine, Molly. Nothing that a few pain killers won't fix," I say, giving her a hug with my free arm.

"I know. It was just the thought of you being brought in with a burn injury." She breathes out.

"Yeah, well, I'll be having a word with Cooper about that. I knew it wasn't serious."

"No, I'm glad he called me. I'm glad that I've seen that you're alright for myself."

Once I'd been examined by Molly's colleague and they went over a treatment plan, she made another call to the nurse's station to ask if they had anyone free to come up to the room and assist her with a burn injury. Then my lovely sister, who could see I was having some trouble keeping my eyes open in the aftermath of a week of bad weather, told me to relax in the recliner chair in the corner of the room while she went to get some supplies and coffee. As soon as I sank into the chair, I knew it was a mistake. I was done for. It felt like every joint in my body was screaming out in appreciation as little snaps and clicks seem to mold my bones into the comfort of the chair as I close my eyes with a sigh of total contentment. The sound of the door opening quickly turns that sigh into a groan at the sudden loss of a potentially much needed snooze.

"I brought you some coffee and something to eat," Molly says as I flick open one eyelid just enough to see her push a table next to me that has a mug of black, steaming liquid on it, accompanied by a plate with two fat, sugary doughnuts.

"Thanks," I say and close my eyes again, listening to the background sounds of a trolley being set up and the pouring of liquids, opening of packages, and plastic tearing, then I hear the door open again.

"Ella, I didn't know you were on shift," I hear Molly say, her voice slightly pitched with excitement.

"Yes, things are a little slow this week, so you have me," an almost soft, breathy voice answers Molly, a voice that makes both my eyes open quickly just to see who it belongs to. May I say I'm not disappointed by the curvy dark-haired beauty standing in the doorway dressed in dark purple scrubs.

"Ella, this is my brother, Jaxon. Jaxon, this is Ella Grey; she'll be helping me with your dressing," Molly introduces us.

"Nice to meet you." She smiles; not just an everyday ordinary smile, but a genuine smile that seems to light up the whole room.

"Likewise," I answer, sitting up straighter in the chair now, focusing all my attention on Ella, because damn, how could I not.

With a faint buzzing noise filling the room, Molly reaches into her pocket, pulls out her phone, and swipes a finger across the screen, bringing it to her ear.

"Dr. Adams," she answers, followed by a pause as she listens. "Okay. I'll be right there," she says, ending the call and pushing the phone back into her pocket.

"I'm needed in the ER. There's a four-year-old having seizures. Will you be right with this?" she asks Ella.

"Yes, fine. You go."

"Thanks. Coffee's on me." She winks at Ella before turning to me. "Sorry, Jaxon."

"No, go, I'll be fine," I reassure her. "I'm sure Nurse Ella, here, will take good care of me."

"She can, so behave," Molly throws over her shoulder sternly as she rushes out of the room.

"Well, we'd better get your clothes off so we can take care of you," she says, walking towards me.

"A little early for that, isn't it?"

"Excuse me?" she says, looking at me, slightly perplexed.

"I mean, normally I at least get to take a woman out for dinner or a movie before she tries to get me undressed," I say with a raised brow.

"Funny guy," she mumbles as she assists me with my heavy coat, making sure the rough material doesn't scrape the very impressive bubble of skin that's now twice as big. Pulling the trolley closer to where I'm sitting, I watch as she pulls on a pair of gloves and starts to bathe my hand in a liquid that must normally have a sting as strong as it's odor because her eyes keep moving between her bathing the burn and my reaction to it. If it did, I wasn't feeling a thing because I was too busy being mesmerized by her gentle hands as they dip a piece of gauze in the liquid then dab it around the burn site, the hands that open packets with a quietness that should not be possible, the hands that apply lotion to the burn then gently wrap my hand in a bandage with perfection. I watch every movement of her small hands and slender fingers as they work almost effortlessly. Finally able to take my eyes away from her hands, I slowly let my gaze move up to the small v of open skin at the top of her scrubs and over the creamy smooth skin of her throat, to her delicate chin and plump lips, a slim nose and eyes that look to be a light color of blue, from what I can see, with dark long lashes that fan out over her clear skin as she concentrates on what she's doing. I can tell by the sudden change in her breathing that she knows I'm studying her, and I am. She is a natural beauty. Her skin is flawless, and all without the need of any make-up.

"I haven't seen you around here before," I manage to say to break the awkwardness that I am pretty sure I'm causing by openly eye-fucking her right now. The last thing I want to do is make her feel uncomfortable.

"It's a big hospital, I'm not surprised," she says without looking up.

"It is."

"I don't work in this part very often," she offers.

"No? Where are you normally?"

"I usually work in the community, but if things are slow, I help out here," she says, finishing up her task and taping off the bandage on my hand, and finally looking up at me. A move that causes my breath to get caught in my throat because under those long dark lashes are the most unusual eyes I have ever seen. It's hard to explain the color, I guess it would be pale grey with a line of vibrant blue around the irises; fucking amazing. Standing up straight and breaking that momentary connection between us, she starts to clean up the trolley, removing her gloves, and washing her hands before turning back towards me.

"That dressing will need to be changed every second day," she says, picking up a clip board to make some notes.

"So, I'll need to come back in here, then?" I ask.

"You can, unless Dr. Adams wants to take care of it herself."

"I think I'd rather come into the hospital. Would there be a special time?"

"Any time, there'll be someone here to take care of you."

"And what about you, Ella? Will you be here to take care of me?" I say, causing her to stop writing and look up at me.

"Well, I can't guarantee that, but maybe."

"I'll take my chances, then." I smile at her, and for just a moment, I watch as the corner of her mouth tilts into a smile I know she's fighting hard to keep contained. That's enough to tell me that I may have a chance with this beauty. Standing, I grab my coat from the bed. "I'll be seeing you soon, Nurse Grey," I say before leaving in search of Molly for a lift home.

"So, Nurse Grey?" I say, looking at Molly as she drives us home.

"What about her?" She asks.

"Exactly, what's her story?"

"I'm not sure she has a story. She's a great nurse, very caring and very experienced."

"And?"

"And she's a friend."

"So, why didn't you invite her to your place for the meet and greet when I first arrived?"

"Well, for one thing, she was on shift and couldn't come, and second, you specifically told me not to try and hook you up with any of my single friends."

"So, she's single then?" I ask, trying to keep a lid on my enthusiasm at the revelation of her singleness.

"As far as I know, she is," Molly says, giving me a side-eyed look. "Why?"

"Just wondering," I say, absently stroking a finger over my chin.

"I'm not sure she's a one-night type of woman, Jaxon."

"I don't think I am any more either, Molly," I say, looking at her honestly.

"Really? When did this happen?"

"You make me sound like I'm some kind of playboy."

"You're right, I'm sorry. I know you have much more respect for women than that. I guess I've just never seen you in a long-term relationship before."

"That's because I haven't met the right one yet." I grin.

"And you think Ella might be the one?"

"Jesus, Molly, I just want to take her out, get to know her, not marry her."

"Okay, I get it, calm down." She laughs and now I know she is just fishing for a reaction. "Look, the only thing I know about Ella, outside of work, is that she's quiet and likes to keep to herself. I have never seen her out with anyone except people from work. I know she loves working on her house; it's her pride and joy. Maybe I can invite her over for dinner one night-" Molly starts, but I stop her in her thoughts.

"No, please don't. I'd rather do my own dating, without a wingman, or in this case a wing sister."

"Okay, just offering."

"Thanks, but no thanks."

When we pull into the driveway, she shuts off the engine then turns to look at me. "Ella is a beautiful person, inside and out, so just be yourself."

Chapter Five

Ella

Wrapping both my hands around the mug of hot coffee, with a need to grip onto something to try and stop the slight tremble in my fingers, I bring it to my mouth and take a generous mouthful without thinking and almost take a layer of skin off my tongue. I have no idea what just happened, or why I have this tremble that's not only in my hands, but running through my body in a gentle flutter. It's an unusual response to a man which I've never encountered before. As soon as I walked into that room and saw him sitting in that chair with his eyes closed, that flutter started deep in the pit of my belly and increased as soon as he opened his eyes and stared right at me. Sure, he was a fireman in uniform, that would make any man have sex appeal, but there was some-thing about his deep blue eyes that seemed to look deep into me, not at me. That, combined with his messy, thick dark blonde hair, a short, neatly-kept beard, and a mouth that looked made for sin, was enough to make that flutter turn into a tremble.

When he stood and I helped him off with his coat, he towered over my five-foot-six frame, and boy, was he built; solid, with thick biceps and one arm totally covered in an array of colorful tattoos that I had to look away from so I could concentrate on the burn on his hand. That's why, when Dr. Adams left us alone, I tried my hardest not to look at his eyes again until I had finished. The problem was, I couldn't ignore his scent that permeated the air in the room, the smell of leather and rain, fresh rain from a sun shower that had that wonderful clean smell, tainted with a small amount of smoke from his clothes. When he spoke, his voice had a deep rich tambour to it that caused the fluttering in my belly to restart after I'd just gotten it to calm, and damn that accent was just the cherry on top.

Looking down at the half-eaten sandwich in front of me, I wrap it back up and toss it into the garbage. I just can't stomach anything but caffeine right now. Hopefully that will clear my head. With that thought, the door swings open and Leah bounces in with an excitement that tells me she's here for the gossip.

I met Leah when I first came to Durandale and she is the closest person I have to family and my best friend. She also has no sense of decorum and loves gossip.

"Okay, spill the beans," she says, sitting down across from me.

"Beans?" I ask staring at her.

"Don't even try with me, girl. It's all over the hospital that Dr. Adams's brother is hot and you got to touch him." She breathes out.

"I attended to his wound," I corrected.

"Whatever. So, is it true?"

"What?"

"That he's sexy as fuck? That, not only does he look like Thor, but he sounds like him as well?"

"Well, he is from Australia, so I guess he would. I mean, Chris Hemsworth, the actor who plays Thor, is from Australia, so?" I say, shrugging one shoulder.

"Stop teasing me and spill it."

"There's not too much to tell. He had a burn on his hand that I treated with-" I start and she cuts me off.

"Stop. I don't want to know the clinical part, I want to know the dirty parts," she says, sounding a little frustrated. Seeing this, I decide to end her agony and sigh in defeat.

"He's tall, well built, and very hot."

"Oh my," she sighs out, pressing a hand against her chest. "He's not the only hot guy in the town, Leah."

"No, but he's new, fresh eye candy, not old enough to be my father, and he sounds edible, unless you're going to make a play for him. In that case, I won't even try."

"Me? No. By all means, go for it," I say, shaking my head at her offer, while trying to look as uninterested as possible. Considering the look of disbelief she is giving me, that doesn't work. "What?" I finally say.

"Nothing. Just wondering why the words coming out of your mouth right now are not matching the glint of something in your eyes."

"No glint, just honest exhaustion," I say, getting up to rinse out my mug and place it into the dishwasher.

"Okay, whatever you say," Leah says, putting both her hands up in surrender.

It was a long shift, and even though I do like working in the wards of the hospital, I love my job working in the community as a hospice nurse. When I moved to Durandale over seven years ago and started work at the hospital, I was determined to convince the hospital board that providing terminal and end of life patients with the choice of being able to spend the rest of their time in the comfort of their own homes with medical support was something of great compassion that we, as not only medical staff, but human beings, can do. I love that people have the choice to be able to spend their last weeks, days, hours in the homes they love, homes full of memories and happiness, places that mean comfort and family. Why shouldn't a person have the choice of being able to take their last breaths in a place that means so much to them, in a calm and peaceful environment? Thankfully, the hospital board didn't take too much convincing, and that's when I began to work in a community where I seem to be known by few different names; an angel, a God send, and the sleep whisperer, on account of being able to talk comfort and peacefulness to someone who is making their final journey. I appreciate them all, but I am really just rewarded by being able to provide support and anything else that's needed by both the patient and their family.

The other thing I'd been determined to do when I moved here was to have my own home. That dream was achieved when I purchase my small Cape Cod style cottage three years ago. It needed some work, but to me it was perfect, from the polished wood floors and original carpentry, to the symmetrical window placement on either side of the heavy paneled front door. I had done most of the home decorating tasks myself, only hiring professionals to take care of the bigger jobs like the electric and plumbing issues worn down by years of use. I even surrounded the yard with a white picket fence and side gardens full of blooms, making my home my haven, my little slice of paradise, my sanctuary, and most importantly mine. Its comfortable homely appearance on the outside and its homely, comfortable furnishings on the inside, were all my choices and no one else's.

Pushing my key into the lock and opening the door, I am startled when a black furry mass jumps off the entry table and straight onto my feet. "Jesus, Walter, you scared the hell out of me," I say to the large black cat that starts to purr as he winds in and around my legs. "Yeah, yeah, I know, I'm a little late. Come on, let's get you fed before I get in the shower," I say, leaning down to give him a scratch behind his ears before dumping my keys and bag at the door and heading for the kitchen to fill his bowl. Once he's fed, I head for a long hot shower followed by some reheated left-over lasagna in front of the TV in my pajamas and fluffy socks – now, this is what I call a night of pleasure. I do occasionally have a night out with Leah, although she complains that it's just not often enough or even healthy for a single thirty-year-old to want to spend so much time at home. I beg to differ. My home is my pleasure. What can I say? I'm a home body. Unlike Leah, who is a self-confessed party animal. Talk about opposites attracting, although I do like to think we both benefit from our friendship. I love her lust for life and living in the moment, and she loves my patience and logical way of thinking, until it comes to trying to wiggle out of a night out with her at Hooligans bar. Then I have a fight on my hands. I do try to spend some social time with her at least every couple of weeks, and this weekend is one of those weekends. Leah managed to sell me on the live band that will be playing there Saturday night. Well, that and her relentless pouting every time I've looked at her this week.

I spent the rest of my working week at the hospital. I don't have any patients to attend to in the community, which is something that happens often, so, at the moment, I'm sitting at the nurse's station looking over some paperwork. When I answer the phone and am asked to come down to triage, I see Leah walking towards me, holding out a chart. I look at her questioningly as I take it from her.

"Your sexy fireman is here for his dressing change," she says, grinning like the cat that got the cream. Looking down at the chart, then back to her, I know she must know what I'm thinking. "Don't ask me? He asked for you and was prepared to wait," she says with the shrug of her shoulders. "He's in room two."

Standing outside room number two, for some weird reason I find myself taking a moment to not only take a deep breath, but to also try to compose myself before I enter. I actually pat my hair and scrubs, making sure everything is in place. "Idiot," I silently chide myself before opening the door and find him standing, looking out the window. This time he's not in uniform, but instead he's casually dressed in a pair of worn jeans that hug his powerful, muscular thighs and wonderful looking ass. With his arms crossed over his chest, I can see his biceps strain against the sleeves of his black t-shirt, the material also showing off wide shoulders and the ripple of muscles over his back.

"Everything alright?" The tone of his deep masculine voice, combined with that delicious accent, breaks through my erotic thoughts like a hammer jolting me back into reality with the embarrassing realization that he's just caught me ogling him. I am sure that's exactly what the cocky smirk at the corner of his mouth and the sparkle in his eyes is confirming.

"Yes, fine," I say, sounding a little breathless as a feeling of warmth tickles at my cheeks. "Please, take a seat and I'll get what I need," I say, turning and opening the supply cupboards, pulling out a clean dressing pack, some sterile saline, and a bowl. After getting everything set up on my trolley, I move it to where he's now sitting on the bed and pull on some gloves. Gently, I take his hand, removing the tape and bandage. "How's it been?"

"Painful, but manageable."

"Have you been taking the pain medication?" I ask, keeping my eyes down while slowly uncoiling the bandage.

"No, just the antibiotics."

"There's no shame in using pain relief, you know."

"I'd rather not if I can help it," he says.

Once the bandage is removed, I inspect the wound which is still red and angry-looking, but looks clean. The bubble of skin has now deflated, leaving the bandage soaking from the serum fluid that it had been containing. Placing his hand in the saline, I gather up the dirty dressing and dispose of it in the garbage.

"You know, anyone downstairs in triage could have changed your dressing. You didn't have to wait for me."

"It's fine, it's my day off. Besides, I didn't want to see anyone else, I wanted to see you."

"You did?"

"Yes, you see, any other nurse could have taken care of my hand, but I didn't want to ask any other nurse if I could take her out...you know, like, on a date." His words cause me to look up at him. A big mistake, because the ocean-blue color of his eyes just sucks me right into them like a vortex.

"I don't think that's a good idea," I say, removing his hand from the bowl of saline and placing it on a sterile pad to let it air dry for a few minutes.

"You don't?" he asks, his left eyebrow rising.

"No, I'm usually pretty busy."

"Hey, I'm pretty easy to please - lunch, dinner, coffee." I could hear the note of sincerity in his voice and when I looked up into his eyes again, I could feel myself crumbling at his request. This man was very tempting, in many ways. "Look, no expectations, just coffee and talk." Yes, he was very tempting, and before I can stop myself, my mouth opens and words come out that I know shouldn't have.

"A friend and I will be at Finnegans tomorrow night, around eight."

"A friend?" he asks, his eyes narrowing slightly.

"Yes, Leah, the blonde nurse you spoke to downstairs," I say, finishing of his bandage with some tape. "There you go, all done," I say and start to clean up the trolley.

"Sounds good. I guess I'll see you tomorrow, then," he says, standing from the bed with a slight flex of the hand that I'd just dressed before walking towards the door.

"Pain medication, Mr. Cane," I remind him. Turning, he gives me a nod along with a grin as he opens the door and walks out, leaving me to sit on the bed. I let out a deep sigh of relief that I'd managed to treat his wound in a professional manner and not embarrass myself, but also at what I had done. I had agreed to do something that I haven't done in years, something I swore I'd never do again...a date.

Chapter Six

Jaxon

After showering, I dress in a pair of jeans and a white button-up shirt, and pull on my boots. Grabbing my wallet, phone, and keys, I head out to the old pick up I purchased yesterday. Jacob, with the help of an old school friend, was able to hook me up with the truck. It's old, but runs great and has a shit load of character to it. Plus, it was a bargain. Having it also means I don't need to rely on using Caleb or Molly's vehicles. Although it wasn't a problem as far as they were concerned, they've already done so much to make my life comfortable here, I felt like if I could do something that involves me not imposing on them to get around then I would. If Molly had her way, I would be with them for every meal and only use the guest house to sleep in. There's no way in hell I'm doing that to a newly married couple, so we seem to have come to an agreement that let's Molly get her fix by me joining them for dinner at least once a week.

Heading out the front, I hop into the truck and start her up. I'm not sure why, but there never seems to be anything more freeing than being in control of your own wheels. Pulling up and parking outside Finnegans, there are cars parked everywhere, and after coasting around for a while I find a spot to park on a grassy patch.

This place is never full, but from the low hum of music filtering out of the door when someone exits, it seems like this is the place to be tonight for a lot of people.

As soon as I manage to find the bar through the crowd of people, I signal the bar attendant for a beer. Taking a mouthful from the bottle, I let my eyes scan around the room looking for Ella. Every table in the place is full and every inch of standing room is occupied by bodies, each one moving at a slightly different pace to the beat of the music. Slipping through the crowd, I finally see her sitting with a blonde woman in a side booth and I take a moment to take her in. She looks completely relaxed and I watch as she brings the mouth of the beer bottle she's holding to her lips and takes a sip, smiling at her friend as they talk. She's wearing jeans and a denim jacket, her hair is long and dark, with gentle waves cascading over her shoulders, and with the minimal amount of make-up she is absolutely stunning. This is also the first time I've seen her out of her hospital scrubs with her hair down, and I'm pretty sure she'd look stunning in anything she wore.

As she lifts the bottle to her mouth again, she spots me. Her eyes settle on mine and I swear her smile just grew that little bit wider. Walking over to the booth, she scoots over, making room for me to sit next to her.

"Hello, ladies," I say, tipping my bottle to each of them in greeting.

"Leah, this is…" Ella starts to say and I finish off for her.

"Jaxon. Nice to meet you again, Leah."

"You too, Jaxon. How is your hand doing?" she asks, nodding towards my bandaged hand.

"Better thanks to Ella, here."

"Yes, she does have a magical touch."

"She certainly does," I say, looking at her.

"Oh, please. Any qualified person could do it. Your sister could just as easily have taken care of it." Ella eyes me with a cheeky grin straining at her beautiful lips.

"I know she could, but like I said, I needed an excuse to come see you again," I say, causing a slight pink shade to flush over her cheeks.

"So," Leah interrupts. "How long will you be staying in Durandale?"

"I have a two-year work visa, so anything up to two years, I guess. It depends."

"On?" Leah asks, questioningly.

"A few things I guess... the job... the town."

"And how is all that going so far?"

"Pretty good; better than I expected, actually. The guys at the station are great and the town has been very welcoming. It didn't take me long to feel comfortable at all."

"That's Durandale for you," Ella says, taking another drink of her beer.

"So, ladies, what can I get you to drink? My treat," I say, rubbing my hands together after finishing off my own beer.

"That's not necessary," Ella says, followed by a squeal from Leah from across the table.

"Shut up, Ella. When a gentleman wants to buy you a drink, just except it with a gracious smile. I'll take another beer, thanks."

"Same for you?" I ask, turning my gaze towards Ella, who seems to have sunken back into the booth a little. "Another beer, wine, something stronger?"

"Beer, please."

"Three more beers, coming up," I say, getting up and making my way back to the bar, which luckily isn't as busy this time. The place is still crowded, but everyone seems to have found somewhere to sit, ready to enjoy the band. Taking the beers back to the table, I sit down just as the lights dim a little and the live band come back onto the small stage, and pick up their instruments. The room is instantly filled with the loud sound of a live band. It was a great night, not very good for having any kind of conversation with Ella, apart from the small talk that we managed to slide in between songs, but as the night progresses, and I guess as the alcohol flows, I was getting more of her attention, judging from the subtle flirty smiles and giggles to elbow bumps and a lot of eye contact. And that right there, that eye contact, is what I was craving from her. I wanted to drown myself in their depth, their color, and the more I looked into them the more I could see of her. This woman had something special about her and I intended to find out more.

Once the band finished, to a loud roar of applause and the stomping of boots in appreciation on the wooden floor, the lights came back up and the crowd started to thin out a little as people start to leave. The live music was replaced with some low background music which starts to filter through the place. When Leah elbows Ella and nods her head towards two men making their way towards us, I see Ella try hard to mask the frown that suddenly crosses her face, and I hope these two guys are friends of Ella and Leah's. It's been a great night and I didn't want it to end in a brawl with some pissed off guys who think I'm trying to steal their women. I mean, don't get me wrong, I've been in a few bar fights and that's not the problem. The problem will be trying to explain to Molly why I got into a fight, which is something I'd rather not do. What can I say? My little sister can be pretty scary at times. As they approach the table, I actually feel myself sitting up straighter. For what reason, I'm not sure; these guys are at least a few inches shorter, and a lot leaner than me. For some bizarre reason, right now I feel a need to puff myself up like a bull frog, making myself look bigger. This is not a conscious act on my part, so I'm just putting it down to some weird male territorial response, I guess.

"Ladies," the dark-haired one says, looking to Leah and Ella before turning his eyes to me.

"Hey, Ash. I didn't know you were here," Leah says.

"Wonder why?" he says, all the time keeping his eyes pinned to mine.

"Ash, this is Jaxon. He recently started work with the boys from station 13. Jaxon, these are the Carter Brothers, Ash and Cole, who I went to high school with," Leah introduces us.

Now, I'm not normally rude when being introduced to people, but the way this prick is looking at me is like he wants to pull his dick out and piss on the floor to mark his territory. I have no intention of putting my hand out first, so I keep my hands by my sides and my eyes on his, narrowing them slightly to subtly convey that I won't be backing away from anything he intends on dishing out. After a few moments of our obvious stare-off competition, his brother has the sense to take a step forward and offer his hand. Even as I shake it, I keep my eyes pinned on the fucker standing in front of me. That's eventually broken into by Leah's voice.

"So, boys, did you enjoy the band tonight?"

"Yeah, they were really good," Cole says. "How are you Ella? I haven't seen you in here for a while."

"I'm good, just been busy with work and the house," she answers politely. I can feel in the tone of her voice that she's starting to feel a little uncomfortable with Ash's eyes still focusing on mine, and I know that I need to be an adult here and smooth the situation down, but I just can't bring myself to do it. There is just something in the back of my throat that tastes foul about this guy, a gut feeling that seems to come from nowhere.

"Yeah, Leah's been telling me about the work you've been doing on the place," Cole continues.

"I wouldn't call it work, it's a pleasure. I love seeing the progress I make every time I complete a room," Ella says, this time her voice smoothing out a little with a sound of pride.

"I bet. You should be proud." Cole smiles.

"I am." She beams at him and the conversation seems to falter into a silent pause until Leah scoots out from the booth.

"Come on, boys, I think you can buy me a drink," she says, standing in the space between them and causing Ash to move, finally breaking our eye contact as he looks at her.

"I thought we were leaving soon," Ella says.

"Really? The night is young, my friend, enjoy," Leah enthuses.

"No, really Leah, I have things to do tomorrow," Ella protests and Leah throws out her bottom lip in an exaggerated pout.

"I'm sure Jaxon wouldn't mind giving you a ride home, would you Jaxon?" she says, turning her gaze towards me.

"Absolutely, not a problem." I smile back at her and think I just found my wingman for the night.

"Leah," Ella almost curses out her name.

"It's fine. I would be happy to give you a ride," I say, looking at Ella and giving her the biggest, most trustworthy smile, I can muster.

"See? Jaxon is happy to take you home."

"Are you sure?" Ella asks, looking at me, her eyes conveying how sorry she is that her friend has put her in this position.

"Very sure."

"Okay. Boys, take me to the bar, I'm all yours," Leah says, slipping her arms through an arm of both men. "Talk tomorrow, Ella," she sings as she turns with a willing and obviously happy Cole and a reluctant Ash over to the bar.

"Close friends of yours?" I ask Ella as she finishes off her drink, placing the empty bottle on the table.

"God no. Cole's a nice guy, he and Leah have been hooking up, off and on, for a few years now, but Ash is just an ass and unfortunately always seems to tag along with him. I'm guessing Cole is the only person around here who likes him."

"And I'm guessing that's probably only because he has to, on account of them being related," I say, causing a sexy snort of laughter to burst from Ella's lips.

"I'm guessing you're right. Sorry about his weird behavior."

"Please, don't apologize for the actions of a neanderthal with zero brain cells like that. So, are you ready to go, or did you want another drink?"

"No, thanks; I'm ready for home. Do you want to share an Uber?"

"No need, my pick up is outside."

"But, what about..." Her words trail off as she gestures towards my own empty bottle on the table. Reaching out, I turn it around to show her the label. "Light beer?" she asks.

"Yep, I drove here and I intended to drive home. It might not seem like it, but I can assure you I'm a very responsible driver." I grin at her.

"Even with the whole driving on the other side of the road thing?"
"Even with that," I say, giving her a wink. Sliding out of the booth, I hold out my hand to her, which she takes without any hesitation.

When we get to my truck, I open the door and help her inside, then walk around and hop into the driver's side, start the engine, push it into gear and pull out onto the road. It's a silent ride, apart from Ella giving me directions to her house. The whole time, my mind is trying to think of something to say without sounding stupid or desperate, which is stupid because I am desperate to get to know her.

Pulling up at the curb of a small house, complete with a white picket fence, I turn off the motor and the cab of the truck is silent for a few moments with a thickness of emptiness in the air.

Just as I open my mouth to say something, Ella says, "Would you like to come in for a coffee?"

"I would love to." I smile at her invitation, relieved that the night is not over.

I swear, as we walk through the gate and up the pathway, the house in front of me reminds me of a dollhouse. It even has window boxes filled with a variety of flowers that fill the air with their fresh scent. Once we step inside, I can understand why she looked so proud when talking about her home earlier. This is not just a house; it is a home that has an instant feeling of comfort and a welcoming warmth. The last time I'd had that feeling was when I'd visit my mum. This house has that same feeling attached to it.

"This is amazing," I say, looking around from the open lounge area on one side, to the opening on the other side showing a kitchen lined in a dark, rich-colored wood.

"Thank you," Ella says, pulling off her jacket and hanging it on a peg behind the front door, then motioning for me to follow her into the kitchen. I sit on one of the stools at the kitchen island as she fills the kettle and places it on the stovetop.

"So, how long have you lived here?" I ask, taking in the kitchen around me.

"I purchased the house about three years ago. It was old and rundown, and needed a lot of work, but for some reason I fell in love with it. I guess I could relate to it in some weird way," she says, spooning coffee into a coffee press then filling it with boiled water before pushing the plunger down and pulling two mugs down from a cupboard.

"That's funny. You don't seem to look old or rundown at all," I say taking the mug she passes to me.

"Well, that's a relief to hear." She chuckles.

"So, were you born here, in Durandale?" I ask, taking a sip of coffee.

"No, I moved here about eight years ago. I was actually born in Madison, that's in Wisconsin."

"So, do you have family here?"

"No, just me. What about you? What's your story?"

"Not too much to tell, you know most of it, but go for it ask me anything." I grin.

"Is Molly your only family?"

Slowly placing my mug down on the bench, I take in a deep breath. "She is. Our Dad passed away some years ago now, but Mum passed away earlier in the year...cancer." I let out that word with the air I'd taken in and immediately see the sorrow in her eyes.

"Yes, I remember when she and Caleb took that trip home. I'm so sorry, Jaxon, it must still be very raw and painful to talk about."

"It was, but it's getting a little easier."

"I always think that, in a strange way, it's good that it hurts. It shows how loved your parents were."

Giving her a silent nod in an effort to close down this conversation, because this is not where I want to go to finish off the evening with this woman, I'm thankful Ella picks up on my silence.

"Okay, you get to ask the next question?"

"That guy, Ash, what was his problem tonight?" I ask her, keeping the question as light as possible. Even though I do, I notice the frown she's trying to hide behind her mug.

"He's just a dick."

"A dick that wasn't too happy about seeing me with you tonight." You and he don't have any history together, do you?"

"No, absolutely not. That man is definitely not my type," she almost chokes out the words.

"Oh, yeah? So, what is your type?" I ask, my words low with curiosity, causing her to look up at me with a smile.

"Now, I see what you're doing. This is where you expect me to say a sexy, Aussie fireman, right?"

"Sexy, huh?" I say with a lifted brow, causing her to chuckle.

"Let's just say that I'm not into the dominant, possessive type."

"That's good to know," I say, giving her a wink.

When Ella offers to show me around her house after we finish our coffee, it was a sign to me that she was starting to relax. As we walk through the place, her whole body language becomes more animated and excited as she explains everything she's done in great detail. She just glows with a pride that I can feel oozing from every pore of her skin.

Eventually, we came to a small room at the back of the house that's been stripped bare of everything, right down to the wood.

"This is what I'll be working on tomorrow. I want to make it into a reading room; it has great light in here and captures the afternoon sun perfectly," she says, walking over to stand at the large window that almost takes up a whole wall.

"This place is terrific. You've done a great job."

"Thanks," she says with a smile teasing at her lips.

"So, I'm guessing that I have zero chance of seeing you tomorrow, then?" I ask.

"Not unless you want to help me sand that Cherry wood floor." Her words come out fast before she covers her mouth with her hand, a slight pinkness flushing her cheeks. "I'm sorry, I didn't mean to rope you into free labor. I'm sure you have a much more enjoyable way to spend your Sunday."

Leaning against the wall across from her, and tucking my hands into the front of my jeans, I let out a sigh. "Actually, I was hoping to take you out for a meal tomorrow, so throw lunch in and you have yourself a deal." I grin.

"Oh, definitely. Lunch is included, with beer, too."

"Now, that I can provide," I say. When I notice her look up at the clock on the back wall, I glance down at my watch and see that it's getting late.

"Well, I'd better get going and let you get some sleep."

Ella gives me a nod and I follow her through the house and down the hall to the front door, taking a step outside when she opens it.

"Any particular time tomorrow?"

"No need to be too early. Is ten alright for you?"

"Perfect," I say and we stand there on either side of the opened door, just looking at each other for a moment. Fucked if I know why I feel like an awkward teenager on his first date, having no idea what to do, but that's exactly how I feel. It's an unusual situation for me. In the past, most dates have always finished up with some mutual hot sweaty sex and an amicable breakfast the next morning, but for some reason, with Ella I feel the need to take things slowly and savor every minute of it. So, instead of going in for a goodnight kiss, I reach out and run the back of my fingers lightly down over her cheek before turning and heading for the truck. Once inside, I feel myself break into a smile as I look up and see Ella standing at the door, her hand on her cheek, touching the place I'd just touched, watching as I start the motor and pull away from the curb.

Chapter Seven

Ella

I'm not sure how long I've been standing in the open doorway, but I do know that I watched as the tail lights of his pickup disappeared into the night and then some, holding my palm against my cheek in an effort to keep the warmth and tingle his fingers had left across my skin. Eventually, the sound of a dog barking seems to pull me out of my almost hypnotic state, and I close the front door and lock it. Walking back into the kitchen, I rinse out our mugs and place them in the dishwasher, then head down to my bedroom, flipping off the lights as I go. After changing into a tank and shorts, I slip in between the sheets as Walter jumps up onto the bed and settles next to me. Running my hand over his soft fur, he quickly starts his rhythmic cycle of contented purring as I lay there with the only thoughts running through my mind revolving around Jaxon. For some reason, I had no problem inviting him into my home. I'm not sure if it's because he's Molly's brother, but for some reason I trust him. I hardly know him, but I trust him. He seems to emanate a warmth and honesty that I've never felt in a man before, or seen in someone who radiates a sexuality that any woman could feel from miles away. It also doesn't help that he's definitely candy for the eyes. I eventually fall asleep with the scent of that sexy man still floating through the house and a strong longing to run my fingers over his short beard, just to feel if it's as soft as it looks.

Of all the mornings to sleep in, it had to be today. I'm usually up as soon as the sun rises, but Jaxon is coming today and when I do crack open an eyelid, the small clock on my bedside table is reading that it's just after nine, causing me to jump out of bed with such speed poor Walter is startled awake, hissing at the shock and not looking too happy. "Sorry, Walter," I yell as I turn on the shower and quickly get under the water. Ten minutes later, I am dressed in a pair of shorts and t-shirt, my hair is brushed out and pulled into a pony tail, and in the kitchen I am boiling some water for coffee. Pulling open the refrigerator door, I scan the contents, hoping I have something decent for lunch and breathe out a sigh of relief when I see the left-over lasagna from last night, together with the ingredients for a salad.

Now, I don't normally go big on lunch and I'm definitely not into entertaining people or hosting dinner parties. In fact, I never have any one over to eat besides Leah occasionally, and then it's normally takeout. But I also don't want to thank Jaxon for helping me today by feeding him a tuna sandwich on the crusty old bread sitting in the bread bin on the counter. After burning my tongue while trying to gulp down my coffee and alternately taking bites of a muesli bar, I am still chewing when I hear the rumble of his pick-up outside. I quickly run to the bathroom, spritz myself with a little perfume, and give my lips a little lip gloss just as I hear a knock at the front door. The first thing that hits me when I open the door, is the smiling face of Jaxon as he holds up a six pack of beer, the second thing I get is the scent of soap and fresh rain. He's dressed in jeans and a t-shirt, and his hair is damp. Maybe someone else slept in this morning as well.

"Hi, come in," I say, making way for him. He heads for the kitchen and places the beer in the fridge as Walter runs out with a loud meow and circles Jaxon's legs. Bending, Jaxon gives Walter a scratch to the top of his head.

"And who might you be?" he asks as Walter rubs his head against his hand.

"That's Walter and he's begging for breakfast," I say, taking the cat food from the cupboard and tipping some into his bowl before filling up his water bowl, which causes Walter to run to the food bowl, leaving Jaxon behind.

"Always a way to a man's heart - through his stomach." Jaxon chuckles as he stands back up and I suddenly hope that my reheated lasagna has the same effect on his stomach.

"So, where do we start?" he asks.

"We'll need to sand the floorboards first before we paint." I say, motioning for him to follow me down the hall to the back room, where I have two wood sanders out.

"Sounds like a plan."

Almost three painful hours later, and they were painful hours, not just on the knees and lower back, but on my poor fingertips as well. I kept catching them on the side of the sander because I was too busy watching Jaxon sanding the floor, instead of concentrating on what I was doing.

What can I say? Every time I glanced up, I was met with his thick biceps twitching as they strained against the sleeves of his t-shirt, the veins on his forearms bulging, or his denim-covered ass moving in front of me. I swear, I must have spent every one of those hours looking the same color as a pink flamingo from my embarrassment at my loss of control at eye-fucking him while he worked. I was so relieved when we finished and I had an excuse to go to the kitchen and prepare some lunch while he went to the bathroom to wash up. I was just slipping the lasagna into the oven when he came in, sliding onto a stool at the kitchen bench. "Beer?" I ask.

"Please," he answers with what sounds like a very grateful tone. Pulling two out, I place them on the bench. He takes them, one at a time, flips off the caps, then hands one to me.

"How is your hand doing? This isn't causing you any pain, is it?" I ask, looking down to his bandage.

"No, it's good. Besides, I've been using my other hand. I thought you would have noticed that while you were watching me," he says just as I take a mouth full of beer which I now cough back into the bottle, while more of it dribbles down my chin. Grabbing a towel, I quickly wipe my face, and cough out, "What?" "It's okay to look," he says with a playful grin.

"How do you know I was looking?"

"Because I was doing the same thing, only with a little more subtleness than you," he says nonchalantly, bringing his beer to his lips and taking a mouthful.

"Oh," I say, pretty sure I have enough heat filling my face right now to combust into flames at any minute. I find myself speechless for a moment before recovering with, "What can I say? The view is nice." Turning to the bench behind me, I start to chop up the vegetables for the salad, glad at the silence, although I can definitely feel him staring at me with what I'm pretty sure is a cocky grin spreading across that sexy face of his.

Thankfully, as we eat lunch, the awkwardness from before is lost in a sea of conversation about everything from music and movies, to me asking endless questions about Australia. So many, in fact, my inner monologue is telling me to shut up because I'm embarrassing him.

"Before you leave tonight, I'd like to change that bandage," I tell him as I wipe down the kitchen bench top.

"No need. I'll be in at the hospital tomorrow, so you can do it then."

"Well, besides the fact that it will be pretty dirty by the time we've finished, I won't be in that part of the hospital tomorrow. I'll be out in the community."

"You did say that wasn't your regular area. So, what do you do out in the community?"

"I'm a hospice nurse; palliative care with terminal patients," I say.

"Wow, tough job."

"It can be, but it can also be rewarding as well." "Rewarding?" he asks, looking a little confused.

"I know it sounds strange," I say, very used to this reaction. "And it's a little hard to explain."

"I'd love to hear about it and I still have some beer left," he says, lifting up his half-empty bottle.

"There are two things in life we all have in common, birth and death. Birth is talked about all the time in a wonderful light, but death is never talked about. It's more a taboo subject that people understandably don't want to think about, but it inevitably happens to us all. Most of my patients are elderly, some have families, some don't, and some have families who just want them to hurry up and pass so they can divide up their inheritance." When I look at Jaxon, he's shaking his head with a look of annoyance.

"So, for me to be present and help them pass away in their home environment, surrounded by people or things they love, peacefully and without pain, is an honor and very rewarding for me. I guess that sounds a little weird," I say, looking at him for an understanding of my job. As his eyes search mine, I see what I am looking for.

"No, not at all. Molly and I were with my mum when she passed. It was painful, but also a relief knowing that she wasn't suffering anymore. It was kind of peaceful for me as well, just to know that at the end, the last thing she saw was her children, the people who loved her the most," he said, a faraway look in his eyes as he was sharing the memory.

The rest of the afternoon was spent painting the walls of the room. It took a little longer than it should have, due to the fact that we played noughts and crosses on the walls with the paint before covering them with the pale green colored paint I'd picked up at a bargain price at a yard sale a couple of weeks ago. Now, looking at the finished walls, the color was perfect for the warmth I wanted to bring to this room. By the time we cleaned up, and I changed the now dirty bandage on Jaxon's hand, it was dark outside. When I saw Jaxon look down at his watch, I felt a small pang of guilt as I realized just how much of his day I'd taken up.

"I'm so sorry, I didn't think it would take so long," I say, holding my hands up towards the walls of the finished room.

"Don't worry, it was fun, but I do have to get up early for a really long shift tomorrow," he says, giving me that perfect smile of his.

"At least let me feed you before you go," I say, walking out to the kitchen with him following behind me.

"No, really, I'm good."

"It's no trouble."

"There isn't anything I would like to do more than to spend more time with you, but aside from needing my beauty sleep, I have a feeling if I stay here any longer tonight, I might not be able to leave," he says, taking a step towards me, so close I have to stretch my head back to look up at him.

"Really?" I breathe out.

"Yes, really. Today has been amazing and I would really like to spend some more amazing time with you," he says with a quirk of his eyebrow as he cups the side of my face with his hand.

"I'd like that too," I say as he bends his head towards mine. Our lips are almost touching when I feel his thumb stroke across my bottom lip before his warm lips touch mine in a brief, gentle, soft kiss. Dropping his hand, he straightens, pulling his phone from his back pocket and hands it to me.

"I need your number," he says, and wordlessly I take his phone and type my number into his contacts list before handing it back to him. He takes my hand in his, threading his fingers through mine as we walk to the front door, only disconnecting our hands when he's standing outside.

"I'll call you," he says, giving me a smile and a wink before turning and walking down the pathway to his truck. This time I close the door as he starts the engine, but I listen as he takes off down the street. Leaning my back against the door, I run my fingertips over my lips where his were just a few minutes ago, then run my tongue over my bottom lip where I can still slightly taste his kiss. I close my eyes in an attempt to capture the feeling of it again, and I do. This time, it sends a warmth flooding through my body that seems to make its way to the apex of my thighs, causing a heat that is unfamiliar, yet has so much pleasurable carnality to it that I feel myself blush with embarrassment. Pulling myself away from the door, I make myself a quick sandwich and a glass of milk, and take them to my bedroom and enjoy them while watching some old black and white movie on the TV before having a shower and sinking into the comfort of my bed, Jaxon Cane's sexiness filling my mind yet again as I close my eyes and fall asleep.

Chapter Seven

Jaxon

Opening the side gate, I quietly make my way up the side path and past the pool to the guest house. All the lights are out in the main house and the last thing I want is to wake Molly and Caleb up, knowing they always have early morning shifts as well. Once inside, I strip down and climb into the shower. Letting the hot water run down my back, I place my palms against the tiles and drop my head. Closing my eyes, I savor the image of Ella's face as I placed that soft chaste kiss on those beautiful plump lips of hers that I so wanted to devour. Fuck if it didn't take everything in me to not take more than I did. Images from the day go through my mind. Watching her as she painted the walls, each stroke of the brush making her stretch up and causing her t-shirt to rise, letting a tempting band of skin just above the waistband of her shorts show, or the way she sanded the floor, her ass swaying back and forth, all while she was on her knees, and with that thought I let out a groan of frustration at the pain that is now throbbing through my balls and hard cock. There is no way I am going to be able to get any sleep tonight with this raging erection, so I take things into my own hands and put myself out of my own misery.

Fisting my cock at the base, I stroke it, and like the filthy bastard I feel like right now, I imagine Ella bending down in front of me with her naked ass swaying as she sands the floor, and that's all it takes.

I have no idea how long I lay in bed, remembering the day and how relaxing it was to be with Ella. It was so comfortable and laid back, apart from a few awkward moments, but even those were smoothed over quickly. I knew this woman was special the minute I laid my eyes on her that first day at the hospital. I'd thought that maybe it was just a spark of lust for a pretty girl, maybe it was that whole nurses uniform fantasy thing she had going on. To be honest, I'd kind of expected her to brush me off, unless she was also up for a quick one-night hook up of what I'm sure would have been a hot night of sex. But once we'd had time to get to know each other, I realized pretty quickly that I wanted much more from this smart, funny, beautiful woman.

Because there is way more to Ella Grey than I first thought. After today, that spark of lust has increased a fuck of a lot, and there is so much more I want to discover about her. I also realize that, with this woman, I really need to take my time and do a little bit of old- fashioned dating. Shaking my head at the shock of my own thoughts, I ask into the dark room, "I must be losing my mind - dating?" That word sounds so foreign, and it's something I haven't done since I was a teenager. I think that once I'd chosen a career and become a firefighter, all my energy had always gone into my job, along with its crazy work hours. Although there are a lot of women who are all too enthusiastic about being with a fireman, not many of them actually want to put up with all the shit that comes with it. The long hours aside, there's the stress and danger of the job. So, it's always been a long line of single nights and odd weekends spent with women for me, never anything more serious. For some reason, I have a feeling that shit is all about to change.

When the alarm on my phone wakes me at six am, I tap it to snooze with a groan of frustration, not only at the small amount of sleep I'd managed to get, but at the painful erection which is causing the sheet to tent in front of my eyes, all because of the rampant carnal thoughts I'd had of Ella before I finally fell asleep. Eventually dragging myself out of bed, I pull on a pair of swim shorts and put a pot of coffee on to brew as I grab a towel and head out to the pool. Diving in, the chill of the water is enough to instantly shock my aching cock back into semi-hardness, which is just what I need right now. Before my mind starts to wander into any more indecent thoughts, I push off the wall and glide into some punishing laps of the pool which I get lost in until I hear the sliding glass doors of the main house open. Looking up, I see Molly standing there, wrapped in a black silk robe and holding two mugs in her hands. Swimming over to the steps, I climb out and grab my towel, quickly rubbing myself down, then wrap the towel around my hips, taking the mug

Molly hands to me. "I bet that was cold?" she says, nodding towards the pool. "Colder than expected, but invigorating," I say, taking a sip from the mug.

"I usually wait until later in the day. I can't stand cold water," she says, letting out a shudder at the thought.

"I remember, but I'm on a forty-eight-hour shift, so I won't be here this afternoon."

"That is one long shift."

"It is if you're on with Cooper and Jacob." I grin.

"Oh, you poor thing. Now, I really feel bad for you. So, what about your dressing change? Are you going to come into the hospital this afternoon?" Molly asks and I hold my hand up, showing her a bare hand. "You took it off?"

"I wanted to go for a swim. Besides, Ella took care of it last night, so I'll just put that one back on."

"Ella?" she asks, both eyebrows raising in interest.

"Yes. Ella."

"Wow." Is her only reaction, although I know she's bursting to say more.

"Is that all you have?" I say with a grin.

"Hey, it's not up to me who you date. You're an adult."

"You're right on both accounts, but you still want to say something, don't you?" I tease.

"Maybe," she says, looking away from me. "Go for it."

"I like Ella. I just don't want to see her hurt."

"And you think I'll hurt her?" I ask in an annoyed tone, which my sister picks up on quickly.

"No, of course I don't. She just doesn't seem your type, that's all."

"Not my type? And what is that?" I ask, getting more pissed off with Molly by the minute, and getting close to ending this conversation before I say something I might just regret.

"Well, she's the type to have a quiet life with a husband and a couple of kids playing in the backyard with a dog, and you don't have a good history of sticking with one woman for more than a couple of nights, Jaxon."

"Just because I haven't had a long-term relationship in the past, doesn't mean that's something I don't want in my future," I say. Finishing off my coffee and standing to walk back to my room, Molly places a hand on my forearm, stopping me.

"I'm sorry, that didn't come out the way I wanted it to. I've known for years, Jaxon, that any woman who catches you would be the luckiest woman on earth. Not only do you have all that good looking stuff on the outside, but you have it on the inside as well. You're the full package." "Please." I cringe.

"You are, and I am thinking I need to leave you and your dating life alone. Just be careful, I think Ella might have been hurt in the past, that's all," she says, putting her hands up in surrender.

"Oh, I know there is a lot more to Ella than meets the eye. That's what draws me to her," I say, pointing my finger at Molly, emphasizing my point and hoping that she understands I have no intention of Ella being a quick night of fun between the sheets When she smiles and gives me a nod of understanding, I give her a side hug and kiss the top of her head. "I have to get ready for work."

"Be careful. Come over for dinner when you have time," she says. "Sure thing." I give her a wink and walk into the guest house and straight into a hot shower.

As soon as I get into the station, I head straight upstairs to the bunk room and shove my back pack into a cupboard before going down to the kitchen area where Jacob is sitting at the table on his phone. He looks up when I join him.

"Hey, Jaxon. How's things?" "Good, and you?"

"Couldn't be better, man." He smiles, looking back to his phone where I know he's most likely texting his wife. I've noticed whenever he's talking to Ruby, he's always got that shit-eating grin going on.

"Has Cooper been baking again?" I ask, nodding at the containers of what looks like home-baked goods sitting in the middle of the table. "No, I haven't," Cooper yells out from the kitchen as he walks out, wiping his hands on a towel.

"It's all from Mrs. Dawson across the road, here. Lovely woman is always baking and bringing pies and slices across. Bless that woman," he says, rubbing a hand over his stomach.

"So, who's on shift tonight?" I ask Jacob.

"You, me, Cooper and Davis, the others are on call."

Nodding, I reach into one of the containers and pull out a brownie. Taking a bite, I just can't stop a moan from coming out around the chewy, chocolaty slice.

"I told you, she's a blessing." Cooper smiles.

"That's an understatement," I say, devouring the rest of it in one mouthful before I continue. "Fingers crossed, it's a quiet night tonight so I can finish those off," I say, pointing to the box of brownies.

"Fuck off, Cane," Jacob growls without even looking up from his phone, which tells me there is definitely going to be a fight over those brownies tonight.

"Hopefully, the only fires we'll be called out to tonight, will be from the meeting over at the community hall," Bowman scoffs.

"Why, what's going on over there?" I ask him.

"It's where they do all the planning for the yearly fundraiser. Durandale has one every year, and this year it's to raise funds for the local school. They need a new gym. When they first start meeting up at the beginning of the year, it's all flowers and rainbows, but the closer it gets to the event, the more arguing they do." He chuckles.

"So, what's the event this year?"

"Well, this year, big Al, who runs the butchers in town, has a friend who owns some fairground equipment, so next month the fair will be coming to town."

"Let's just hope the rides are safe and well maintained," Jacob grumbles under his breath.

"That's why we're going to check them over first," Cooper says, slapping Jacob's shoulder. "You're just pissed because it'll make more money than the calendar." "Calendar?" I ask.

"Shut the fuck up," Jacob growls, looking up and throwing daggers at Cooper, which only causes Cooper to chuckle before he continues.

"A few years back, the fundraiser was a sexy fireman calendar, and Jacob here, well, let's just say, he was the star." "Cooper," Jacob growls out a warning.

"What? Nothing to be ashamed of, man; it raised a lot of money." "So, you were a centerfold, then?" I say, smiling and pointing at Jacob, who actually starts to look a little uncomfortable. "Fuck, don't you start," he groans.

"Hey, no judgment here. What red-blooded male wouldn't like to know he's in some woman's fantasy?" I grin.

"I'm done," Jacob says, standing up and heading into the lounge area, flipping on the TV and surfing the channels until he settles on the sports channel, leaving me and Cooper chuckling at his fast exit.

The night turned out to be a quiet one, thankfully, until the station alarm blared through the place just after four am, calling us to an out-of-control grass fire down on South Street. It was a good distance from any homes and was quickly under control, and most likely caused by a careless driver discarding a cigarette out of a car window. On our return, Cooper cooked us up some breakfast, which was amazing as usual. I swear, he should ditch the fireman thing and open a restaurant. He cooks like a beast. Just as I wipe up the last bit of egg on my plate, my phone pings with a text. Swiping the screen, I smile when I see it's from Ella.

ELLA

Just wanted to thank you again for your help, the room looks great.

ME

Anytime, how is your day?

ELLA

Just starting, but I can see it's going to be a busy week. You?

ME

Quiet at the moment, let me know if you need my help again.

ELLA

Sure will, have a good day.

ME

You too.

"Someone special?" Jacob asks, nodding to my phone.

"Huh?" I say, looking up at him questioningly until I realize he's talking about my texts. "What makes you think it's a woman?" I grin. "Because the only time a text puts that kind of smile on a man's face is when it's from someone special," he says with a shit-eating grin spreading across his mouth. "Could be," I tease.

"Someone I know?"

"Maybe."

"Are you going to give me a name?"

"Not sure."

"You do know that I know just about everyone who lives in or near Durandale, right? It wouldn't take me long to find out."

"She's a nurse at the hospital - Ella."

"I know Ella, she's a good woman. Too good for you," he grins. "Fuck off," I say, throwing my used napkin at him, which he dodges.

"No, really? Ella?"

"I helped her out painting a room at her house." "And?"

"And I plan to get to know her better," I say as nonchalantly as possible.

"I know she moved here about eight years ago. She likes to keep to herself mostly, you know, she's not one of those in-your-face party girls. Your sister probably knows more."

"I know, but I think I'm going to enjoy getting to know her my own way," I say and he nods his head.

"That is the only way, man."

By the end of the week, I am ready for a weekend break. The week that had started on a quiet note had just snowballed into crazy. Collins and Ethan called in sick with the flu, which would have left the station short staffed, so I ended up spending the whole week at the station. Thankfully, the guys were feeling better by the end of the week, which means I get the weekend to myself, and Ella, if I'm lucky.

My week was definitely made more enjoyable by the random texts she sent. For me, this was a relief because when she didn't answer the first text I sent her until around five hours later I'd thought she might have been ghosting me already. Once she'd answered, letting me know that while she's with a patient in palliative care her phone is on silent, I felt like smacking myself in the back of my head for acting like a lovesick teenager waiting for her response. I did try to subtly drop hints about meeting up again on the weekend, but she couldn't give me a clear answer as she was unsure of her schedule until Friday. So, when Jacob invited me and Caleb to meet up with him and his brothers on Friday night for a beer, I was so ready.

Chapter Nine

Ella

Walking into the hospital this morning, I had tired eyes and weary limbs from all that floor sanding yesterday which had really stretched out some muscles I didn't even know existed. Even after taking a hot shower last night, I had still lain awake for most of it, just remembering the taste of Jaxon's kiss. Just that small, light brushing of his lips across mine was enough to set every nerve in my body into a lustful spark of longing I haven't felt for such a long time. As I lay in bed last night, I'd found myself starting to dissect Jaxon Cane's obvious interest, which I quickly stopped because for the first time I didn't want to analyze a man's intentions; I just want to free fall into everything he has to offer me. I'd felt an instant trust in him, and I'm not sure if it's a combination of my sexual desire and excited libido that's talking and drowning out my always logical and guarded voice, or if I'm actually choosing to take a chance for once. Either way, it feels, good.

As soon as I pull the folder from my little pigeon hole, I leave my thoughts of Jaxon behind and take a seat at a desk in the nurse's station, opening the folder of the patient who has been assigned to me and start to read.

Jean Garner an 83-year-old female who's been battling cancer for at least the last five years, was brought into the hospital five days ago with an increase in pain as the cancer which started in her kidneys had now spread through her body like a wildfire. She has been diagnosed as terminal and is now in palliative care with a prognosis of deterioration over the next week. Picking up the file and a pad of paper, I make my way down the hall to room six where I find a frail, grey-haired woman laying in the hospital bed and another woman with a head full of tight grey curls sitting on a chair next to the bed, holding the other woman's delicate hand in her own. When I enter the room, I notice that Jean has been hooked up to a drip of fluid, which I know will also contain a concoction of pain relief medication to help with her pain. The woman sitting next to the bed looks up and stands when I move closer to the bed.

"I'm Ella Grey, the palliative care nurse who'll be looking after Jean," I say, holding my hand out to the woman, which she slips her own frail, but warm, hand into.

"I'm Maya, Jean's other half," she says, giving me a weak smile. "Shall we grab a coffee and find somewhere to talk while Jean is sleeping?" I ask. She gives me a nod before taking another look at the sleeping woman in the bed, then follows me out into the hall and down to the empty family room, where I make her a coffee and we sit down at a small table.

"I know this is hard, but I will be here to make things a little easier for you and Jean. So, if you have any questions, I'm here to help, okay?" I say, opening up the file and placing the pad on top of it as Maya slowly nods her head.

"Have the doctors explained everything to you?"

"Yes, they did, but we've known it's been coming for a while now," she says, giving me a wistful half-smile.

"So, you and Jean have talked about what she'd like to happen." "Yes, and this place is far from it."

"The hospital?" I ask her and she nods, taking a sip of coffee. "We were hoping it would take her in her sleep, in her own bed." "We can do that," I tell her, writing down some notes on my pad. "Really?"

"Yes, I can arrange for Jean to be transferred home today."

"I thought...I didn't..." she sputters out in shock and slight confusion.

"That's what I'm here to help with, Maya," I say, taking her hands in mine and giving them a gentle squeeze, letting her know that she isn't on her own.

"But what about her care and medication? I don't want her to be in any pain."

"I'll be there with you both to help with all of that. The most important thing is that Jean will be where she wants to be, at home with you."

"Thank you so much. I don't know what to say," she says, looking at me with wide, watery, hazel eyes.

"It's my honor, Maya. Now, let's go arrange for Jean to go home." The rest of the day was all about paperwork, talking to Jean's doctors, seeing the pharmacist, and even though it was a crazy scramble and took most of the day to organize, it was worth every second just to see the look on Maya's face as she sits on the bed smiling down at Jean, gently chatting to her while brushing out her long hair then carefully braiding it into one long plait. Jean looks comfortable and peaceful now in her own bed, not hooked up to drips and loud machines that beep incessantly. Now she's in a quiet and loving environment that has the smell of freshly washed laundry and just-baked cookies, instead of the antiseptic, disinfectant smell of the hospital. That, together with the warmth and love from Maya, leaves me in no doubt that Jean is already in a much better place.

That's how my week started, and apart from going home to feed Walter and give him some loving, I spent most of my time with Jean and Maya. Normally, I go home for meals and sleep breaks, but this time I chose to stay with Maya, especially after she convinced me how much it would mean to her if I let her cook me dinner. With the house smelling of the freshly baked chicken pot pie which melted in my mouth, I can only say that I'm sure my scales are not going to be very happy with me this week.

Our nights were spent with Maya holding Jean's hand and stroking her delicate paper-thin skin with soft strokes, talking to her about their lives together, straightening the blankets on the bed, and showing me photo albums full of the history of their life. I noticed a change in Jean's breathing pattern late Wednesday night, and I sensed that Maya did as well by the change in her demeanor; not because she was showing any signs of anxiety, but because she became calm, content, and excepting. Making her a cup of tea, I take it to her and sit next to her at Jean's bedside.

"Sixty years, we've had together," she speaks in a low voice.

"That is so wonderful."

"They weren't easy years. We met just before the 1960's, in a time that unfortunately wasn't very accepting. Even though we were shunned by our families, our community, and even total strangers, we knew our love was bigger and stronger than anything society could throw at us." Maya took a sip of her tea and paused for a moment before she continued.

"Even in the late sixties, the era of free love, we were still shunned. I mean, it was alright to sleep with anyone, or as many people as you wanted, as long as they were of the opposite sex. So, we left everything behind and moved here, Durandale was pretty small, but everyone just thought we were a pair of spinsters and that's the way we liked it. Because, inside the walls of this house, we were free to show our love for each other without fear or judgment, we made this house our little slice of heaven."

"I'm sorry you had to live through that," I say, genuinely feeling her pain.

"I guess it was all worth it in the end. I got to spend sixty years with someone I loved unconditionally." Maya finished off her cup of tea in silence then, putting the cup aside, she took Jean's hand in hers again, bringing it to her lips and placing a kiss on it. "We'll always be together, my love. I know we'll be together again soon, but I need you to let go now. I need you to let go of the pain and find your peace, my darling," she says, placing gentle kisses over her fingers. "If only you could pass in my arms," I hear her whisper.

"Is that what you want?" I ask her.

"More than anything," she says, her eyes now swollen with tears.

And so, while Maya got ready for bed, I made some adjustments to the bed Jean and Maya had shared for sixty years. Maya had chosen not to get into that bed since we'd brought Jean home as she feared she would somehow cause Jean discomfort or pain. But tonight, Maya knew it would be their last night together. When she came out of the bath-room in her nightgown and slipped in and under the covers, I helped her place her arms around Jean. With Jean's head now laying on Maya's shoulder, they looked beautiful and I left the room, with Maya placing kisses to the top of Jean's head as she quietly sang 'You are my sunshine' to her.

Later, the next morning, when I got home, I fed Walter then slipped into the steaming-hot water of my bath, exhausted. Jean had passed away peacefully, wrapped in the arms of her loving wife, in the early hours of the morning. After doing the necessary paperwork, and calling the funeral director, Maya insisted on cooking me a hearty breakfast before I went home. Over pancakes with melted butter and warm syrup, she thanked me for helping Jean pass away painlessly and at home.

"You are truly an angel," she said, reaching across the table and placing her hand on top of mine.

"Thank you, but I'm just a nurse."

"There is nothing 'just' about what you did for Jean, and for me, I can assure you. I will be forever grateful for that memory."

"You have my phone number and you can call me anytime you want to share a cup of tea and a chat. And you can always call me to come pick up one of your delicious pies, if you cook too many," I said with a smile and a wink.

"You have yourself a deal."

"Now, let me help you with these dishes before I leave," I said, getting up from the table and picking up the breakfast dishes.

Now, leaning back in my deep bath with my eyes closed, I can feel my body start to relax, piece by piece, each tight muscle, from my toes to the top of my head, as I breathe out the physical and emotional stress of the last few days. Although hard, it always leaves me with an added sense of deep calmness and serenity.

Relaxed and languid from my bath, as soon as I pull down the blinds in the bedroom and slip into bed, I pick up my phone to put it onto silent mode, when I notice a text from Jaxon waiting in my inbox.

JAXON

Hey, I know your week has been busy, but I would really like to see you again.

Reading his words with a slight feeling of butterflies in the pit of my stomach, I realize that it didn't matter how much I needed to keep my life simple and uncomplicated like it has been for the last several years, I really wanted to get to know this man who, with one kiss, had knocked my need for seclusion and solitude off its axis. All I want to do is open myself up to him and take that chance. The fluttering in my belly right now, is enough to tell me that there is something there that's just too big to be ignored.

ME
Dinner tomorrow my place around 7pm?

As soon as I send the text, the little grey bubbles appear on my screen.

JAXON
See you at 7.

Chapter Ten

Jaxon

All I've been able to think about all week is Ella, which means I've also had to adjust my aching dick a lot as well. I know her week has been just as busy as mine, and we did manage to throw a few text messages at each other through the week, but they were few and far between. I know she'd explained to me that she was with a palliative care patient, and I fully understood, but I didn't have to like it. When she invited me over for dinner tonight, I'd agreed on the spot, but had texted her again earlier this morning letting her know that I'd bring dinner over so there was no need for her to cook. If her week had been as bad as I think it had, then takeaway in front of a movie beats out her having to cook. Nope, tonight I want her to relax.

Grabbing my phone and wallet, and pushing them into the pockets of my jeans, I pick up my keys and head for the door just as there's a knock on it. Opening it, I find Molly standing there.

"Hey," I greet her with a smile, but notice that the smile she gives me in return is not as big as normal. In fact, she looks nervous.

"Oh, are you going out?" "Yeah. Going over to see Ella."

"Another date? Getting serious now?" She grins at me, but still not enough to hide that she's clearly hiding something.

"Is everything alright?"

"Yeah. I wanted to talk to you, but it's okay; it can wait," she says, turning, and I follow her, closing the door.

"Hey, I always have time for you. What's going on?" I ask, a little worried about her behavior. When she turns to face me, looking a little flustered, I know there is something going on. "Molly?"

"Everything is fine. No need to worry."

"Then, what is it?"

"Just come inside for a few minutes, okay?"

"Sure," I say, following her around the pool and through the sliding glass doors to her kitchen, where Caleb is sitting at the kitchen table scrolling through his phone, which he instantly puts down and looks at me with the same strange look that Molly has. Now, I really want to know what's going on. Standing, Caleb stands next to Molly, placing his arm around her waist.

"What is it? Is there something wrong?" I ask, a little disturbed by their behavior.

"Calm down, Jaxon. Everything is fine. We just wanted you to be the first to know that I'm pregnant," Molly says, looking up at Caleb like a love-struck puppy. I let out the huge breath that I'd been painfully holding in at the thought of something being wrong with Molly.

"Holy fuck, Molly, what are you trying to do to me? I almost had a heart attack," I say, frantically scrubbing my hands through my hair.

"I'm sorry," she laughs.

"So, your pregnant?" I ask, making sure I heard exactly what she'd said.

"Yes."

"So, I'm going to be an uncle?" I say, a smile slowly starting to spread across my mouth at the thought of Molly being a mum. My little sister is having a baby. "That is fucking awesome. Congratulations," I say, stepping forward and shaking a proud looking Caleb's hand before taking Molly into my arms. "I am so happy for you both."

"Thank you," Molly says with a slight emotional crack in her voice. Pulling her into my arms again, I whisper against her ear, "She will be with you all the way." I needed to give her something because I know, at this moment, she will be thinking about our mum not being here to see her first grandchild. She gives me a slight nod in understanding of my words, then squeezes me a little tighter before releasing her arms and stepping back to wipe away the tears that are forming in her eyes. "Go, you don't want to be late for your date." She smiles at me, and with a smile, I turn and head for my truck.

It didn't take me long to pick up a pizza and a six pack, and then I was standing at her front door in anticipation of seeing her again. When the door opens, and I'm welcomed by her beautiful smile and her casual look of yoga pants and a long sweat-shirt, I can't help but smile at the simplicity of her presence. Walking in, I place the pizza and beer on the kitchen table, then turn to do something I hadn't planned. Sliding my hands around her waist, I pull her body into mine, her curves molding against me, and when she looks up at me with those incredible eyes that show a little shock at my actions, I lean down and take her lips with mine. They are exactly how I've been imagining them to be all week - soft, warm, and so fucking tasty. She opens for me, allowing our tongues to gently explore each other, and I feel her arms slide up and around my neck, the action letting her press into me harder. The feeling of static crackling between us ignites, our kiss deepening. She tastes like mint and honey, so sweet and fresh, and when that pleasure starts to trickle through my body, I know I need to stop before I take her right now, right here in her kitchen. If there's one thing that I don't want with Ella, it's a quick fuck. No, I want to savor everything she wants to give me. So, making a very painful and reluctant decision, I slowly bring the kiss to a slow end, bringing my hands up to her face and letting my thumbs caress her cheeks.

"I brought pizza," I breathe out as I search her eyes for an understanding that I am really trying to restrain myself here. When her eyes crinkle at the sides and she smiles, I know, without any spoken words, that she gets why I needed that stolen kiss.

"Me too," she whispers then moves into the kitchen, pulling out a couple of plates and napkins, then nodding to the pizza and beer. With a lift of her chin towards the living room, I scoop them up and follow her. We sit on the couch as she opens the pizza and we each take out a slice, followed by huge bites and groans in unison at the warm melted cheese. As we devour the pizza, we make aimless chatter about our weeks between mouthfuls. My week was mostly busy because of the guys who'd called in sick, but when Ella starts telling me about her week, being careful not to go into too much detail in what I know is a practiced way of protecting her patient's confidentiality, which I respect, I suddenly see just how tired she really is. Flipping the caps on two beers, I hand her one, then lean back and take a long pull from my bottle.

"I don't know how you do it," I say.

"Sometimes, I wonder that myself, but once I get over the exhaustion and have some quiet time to relax and reflect, I feel so much better," she says, bringing the beer to her mouth and taking a sip.

"Now I see how tired you are, I'm sorry if I pushed to see you tonight. I just needed to," I say, turning to look at her.

"No, I'm glad you did. I needed it, too."

"I did get some good news tonight before I left home." I grin.

"You did?"

"Yep. I'm going to be an uncle," I say, my grin now spreading into a proud smile, so big it makes my cheeks hurt.

"Molly's pregnant?" she gasps.

"Yes, but you didn't hear it from me, right?" "That's great news. I'm so happy for her," she says.

"So, what about your family? Do you see them much?" I ask, then regret it as I see Ella's smile fade as she leans forward, placing her beer on the coffee table and pulling her legs under her as she seems to sink deeper into the couch.

"No, not for a long time"

"Is this a hard subject?" I ask, now curious at her reaction at the mention of her family, but still not wanting her to talk about something that's obviously uncomfortable.

"A little. Let's just say I walked away years ago and it was the best thing I ever did."

Putting my own beer down on the table, I move closer to her and pull her onto my lap. It takes only seconds for her rigid posture to relax as she sinks into my arms and I stroke a hand up and down her back. "Message received...subject closed," I breathe softly into her hair, as her fingers draw tiny circles on my chest. It feels like tiny prickles of static electricity against my skin and I am content to stay like this for the night and hope that my dick can behave, as long as Ella doesn't move around too much in this position, I might have a chance.

Sitting here on her couch, with her cradled in my arms and our breathing the only sound in the air, she tilts her head up, her beautiful eyes searching mine, her pupils dilating as I watch them. Moving a hand up to the back her neck, I hold her there as I press my lips against hers. With that first touch, the parting of her soft lips, the warmth of her tongue as it sweeps out to taste my own, and that low groan deep in her throat, I am lost in a hunger for this woman. Moving my hand around to the front of her throat, I gently stroke the soft skin there, letting my fingers slide down and across her collar bone, enjoying the feeling of her smooth, silky skin. The ferocity of the kiss turns into small nips and bites to her bottom lip, which she returns with a starving hunger of her own. When she turns in my arms so she is straddling me with her hands running through the back of my hair, all I can do is enjoy the friction of her sex as it rubs against my hard cock, which is straining against the material of my jeans in a painful but very pleasurable way. All I want to do is sink into her with no barriers between us at all. Gripping her hips, I pull her down harder onto my throbbing shaft. If she's intending to dry hump me, then I want to feel her wetness seep through onto my jeans. The once-silent room is now filled with the panting breaths of lust and moans as we become lost in each other, until I feel a large, warm, hairy body plop onto the back of my neck. With a smack of our lips as they break apart, Ella begins to chuckle as she grabs her cat, Walter, and places him down on the floor behind her.

"I guess he wants his dinner." She looks at me with heat and lust-filled eyes.

"Great timing," I say, reaching up and moving a long lock of her hair away from her face.

"Maybe it was a good thing," she says, looking at me with a slight grimace. When I give her a puzzled look, she continues, "I got a little carried away and I don't think I'm ready for..." Her words trail off as she motions with her hand between us.

"It's okay."

"Really?"

"Absolutely," I tell her and I mean it. I will wait until she is ready, even if my dick is going to hate me for it. The last thing I want is for her to feel uncomfortable. After a moment of slightly awkward silence, Ella stands and picks up the remote, handing it to me.

"Why don't you find a movie while I feed Walter and make some popcorn," she says, picking up the cat that just fucked up my night and taking him into the kitchen.

What started out as us both sitting, watching a movie while munching on popcorn and laughing at the stupidity of the movie that turned out to be a B grade drama, ended in her turning the volume down while we gave the actors on screen our own voices, with our own dialogue, which improved the movie tenfold. Ella picked the next movie, a survival story set in the snow of Alaska, and I'm not sure if it was the dimmed lights in the room or the glow of the TV, but we both ended up laying stretched out on the couch. With Ella's back to my front and my arm draped over her waist, I feel myself settle into a warm and blissful place, where all I can do is pull her body closer into mine, close my eyes, and inhale the scent of fresh green apples that permeates her hair.

Slowly opening my eyes, they are assaulted by bright sunlight shining through a small gap in the curtains that cover the large window. Lifting my arm up to cover my eyes, I feel the brush of a soft blanket dropping away. Waking up more, I realize that I am still laying on Ella's couch and the spot next to me where she was before falling asleep, is now very empty. Closing my eyes again, I silently kick myself for unintentionally spending the night after she told me that she wasn't ready, even though her body was telling me something completely different. Her mind is telling her something that I sense is deeper than she's willing to share with me. With that thought comes an indescribable feeling of instant protectiveness for this woman, and the need to find out what is going on in that beautiful head of hers. The sound of movement coming from the kitchen causes me to get up from the couch and stretch out the muscles in my back. Making my way toward the kitchen, the smell of bacon frying assaults my nostrils, causing my mouth to water instantly. As I turn into the kitchen, there she is, her back towards me, her head slightly bent as she concentrates on the frying pan on the stove in front of her.

"Something smells good," I say and notice how she jumps at the sound of my voice then turns around to face me with that beautiful smile of hers.

"Good morning," she says, pouring some coffee into a mug and sliding it across the kitchen bench towards me. "Are you hungry?"

"Starving," I say, looking at her and trying not to show that the huger I'm feeling is not just for food.

"Yeah, about that, I'm sorry about last night, I got a little carried away," she says, looking away and back to the pan full of bacon and eggs.

"Don't ever be sorry for stopping something that you're not ready for, Ella."

"I know, but I was, if Walter hadn't cock-blocked you." She grins. "Honestly, I'm happy for Walter's interruption, because the last thing I want is for you to feel uncomfortable. The ball is in your court, so you just let me know when you're ready," I say with a waggle of my brows causing her to laugh. "Besides, at least I'm half way there now."

"Really? How is that?" she says, leaning one hip against the kitchen bench.

"I did spend the night and you're making me breakfast, right, so I'll take that as a win."

"Smartass," she says, turning back to the stove, serving up two plates and placing them on the bench before fishing cutlery out of a drawer and handing me some, then pulling herself up onto a stool beside me.

"So, what are your plans for today? Any more painting to do?" I ask before shoving a forkful of food into my mouth.

"Not today. I have a feeling it's going to be too hot to do anything today, other than relax and stay cool."

"You could always come over to my place and we could spend the day cooling off in the pool," I say. When she doesn't answer straight away, and I can see her clearly thinking about my invitation, I continue with, "Molly and Caleb are out for the day, visiting some relative of his," I try, thinking that she might feel uncomfortable about being at Molly's house, and bingo, I was right.

As soon as I share that little piece of information, she smiles and says, "That sounds perfect."

By the time we get to Molly's house, they have already left. Taking

Ella by the hand, I lead her to the side gate and into the back yard, following the path until we reach my place. Opening the door, I stretch out my arm for her to enter and say, "Welcome to my little abode."

As Ella steps in, I hear a small gasp as she looks around. Stepping deeper into the living room, she places her bag on the couch, turning around to look at every room, which you can do from the living room.

"This is amazing. Did you say Molly and Caleb did all this?" "Yeah. Molly said it was already a guest house, but they gutted it and made it into a small apartment with all the mod cons."

"They did a great job."

"They sure did. Now, the bathroom is in there, if you want to change," I say, pointing towards the bathroom door. I watch as Ella picks up her bag and takes it into the bathroom while I go into the bedroom. I change into a pair of shorts then head out to the pool, grabbing a couple of towels on the way. Once outside, I lay the towels on a sun lounge and dive into the pool, the water cooling my skin instantly. Coming up on the other side, I start to leisurely do some laps while waiting for Ella. When I get to the other end of the pool, a flash of red catches my eye and I stop. Standing, I run a hand over my face to get rid of the water there, my eyes focusing on her. Fuck me, what I see through my waterlogged eyes right now is absolute perfection. She has curves in all the right places, which are hugged by the dark red, one-piece swimsuit, with the elegance of a model. All I can do is watch as she pulls her long dark waves into a pony tail and walks to the edge of the pool, before sitting down and effortlessly sliding into the water. As she moves through the water towards me, I find myself moving towards her, our eyes fixed on each other's until our bodies connect in the middle of the pool. I instinctively reach out and slide my arms around her waist, drawing her into my body with a perfect fit, her skin against mine feels warm and supple, even through the cool water. "Hey," I say, looking down into her beautiful eyes.

"Hey," she replies as she moves her hands up over my naked chest, letting her fingers slide over the grooves of my muscles.

"The water feels nice."

"You feel better," I groan.

"You feel pretty good yourself." She grins at me.

"If you keep touching me like that, I feel the need to apologize in advance."

"What for?" She looks up at me, looking puzzled.

"For the actions of my dick, because I can assure you it's going to have a hard time behaving itself today." I grin at her and she gives me a playful slap on my chest. Her beautiful laughter filling our enclosed private slice of paradise sets the perfect atmosphere for the day. A day filled with flirty water play and lots of opportunities for me to hold and feel her as much as I want, and I intend to get my fill. From playing in the pool, to lazing together on a sun lounge, to watching her forage through my refrigerator until she'd gathered enough ingredients to cook us a meal of stir-fried chicken. As I had the pleasure of sitting and watching her every move as she almost danced around my kitchen in that sexy as fuck red swimsuit, I was sure I was one lucky man today. When it got late, I drove her home and left her at her front door with only a small brush of my mouth across hers because, honestly, after the cock-hardening day I'd endured today, I don't think I could have trusted myself to stop at just one kiss from those succulent lips of hers.

Chapter Eleven

Ella

The next day at work was busy and considering the hard time I'd had pulling myself out of bed this morning only made the day drag more. All the time spent in the pool with Jaxon had turned out to be a great source of exhausting exercise because this morning, when my alarm went off at the crack of dawn, I really wanted to call in sick. It wasn't until mid-afternoon that I actually bumped into Leah and we arranged to meet up after work. Once we were seated at a table in the corner at Lilies coffee bar, with a coffee and banana muffin each, Leah began her inquisition about my weekend.

"So, you spent the whole weekend with him?" she asks, looking a little shocked.

"Yeah. Well, Friday he brought over pizza and ended up staying the night, and Saturday was too hot to do any work on the house, so we spent it at his place," I say, taking a bite from my muffin.

"Hold on, he stayed over?" "Yep."

"Like in sleep over, the whole night?" she asks.

"Yep, I even cooked him breakfast in the morning," I say, trying to hold back the grin which is trying to burst through my lips at the thought of how hard her dirty mind is working overtime right now, yet enjoying teasing her.

"Holy shit, Ella. I can't believe you actually banged the guy."

"I didn't say anything about banging him," I answer, continuing to devour the rest of my muffin.

"Wait, what?" she sputters out, eyes now wide in disbelief. "I didn't say I banged him, I said he spent the night."

"Now I'm confused," she says with a shake of her head, looking even more confused, and I know it's time to end her suffering.

"Like I said, he brought over a pizza and some beer. We watched movies and fell asleep on the couch."

"That's all?"

"Yep."

"No sex? No nothing?"

"Well, we did make out a little."

"What the fuck? Make out? What are you, in high school? You have this amazingly hot man in your house, and you don't think of fucking his brains out?" The incredulous look she has on her face at my words is beyond funny right now.

Holding my hand up to stop her, I say, "Now, I never said anything about not wanting to fuck his brains out. I just want to get to know him better, that's all."

"Okay," she drags out the word. "And how has that worked out for you?" "Not too well, because even though my brain is telling me to take it slow and get to know him before jumping in the sack with him, my body wants a lot more." I sigh.

"Then just go for it, Ella. Enjoy it for what it is - some incredible, hot sex with a sexy Aussie fireman. What do you have to lose?"

"Nothing, everything, who knows?" I shrug and feel her soften as she reaches across the table, placing a hand on top of mine.

"Look, I know something must have happened in your life to make you build this security fence around yourself. Even though we've been friends for years now, you still won't share anything about your past with me."

In her voice, I hear a small amount of sadness from her wanting me to share with her, and it makes me feel like a second-rate, terrible friend right now. I mean, I know friends are there to confide in, but when I moved here all those years ago, I left everything behind, and that included sharing with anyone. Looking at her now, I feel like the scum on the bottom of a pond, because I know she just wants to help. I try to relay to her, with my softened tone and reassuring smile, that I'm sorry and I appreciate her friendship and understanding, when I say, "Leah." But she quickly holds up her hand to stop me.

"No, let me finish, okay?" she asks and I give her a nod. "I don't need to know what happened, but I do know that something happened. You know, if you ever feel the need for a shoulder to lean on, it's always here," she says, patting the top of her shoulder. "But whatever did happen, please don't let it spoil your enjoyment of life. You need to live, Ella. Take chances, otherwise whatever shit thing happened to you has won. You're stronger than it, you've already proven that to yourself. Now, it's time to live for yourself." Her touching words bring tears to my eyes, because I've always known she's been there for me, but in this moment, I realize just how much.

"You're right."

"What's new? I'm always right. Haven't I been telling you that for years?" She chuckles, and the seriousness and tension of our conversation is instantly broken and I feel a little lighter. "Now, how heavy was the petting?" She grins at me.

"Well, if you take into consideration dry humping his leg until I almost came? Pretty heavy." I grin back at her.

"You dirty girl."

"I felt dirty. I couldn't help myself. He's so gentle and caring, it feels so right when I'm around him." "Not to mention, he's hot," she says, taking a bite of her own muffin now and looking just as relaxed as I feel.

Over the next couple of weeks, I found myself falling deeper under the spell of Jaxon Cane. Even though we both had crazy work hours going on, we still managed to spend our weekends together. This consisted of anything from going for a simple walk in the local park, to sharing a meal and a movie. It seems as though we don't feel the need to do anything other than enjoy each other's company. Everything about him is so warm and comforting, it's almost like he's in a permanent relaxed mood. I'm sure if he'd just pulled a forty-eight-hour shift at the station with a minimal amount of sleep, he'd still be relaxed and fun to be around, and completely different than what I'd imagined him to be like when I first saw him at the hospital that day when he injured his hand. With his smoldering looks and wicked grin, I thought he was just another cocky, sexy fireman, who thought his uniform would get him any woman he wanted. Yet, he's the complete opposite.

That small flutter of excitement I used to feel in my belly when we first met, has now grown into a kaleidoscope of butterflies frantically beating their wings in what feels like every part of my body whenever I see his beautiful smiling face. That smile which causes small creases to form at the corner of his eyes as soon as I open the door to him. He makes me feel things I haven't allowed myself to feel for so long; things that, until he came into my life and awakened them, I'd forgotten ever existed.

"So, will I be seeing you at the fair tomorrow?" Leah asks, breaking into my thoughts.

"You sure will. I can't wait to see how much money is raised."

"Me too. Plus, I get to eat all the cotton candy I can stomach." She chuckles as she pops the last bite of muffin into her mouth and finishes off the rest of her coffee.

Once home and showered, I make myself a mug of hot soup and curl up on the couch. This is just one of those nights when all I want to do is relax with something simple for dinner. Flipping through the channels looking for something to watch, I find my favorite home decorating channel and sigh out in bliss as I lean back into the comfort of the cushions and sip from my mug. After locking up and getting into bed, I had just turned off the lamp when my phone beeps. Looking down, I see a message from Jaxon.

JAXON

Hey beautiful, can't wait to see you tomorrow. What time do you want to leave?

ME

That depends.

JAXON

On?

ME

What time your shift finishes.

JAXON

About 9 in the morning.

ME

Then I'll see you in the afternoon, you need some sleep.

JAXON

No need for sleep when I'm coming to see you.

ME

You say the sweetest things.

JAXON

Only to you.

ME

I would feel better if you get some sleep first.

JAXON

I would get a much better sleep in your bed lol. ME: Nice try, see you tomorrow AFTERNOON.

JAXON

OKAY. Sweet dreams.

ME

You too, be safe xx

Placing my phone on the bedside table, I snuggle up under the covers just as Walter jumps up onto the bed and takes up his favorite position on the pillow next to mine, turning around several times until he finds a comfortable position, then curling up with a soft purr of satisfaction which lulls me to sleep.

Chapter Twelve

Jaxon

After ending my messages with Ella, I can't seem to wipe the smile from my mouth. Something which Jacob notices then makes kissing and moaning noises from the other side of the lounge area. Ignoring him, I give him nothing, no reaction, because if there's one thing I've learnt about Jacob Miller, it's that if you give him an inch, he will take a mile, and once he starts stirring the pot he just can't stop. He's a funny guy under all of that tough exterior. I can't wait to see Ella tomorrow. I know we've swapped text messages and talked throughout the week, but it's not the same as having her close to me so I can look at her beauty, feel her warm skin, and taste her delicious mouth. Believe me, these are things I've been thinking about constantly this week. So much so, I'm pretty sure I'm getting a serious case of chaffing in the groin area, because every time I leave her for the evening, my balls are definitely blue and I'm painfully hard. She's on my mind twenty-four hours a day, every day until I see her and it is driving me to the edge of destruction. It has nothing to do with her hesitation about sex either, because I respect her for that, I love that she's been honest with me about being unsure and just not ready. On the other hand, I'm also a little worried that the feelings behind her hesitation are from something more sinister which happened in her past. I have to admit that this thought has unfortunately crossed my mind lately due to her reluctance to talk about anything to do with it or her family.

I'm not sure what happened, but I have a strong feeling it must be something pretty painful if she has it so deeply hidden that even the people around her, some who've known her for years, have never noticed. Fuck, it didn't take me long to work out that something was going on with Ella. Yes, maybe that has to do with the fact that we're on a more intimate level with each other, but still, I'm no therapist. And this is how my week has been, moving between carnal thoughts of Ella and trying to work out her deepest secrets, when maybe I need to just enjoy what we have and hope she learns to trust me enough to let me in. And is this beautiful woman who seems to not only have my body, but also my mind, in a twisted mess right now worth all of the torturous thoughts I'm having? Fuck yes, she is, and much more. Stepping up the stairs to Ella's front door, I knock and take a step back, pushing my hands into the front pockets of my jeans, and hoping to keep them there long enough to at least get inside the house before I touch her. I hear her footsteps as she approaches the door from the inside, and when she opens it, all I can do is take her in. With her freshly washed make-up free face and her long dark hair loose and laying in waves which cascade over her shoulders like a waterfall, her wide smile and the sparkle in those magnificent eyes of hers, she leaves me breathless. She's a vision of beauty and all she had to do was open the door.

"Hi, come in," she says, moving to the side for me to step in. "Did you get some sleep?" she asks, lifting one delicate eyebrow at me.

"I did, but seeing you now, I wish I would have just come straight here," I say, removing my hands from my pockets, finally pulling her into my arms and burying my face into the side of her neck so I can breathe her in.

"Is that so?"

"Hmm." Is all I can manage to get out as I run a hand up between her shoulder blades and gently press her in closer, placing a kiss on the soft skin just below her ear.

"Now you're making me wish you had, too," she breathes as I take advantage of our position by pressing more kisses up and across her delicate jaw line until I reach her mouth. Her lips are slightly parted and waiting for me to take, and I do with a hunger I've managed to keep under control until now. Sweeping my tongue into her warm mouth, she tastes of coffee with a slight mint flavor. As her tongue tangles with mine in a dance of want and need which quickly grows hot and needy, as it always does when our mouths fuse together. It's like an instant greed we both have which explodes when our mouths touch, and honestly, I don't know how much longer I can control this deep burning need I have to take her body and devour every last inch of it. I just want to bury myself inside her so deeply that we become one. Thankfully, Ella slowly breaks the kiss before my dirty thoughts take over.

"We need to stop or we won't be going anywhere," she says, her breath lightly feathering over my lips before she places a chaste kiss on my mouth and I begrudgingly let her go.

"And that would be bad, because?" I trail off as she heads into the kitchen.

Turning her head to look over her shoulder, she throws a word I've been longing to hear.

"Later."

Taking Ella's hand in mine, we stroll down the road to where the fair is being held in a large field at the tail end of the Jackson farm that he's made available for the event, including portable bathrooms and plenty of bales of hay scattered around for makeshift seating. As we get closer, we can see the whole field is lit by the bright lights of all of the attractions and I'm amazed at how big this thing is. I was expecting a small-town fair with some of the locals manning the rides and stalls, but this thing is huge with a Ferris wheel, dodgem cars, and lines of booths and tents set up with carnival games and food; lots and lots of food. The smells of fried foods and meat juices permeate the air, making my mouth water and my stomach groan in protest. Walking through the gates and dropping a donation into the bucket hanging from the fence, I take Ella's hand in mine again, gently pulling her in the direction of the smell and sound of meat sizzling on a barbecue.

"Let's eat," I say with enthusiasm, making her chuckle at my seemingly impatience to find some food.

Half an hour later, my stomach is now groaning at being too full from eating the biggest steak I've ever seen, accompanied by a bunch of sides including deep fried chicken wings, all washed down with a cold beer. Ella finished off the rest of my fries as she laughed at the after effects of my glutinous feast. She did take pity on me though, and we sat for a while, letting the food settle before she dragged me over to the carnival games where we purchased a roll of tickets and had fun spending hundreds of dollars in an attempt to win something that was probably worth two bucks at the most. It was all for a great cause, and even though Ella's arms were starting to fill up with stuffed toys as we walked towards the Ferris wheel, she indicated she wanted to go on with an excited squeal which was just totally adorable. She managed to get the wheel operator to babysit all the toys as we climbed aboard and started to move upwards. The look on her face when the wheel stopped with us at the highest point while others got on below was wonderful. Watching her eyes dart around, taking everything in, sparkling with the shimmer of lights from the fair as she glowed with excitement was mesmerizing. With my arm around her shoulders, she leans back into me, letting out a sigh of contentment. And that's the way we stay for another three turns of the wheel until our ride is over and we get off, pick up her toys, and make our way over to the ice cream stand where I manage to talk Ella into sharing a large chocolate hot fudge sundae with me. Boy, am I glad she agreed, because I got to watch those perfect lips of hers as they wrapped around a spoon covered in cream, which she sucks on, driving me insane.

And after that self-torture, we went back to the carnival games because Ella stated that she needed more stuffed toys so she could take them into the children's ward on Monday and donate them to the kids. The atmosphere of the fair is pumping with the loud beat of music from the rides and the sounds of excited kids laughing and running around, stuffing their faces with huge chunks of cotton candy and corn dogs, the squeals of teenage girls piercing the night air as the teenage boys try to impress them with their mad driving skills on the dodgem cars, or by rocking the cars while riding the Ferris wheel. The place is so crowded, I'm pretty sure the whole of Durandale is here. At some point during the night, we bumped into the Miller clan, which is exactly the right word to describe them; Chief Miller and his wife walking around, surrounded by all three of the Miller brothers, their wives and kids. We managed to stop and talk for a few minutes before they were all pulled away by eager kids wanting to go in all directions.

Stopping at the bar area, Ella takes a seat on a hay bale while I grab us a couple of beers. By the time I get back to her, she's been joined by Molly and Caleb.

"Hey," I greet them as I hand a beer to Ella. "Do you want me to get you something to drink?"

"No, we're good. We just ate at the barbeque stand and honestly, I don't think I can fit another thing in," Molly says, rubbing at her belly. "So, what do you think?" she asks me, motioning to the fair around us.

"I think they certainly know how to do things big in Durandale." "It turned out better than the committee expected too, I think. Seems to have drawn in a lot of people from the surrounding areas."

"That's great," Ella says.

"I know. The only trouble is, I'm not sure we'll be able to top this with something better for next year's fundraiser." She chuckles.

"And you might be too busy next year," Ella says, nodding towards Molly's stomach.

"That's true. I hope I can though, I really enjoyed it. I'm glad Caleb talked me into helping out this year."

"I knew you'd be perfect for the job," Caleb says, smiling at Molly. "Thanks, babe."

"Yeah, he knew he could put your need for control and organization skills to good use somewhere," I say with a grin as I take a pull from my beer bottle.

"Real funny," Molly says with a roll of her eyes.

"What can I say? I'm a funny kind of guy," I say, giving my little sister a playful wink.

"Hey, why don't you come over for dinner Sunday night? I'm sure I can tell you lots of stories about this funny guy, here, that you will love," Molly says, and Ella's eyes shoot straight to mine. I am momentarily confused about the look she's giving me; not sure if it's wariness, apprehension, or if she's looking for my permission to except Molly's invitation. What the fuck?

Giving her a reassuring smile, I say, "If you don't have any plans tomorrow, and you want to listen to my little sister tell fairytales, it's up to you." Giving me a smile, she turns to Molly.

"I would love to."

As it gets later, the night air starts to turn a little chilly, and with bellies bursting at the seams from all the food we'd consumed, not to mention the huge pile of stuffed toys we had accumulated, I look down at Ella.

"You ready to leave?"

"So ready," she says. Taking her free hand in mine and threading our fingers together, we take a slow walk back to her house with great timing, because as soon as we stepped up onto her front porch the fair put on a firework display and we had a great view of it. Placing the toys on one of the chairs, I sat in the other and pulled her into my lap. We watched the sky fill with all the colors of the rainbow for several minutes and as I held her there, my chin on top of her head and with the warmth of her body against mine, I felt a soothing swell of calmness grow inside my chest.

We stay like this for a long time after the last sparkles from the fireworks have floated down through the night sky and the sounds coming from the fair slowly dwindle to silence, then Ella looks up at me and says, "Let's go to bed," before standing and taking my hand, giving it a gentle tug as she leads me inside and down the hall to her bedroom. Closing the door and turning to stand in front of me, she places both hands against my chest, her face tilted up towards mine, her eyes glistening in the light from the moon which is coming through the window.

As I search her eyes, looking for a sign of affirmation from her, I see it the instant her eyes become hooded. In those radiant, intense, blue eyes of hers, I see a lustful heat and hunger, almost as consuming as my own. Sliding a hand around to the back of her neck, I pull her head gently towards me as I lean down and take her mouth with mine, greedily running my tongue over the seam of her lips, parting them so my tongue can slide inside and taste her. Devouring her mouth, I move between deep and penetrating to soft bites sucking on her bottom lip. Slipping my other hand around her waist, pulling her closer into my body, the room fills with our heated breaths and the furious movement of our bodies trying to consume each other, trying to get even closer than we already are, and I'm completely lost in her until she breaks the kiss. Taking a step back, I watch as her hands grasp the hem of her shirt and she pulls it up over her head, revealing delicate pink lace encasing those beautiful plump breasts which are heaving up and down. Looking from her breasts and back up to her face, I manage to breathe out her name. "Ella".

Her hair is mussed from my hands, her lips are swollen from my punishing mouth, and her skin has taken on a light blush-pink color. She looks totally stunning like this. When she reaches for the button of her jeans, I place a hand over hers, stopping her so I can take over. Kneeling before her, I slowly unzip her jeans and slip my hands inside to her hips. Slowly removing them, one leg at a time, feeling the soft warm skin of her thighs and legs, lifting each foot from the jeans until I am faced with a pair of white lace panties along with a visible damp spot at the front which makes me groan at the thought of her being this wet for me. Wrapping my hands around, I slip them both under the material and grab her ass, pulling her closer to me and burying my face into the silky material so I can smell her wonderful sweet scent of arousal. Placing my lips on the tiny spot of wetness on the lace in an open mouthed kiss which causes a deep groan of utter pleasure to escape from deep in my throat, I pull her deeper into my face.

Slipping my fingers into the sides of her panties, I slowly pull them down to where they pool at her feet, then run my palms up her inner thighs to the apex of soft skin and a small strip of soft hair and lay my cheek against it, and I feel like I have found my happy spot, right here. Closing my eyes, I take my time, just breathing in her addictive scent. When I feel her fingers stroke through my hair, I look up and find her looking down at me through a curtain of long, silky, black hair which emphasizes the brightness of her blue eyes. With my hands on her hips, I move her backwards until the backs of her legs touch her mattress and she sits. With our eyes still locked on each other's, I run my palms down the outside of her legs to her ankles, then up the inside of her legs gently pushing them apart so I can let my eyes feast on that beautiful pussy. With my hands splayed out on the inside of her thighs, I let my fingers move down to the lips of her sex and gently stroke the soft wet skin that feels so silky and warm, I need to taste her more than I need my next breath. As I bring my mouth closer to taste her, I feel her hands grip my head and bring it up to look at her lust filled eyes marred with, what? Hesitation? Fear?

"You don't have to," she says, her words trailing off with what sounds like embarrassment. "I've never…"

"Then you'd better get comfortable, baby, because you're about to, right now," is all I can get out, because the thought of no-one ever giving her pleasure this way makes my mouth water even more. Running my face up her inner thighs, letting my beard run over her skin, I press light kisses as I trail my way up to the center of her core and just breathe.

All I want to do is just look at her, with her legs spread before me as she lays back on the bed, I can hear her ragged breathing in anticipation of what I'm about to do with her in this exposed position. Stroking the soft hair of her pussy with the back of my knuckles, slowly up and down, I hear her sharp intake of air. With my thumbs on the lips of her sex, I open her up to me, and she's glistening with the wetness of her arousal, and when I run my tongue from the bottom to the top of her dripping folds, I let out a feral groan of appreciation for her sweet honey-like taste as it coats my tongue. Taking her clit between my lips and sucking it into my mouth, I feel it swell and pulsate as she squirms her bottom around with a small moan. Placing my palms back onto her inner thighs, I hold her legs open, pressing them back into place and holding her still. The more I suck and lick, the more I want. I feel an insatiable hunger take over as I place my open mouth over her pussy, spearing my tongue deep inside her heat, causing her to buck her hips upwards. When I feel her hands touch my head, her fingers scraping through my hair as she pulls me in closer, I continue to feast on her, sucking and licking with small, soft bites to her clit. Sliding a finger into her while my lips are sucking hard on that little bundle of sensitive nerves, she starts to writhe on the bed, her hands frantically grasping at my hair, her breathing and moaning now a desperate chant for me to push her where she need to be and as she moans out my name. With a lift of her hips, I feel the shudder of her orgasm as her legs tremble and I taste the evidence of her juicy release on my tongue. Slowing down the eagerness of my mouth against her pulsating sex, she rides out her orgasm, and once I feel her body relax from her release, I place soft gentle kisses up her stomach until I reach her beautiful breasts and watch as they heave, still confined in her bra until I flip the fastener in the middle and watch as they spill out. Moving the material of the bra aside, I continue kissing the underneath swell of her breasts, the skin so soft and delicate. Taking one of her taught nipples into my mouth to gently suck it, then letting it go with a slight pop as I do the same to her other nipple, rolling the cherry-like nub between my lips as I hear her moan is driving me to the edge of insanity. Letting my tongue trail a path up to her neck, I take small nips along her jawline until my mouth crashes onto hers. Running my hand down to the apex of her thighs so I can palm her wetness, I feel her fingers fumbling at my belt until she opens it, then my jeans. When I feel her hand slip inside and wrap around my cock, I groan into her mouth with the pleasure of finally feeling her soft skin wrapped around my shaft as she strokes up and down while trying to push my jeans down with her other hand.

"I need these off," she breathes into my mouth.

"Me, too," I say, pulling back and giving this sexy siren what she wants, pulling off my shirt and toeing off my boots and socks at the same time, followed by my jeans. Moving between Ella's open legs, I push my hands under her back and move her up the bed a little. As my fingers glide up her thighs, I feel her fingers trace the lines of my chest, the soft feel of her fingertips moving over every muscle and dip, trailing down over my stomach.

"You're so beautiful," she says and I chuckle at her words. "Now, that's my line."

"Come here," she breathes out, pulling me down so our bodies are finally touching, my chest pressed against her breasts, our stomachs and thighs pressed together, and I swear it's the best fucking thing I've ever felt. Her warmth, her scent, her softness.

"I need you inside me," she whispers, taking a gentle bite of my chin.

"Mmm, great minds think alike," I hum into the side of her neck. "Side table, left side."

"Hmm?"

"Condom," she says, breaking into my brain which was completely lost in the feel of her. Leaning up, I open the drawer. Shoving my hand inside, blindly searching until I feel the foil packet. Pulling it out, I lean up, tear it open, and have my cock sheathed and poised at her opening. Lifting her legs up to drape over my thighs, I slowly push inside her heat, watching her eyes as I take my time. I feel the tight walls of her sex stretch and relax to take me all the way in, until I'm so deep inside her that I don't want to move, I just want to stay in this position forever, with her heat surrounding me. When Ella starts to move her hips under me, I move with her, slowly at first, pulling out then pushing back in, taking long, deep strokes, even taking a moment to look down at where our bodies are connected.

Leaning down, I press my mouth against hers, sucking at her bottom lip and causing her to moan into my mouth. Sliding my tongue against hers as she lifts her hips up, meeting my thrusts as she pants her hunger for more into my mouth, I feel her inner muscles start to clamp down around my cock with a pulsating squeeze as she drawls out my name on a long breathy moan. I feel it travel all the way down to my balls as they tighten and tingle with a spark of electricity that runs up my spine, and with a final jolt of pure ecstasy and a growl of pleasure, I join her with my own release.

With my forehead against hers, I take her panting breath into my mouth with a soft kiss as we continue to rock against each other, drawing out every last second of our pleasure.

Chapter Thirteen

Ella

With heavy eyelids, I open my eyes and have to blink several times to fully wake. I realize that my cheek is pressed against a hard, warm chest with a steady heartbeat, and the muscled arm that's around me, pulling me into the side of that warm body, makes me feel safe, and the ache in my body certainly makes me feel very satisfied. Looking up at the sleeping, serene face of Jaxon makes me smile and I take a moment to appreciate this man who, over the last month, has managed to break down the walls which had taken me years to build, causing them to crack, just a little. With his dark blonde hair messy from our passion-filled night and his neatly trimmed beard, the angles of his strong jaw line and those ocean-blue eyes which are hidden behind his closed lids, eyes I could fall into and lose myself in every time I look into them. Last night was the first time I'd seen his body in all its beauty, after only imagining what he had going on under his clothes every time we'd met, and it was perfect. Wide shoulders and thick biceps, well defined chest and abs, not to mention the slim waist and those perfect V lines that trail a path straight to his magnificent manhood. In all the times I'd lain in this bed alone at night and pictured him naked, it was nothing compared to the reality that is Jaxon. Looking at him now, and watching him sleep, causes a warmth to rush through my body that feels exciting and scary all at once. This crazy, Aussie fireman has certainly popped a hole in the security bubble of the life I've been living. He also seems to have let in some fresh air, and breathing it in feels wonderful.

Inhaling a deep breath of total contentment, I close my eyes again and am settling back into the warmth of his body when I feel the deep rumble of his voice.

"You know, I don't mind you looking, but I'd much rather you climb on top."

"How long have you been awake?" I chuckle.

"From the minute I felt your eyes on me," he says, lips lifting slightly at the corners with a grin.

"I didn't mean to wake you," I say, lifting my head to look at him placing my hand on his chest.

"You didn't, it's just a professional habit," he says, letting his fingers stroke up and down my back while my own fingertips brush over the lines of his chest, swirling around a nipple before moving down over the ridges of his stomach. Following the line of hair from his navel, down under the covers to his semi-erect cock, I take my time stroking up and down the silky length of him, rubbing my thumb over the head, now moist with pre-cum. In an instant, he reaches into the bedside table, pulling out another condom and placing it on his stomach.

"Whenever you're ready, babe," he breathes out. I see a slight tremor ripple across his abs and I know he's more than ready. Opening the foil packet, I slide the latex down his impressive morning wood and as soon as he's fully sheathed, he pulls me up to lay on top of him.

"You going to torture me, or ride me?"

"Torture," I say, pulling my legs up to straddle him and rubbing the wet lips of my sex over his cock.

"I don't think so," he says, placing his hands on my hips and lifting me effortlessly up until the head of his cock is poised at my entrance before slowly lowering me down onto it. It's wickedly hard, and I'm deliciously wet as I take him in, right down to the base. Giving myself a minute to revel in the sweet stretch and burn of adjusting to him, I start to move in a slow circular motion while he's buried deep inside, causing him to grip my hips and growl, "You feel so fucking good." "So, do you," I manage to breath out because he does. So good, that I quickly lose myself in a rhythmic chase after an orgasm which comes very quickly with the hard upward thrusts of Jaxon's hips. As I feel the slow burn of my orgasm move down my spine and burst deep inside my core, I arch my back and let my head fall back, moaning out his name over and over as I continue to rock back and forth, languid moans slipping from my lips. As my legs start to tremble, I'm quickly flipped onto my back with him still buried deep inside me. As he moves my legs up onto his shoulders and starts pumping deep hard strokes into me, the after-shock of my orgasm continues to run through my body and climb again. All I can do is look at where our bodies are connected and watch with an erotic hunger as he moves in and out as sweat starts to trickle down the line in the middle of his chest. Feeling the heat and tingle spreading through my swollen clit as the muscles of my sex start to squeeze and contract around his hard shaft, his eyes shoot to mine.

"I want to see you come again," he pants out and those words push me over the edge. This time, when I come, I keep my eyes locked onto his. I want him to see just how he makes me feel as I moan out my orgasm through the perfect O of my lips. The blue of his eyes seems to darken with lust as he growls out my name with another deep, hard thrust as he releases his own orgasm. With his face so close to mine, our noses almost touching, holding himself up on his elbows, and running a thumb over my bottom lip, all we can do is gaze at each other with panted breaths that slowly calm. He presses a kiss against my lips before pushing up from the bed and disappearing into the bathroom, returning almost instantly to slip back into the bed, pulling the covers up over us both as he pulls me into his side, placing another kiss to the top of my head.

The next time I open my eyes, it's to the sound of Walter meowing at the bedroom door. Reaching over to look at the time on my phone, I instantly feel guilty. It's almost eleven am, poor Walter must be starving. With a gentle extrication of my body from the bed, including the warm body spooning me with a possessive hand on my hip, I manage to slip from the bed, picking up my underwear and t-shirt before getting out into the hallway. Heading for the kitchen with Walter weaving around my legs, I manage to get my panties on and the shirt over my head while grabbing his food from the cupboard and filling his bowl and putting on a pot of coffee. Sitting on a stool at the kitchen bench, I watch Walter inhale his food like he hasn't been fed for a month, then pour myself a coffee. I just sit with it cradled in my hands; the house quiet apart from the bird sounds coming in from outside. Then it hits me that for the first time in years, there's a man asleep in my bed. It's not just me sharing the morning with Walter, there is another person in the house, and not just any person. He's a kind, funny, caring man, a man who respected my boundaries and feelings, and was so patient and understanding with me.

Picturing Jaxon's wide smile causes a flutter in the bottom of my stomach, one of excitement and unfamiliar feelings towards this man who seems to have blown into my life like a tornado and swept me off my feet. Even though I didn't want to fall for him, I find that I just can't help it, and that thought scares the shit out of me. To think it took a man to come here from the other side of the world for me to relax and let go of my fears of intimacy and trust, and let him in. My thoughts are interrupted by the sound of the bedroom door opening and when I look up, Jaxon is standing in the kitchen doorway, barefoot, bare-chested, wearing only his jeans from last night and looking edible.

"Good morning." His low, sleepy voice causes goose bumps to run over my skin.

"Morning. Coffee?" I ask, getting up and pouring him a cup before he answers, and placing it on the kitchen bench. Moving into the kitchen, he catches me around the waist with his arms from behind, burying his face into my neck.

"You smell wonderful."

"Thank you."

"You're welcome," he says, kissing the side of my neck as he breathes me in. We stay like this for a few minutes, just enjoying the feel of each other's warmth, then I hear a deep rumbling sound and turn my head to look at him.

"Was that your stomach?" I smile.

"Sorry." He mumbles into the side of my neck.

"No, I'm sorry. Sit down and I'll make you some breakfast," I say, pulling away from him and moving quickly to grab some bacon and eggs from the refrigerator, almost dropping them on the floor in my haste to place them on the bench.

"Hey, slow down, my stomach will wait," he says, pulling me back into his arms and stroking my hair away from my face.

"No, really. I should have had it cooked already for you." "What? Wait a minute. You don't have to do anything for me. I'm a grown man and you are not my maid," he says placing two fingers under my chin, tilting it to where I am forced to look into his eyes as they search mine for understanding. As I look into the depths of his eyes, I seem to feel an instant calmness and let out a deep breath and smile at him.

"I'm sorry. I think, maybe all the sex has fried my brain," I say with a chuckle, in an attempt to shrug off the intensity in his eyes. Finally, he places a soft kiss to my forehead, then leads me to sit on a stool.

"Now, you sit and enjoy your coffee, while I cook you up some breakfast."

"No, really. I can make it," I start to protest, but he holds up a hand to stop me.

"I can assure you, I not only have skills in the bedroom, but in the kitchen as well," he says with that wide and captivating smile that makes me instantly relax and watch as he pulls cooking utensils from the cupboard, looking to me for direction on where to find what he needs. Over breakfast, that slightly awkward moment we had is quickly forgotten as Jaxon teases me after receiving a text message from Molly, reminding him about dinner tonight.

"So, you all good about dinner?" he asks as he rinses off our plates and places them into the dishwasher.

"Sure, I haven't had a chance to catch up with Molly for a while.

It'll be good, unless you don't..."

"Stop, don't even go there. I just wanted to make sure you were ready to hear all her freaky stories about our childhood, not to mention the questions about us seeing each other."

"I cannot wait to hear about little Jaxon and all the naughty things he got up to." I grin at him and I mean it. I want to know what he was like growing up. In fact, I want to know everything about this man.

"Well, I can tell you there is nothing little about me, but I have always been naughty," he says with a cheeky wink as he wipes his hands on a towel then drops it onto the bench. "In fact, I think we should get naughty in the shower right this minute," he says, walking over to where I'm sitting at the kitchen bench on a stool. Nudging open my thighs and moving between them, placing his hands on my waist he lifts me in one quick swoop. I instinctively wrap my legs around his waist and let him carry me down the hall and into the bathroom with a squeal of laughter.

Placing me on the counter in the bathroom, I watch as he turns on the shower, running his hand under the water until he seems satisfied with the temperature. He then proceeds to pull off his jeans, before getting between my legs and pulling of my t-shirt, followed by my panties. Picking me up, he walks into the shower before letting me place my feet on the floor. One of the best things I installed in this old bathroom was a big shower, with a bench and three shower heads that let the water accumulate into a waterfall in the middle. The steaming hot water that's running over our naked bodies right now feels so decadent.

Chapter Fourteen

Feeling the stream of hot water running between our naked bodies is almost like an aphrodisiac, and even though I know this was a torturous idea, I need to restrain myself from fucking her again right here, right now, against the shower wall. Squeezing some body wash into my hands, I start to run my palms over her shoulders and arms, and as I watch the soap bubbles slide down and over her breasts, I start to wonder why in hell I thought this was going to be a good idea. By the time I've run my hands over every inch of her beautiful body, bending down to wash the apex between her legs and right down to her feet, my cock is rock hard. Moving Ella around, I continue to torture myself by washing her hair, letting my fingers slide through her silky dark strands which run slick down her back under the water, making it look like a dark curtain of silk. Once I finish, thankfully, and rinse us both off, I turn off the shower, stepping out to grab a towel. As I start to dry her off, I notice a small white scar just under her breast, over her ribs.

"How did you get this?" I ask, running my thumb gently over the raised skin.

"What? Oh, that. I got it when I fell off a horse when I was a kid. I broke a rib and it came through the skin," she says casually.

"Ouch."

"It sure was, but at the time, I was more annoyed that I couldn't ride my friend's horse again."

"What? Ever?"

"Yep, my mom was pretty strict," she says, shrugging her shoulders as she turns and takes the towel from me, gently rubbing it over the water on my chest.

"My parents were the opposite."

"Ah yes, hippy parents, you said." She grins up at me. "Something like that. They just believed that kids should be kids."

"They sound like very loving parents."

"They were. What about yours?" I ask and notice her wince at the question.

"Mine were something I'd rather not talk about," she sighs, giving me an apologetic half-smile. I can see that the subject of her parents is obviously a touchy one and not something she wants to talk about by the way she turns and walks into the bedroom.

By the time we head over to Molly and Caleb's for dinner, we'd spent the day in Ella's small back yard, where I helped her plan out some garden beds. Not sure what I was thinking, because I have no idea what to do when it comes to growing anything. I only know how to buy fresh vegetables, which is how we ended up taking the short drive out of town to a local farm that sells a healthy selection of home- grown fruit and vegetables, where we picked up a few things. But really, I just love spending time with Ella. I love the way she smiles when she looks at me, her laugh when I say something in what she considers a foreign language and then have to explain the meaning to her, the way her eyes light up when she talks about the work she's done on her house; a house that any idiot can see she's really proud of. In fact, almost everything she does and says is almost like a magical experience to me, especially when I catch glimpses of her carefree spirit that's a contradiction to those small moments when I see something darker behind her eyes, something I'm guessing she's been carrying around with her for some time. I promised myself that I wasn't going to push her, but fuck I need to know everything about her.

Opening the glass sliding door that leads into Molly's kitchen, I am instantly hit with the aroma of garlic and tomatoes, and my mouth waters. Molly's standing at the kitchen bench, stirring something in a bowl, and when she sees us, she quickly wipes off her hands on a towel and moves around the bench, giving Ella a hug first, then me.

"You're making pasta?" I grin down at my little sister.

"Of course, your favorite."

"Smells wonderful," Ella says.

"Believe me, if there is one thing Molly can cook, it's pasta."

"Come, sit down. Why don't you grab us something to drink?" Molly smiles at me and takes Ella to sit at the kitchen table, while I take out a large glass jug of juice from the fridge, snatching three glasses on the way back to the table.

"There's beer in there," Molly says, glancing at the fridge.

"Juice is fine." I wave her off, pouring out the juice and taking a seat.

"It's so good to see you, Ella. We just don't seem to get any time at work to stop and chat anymore." Molly beams at Ella.

"I know, it been crazy, and it doesn't make it any easier that I have no idea when I'm working in the wards or out in the community."

"How's that going?"

"It's going good. I've had some great feedback from the hospital board."

"That's great, you should be proud of yourself. That community hospice program would still be a footnote on an agenda if you hadn't put so much work into getting it up and running."

"Thanks. I'm just glad it's helped so many people and their families," Ella says, looking a little embarrassed by Molly's praise.

"So, you were responsible for the whole hospice at home program?" I ask, looking at Ella.

"She was and she runs it like an angel." Molly smiles.

"That's because she is an angel," I find myself saying. But seeing the blush of color on Ella's cheeks, I kind of wish I hadn't because it seems to have caused a weird awkward silence at the table as Molly looks between me and Ella with a huge smile growing by the second, which she can't even cover with the glass of juice tilted to her lips.

"So, where is Caleb?" I ask, finally breaking the silence and putting an end to the weirdness.

"He shouldn't be long. He just took George out for a walk," Molly says and Ella gives me a quizzical look.

"George is their giant beast of a dog, with a heart of gold," I say as I hear the front door open, followed by the tell-tale ticking sound of the fast-moving paws of the so-called beast in question on the wood floorboards. He skids to a stop when his bulking body enters the kitchen, where he sits and looks from me to Ella, obviously wondering which one to slobber over first. Thankfully, he chooses Ella and within seconds he's smooching and sniffing her all over, his tail wagging so hard that if it hit you, it would most definitely knock you the fuck out.

"You are so sweet," Ella coos, scratching George behind his ears, causing his body to shake and bounce with excitement.

"Calm down, George," Molly yells at him from the kitchen where she's now standing, stirring the pot on the stovetop.

"He's fine," Ella giggles, continuing to stroke the dog.

"Sit," comes a command in a deep voice as Caleb enters the kitchen from the hall, and George quickly looks up at Caleb and sits.

"When he gets too excited, he tends to try and climb onto your lap. For some reason, George thinks he's a Chihuahua, not a Mastiff mixed with a great Dane," Caleb says, crossing to Ella and holding out his hand. "I'm Caleb. Molly has spoken of you, Ella, and it's good to put a name to a face, at last."

"Good to meet you, too." Ella smiles, taking Caleb's hand. "Caleb, can you set the table please?" Molly shouts out from the kitchen.

"Sure, babe."

"Do you need a hand?" Ella asks, standing.

"Nope. You are a guest, so sit and relax." Caleb says, heading for the kitchen.

Within minutes, the table is full of food; freshly baked garlic bread, salad, and a huge platter of steaming pasta, with sliced chicken covered in a creamy tomato sauce. There wasn't much time for talking as we filled our plates and enjoyed the meal, until everyone slumped back and groaned with satisfaction in unison. When Caleb stands and starts to clear the dishes, I help him and join him in the kitchen, leaving the ladies at the table as we fill the dishwasher and put a pot of coffee on to brew.

"She seems nice," Caleb half-whispers.

"Yeah, she is," I say, letting my eyes wander over to where Ella is smiling while deep in conversation with Molly.

"Oh, man, you have it bad." He chuckles. "What?"

"You're looking at her with the biggest puppy-dog eyes I've ever seen. Jaxon, you are done, man."

"You might be right there, mate. I think I may be addicted." "Well, at least it helps that Molly already likes her. You just won half the battle."

"I know, right," I say with what I know is a goofy grin on my face which drops slightly when I think about the things I don't know about Ella. Caleb, being true to his profession, calls me on it in an instant. "What is it?"

"Nothing."

"Bullshit," he scoffs.

"Not sure, just a gut feeling."

"About?" Caleb asks, raising an eyebrow.

"I don't know...her family, her past...she's open about everything except when it comes to that."

"Maybe she grew up in a place she would rather forget." "Yeah, maybe."

"Do you want me to do a background check on her?"

"No, absolutely not, Jesus."

"Just kidding, calm down." He grins, holding up his hands in defense at my sharpness.

"Then, just enjoy the lady's company," he says, giving me a slap to the shoulder as he takes the pot of coffee out to the table while I grab some mugs.

Later that night, I drive Ella home and we stand at the door, my mouth on hers, my hands grabbing her ass and pulling her into me. With a groan, I finally end the kiss, which is a painful decision, but with both of us on early shifts in the morning, I know if I stay the night in her bed, neither of us would get any sleep.

It's just after midnight when I open the side gate and make my way past the pool, but as I get to the guest house, I notice movement at the outdoor table through the dim garden light. Narrowing my eyes, I see Molly wrapped in a blanket, with her legs curled up, in a chair.

"Molly?"

"It's just me."

"What are you doing? Is everything alright?" I ask, now changing direction to go to where she is sitting. When I get to her, I notice she's holding a mug in her hands.

"I'm fine. Just hoping a mug of hot chocolate and doing a little star gazing will help me sleep better."

"You're not sleeping?"

"Not much," she says with a sigh.

"Is it just a pregnancy thing, or is there something on your mind that you're not telling me?" I ask with some concern.

"No, everything's fine. I'm just a weirdo." She smiles at me and it makes me chuckle.

"Well, I've known that for years."

"Funny guy. So, you and Ella look smitten with each other." "Not sure if smitten is the right word, but yeah, I like her a lot. She's comfortable and easy to be with."

"I don't know. The way you two were eye-balling each other all night looks serious to me."

"It's a little early to throw the word serious out there, isn't it?"

"Sometimes these things just hit you when you least expect them."

"Honestly, I wouldn't know."

"That's because you've never dated anyone long enough," she teases.

"True. Ella is different," I say, scratching my beard in thought. "And that's a bad thing?" Molly asks.

"No. I guess I'm just new to all this."

"What's going on in that head of yours Jaxon Cane?"

"I don't know. On one hand, I think I should slow down a little, and on the other, I want to spend every minute of the day with her."

"You just don't want to fuck it up," Molly says knowingly. "Exactly. I mean, is it normal to think about someone so much, and want to be with them all the time, or am I moving into stalkerish behavior?"

"Oh, my god. You are so funny, right now," she laughs out. "Well, I'm glad you're amused by my love life."

"And Boom. That's it, right there." She stabs a finger in my direction. "You, my dear brother, are falling in love."

"Now, you're just taking the piss."

"You are showing all the signs. You're just too inexperienced to see them. Think about it. You love being with her and when you're not, you're thinking about her, and you're nervous because you don't want to do anything to jeopardize it. Tell me, when you first see her what happens? Let me guess, you get butterflies in your stomach, an ache in the middle of your chest, and when she smiles you feel like nothing else matters, right?"

Sitting back in the chair, I think about her words for a moment before letting out a deep sigh as I scrub my hands down my face, giving her a reluctant nod.

"Ha, I knew it." She beams at me, throwing up her hands in a victory wave and wiggling in her chair.

"So, what do I do now?"

"Enjoy it, let it happen, and stop trying to dissect it like it's a math problem, Jaxon."

Standing, I move to where she's sitting, lean down, and kiss her cheek. "Thank you for your wisdom, but I have an early shift tomorrow and you need to go to bed and get some sleep."

"You're right," she says, standing and pulling the blanket up around her shoulders, then picking up her empty mug. "Night Jaxon, love you."

"Love you too, weirdo," I say, giving her a wink as I watch her go inside before I head for my own bed.

Over the next couple of weeks, I try to spend every free minute, hour, and day with Ella. This may sound like a lot of time, but with our different shift times clashing, it's mostly on the weekends. The rest of the time was spent texting or talking for sometimes hours on the phone, and when we do this, I know I'm gone because talking on the phone for long periods of time is not in my forte. Sometimes we'd go out driving around in the truck as Ella shows me everything from the local vineyards to small open markets. Sometimes we'd just spend the day at her house, sharing a meal, talking, watching movies, leading to having wild hot sex in every corner and on every surface in her place. It felt like I was lost in the vortex of a romance movie, where I could just spend endless hours caught up in watching her, touching her, and inhaling her like a drug. She's taken over my body so much that when we're not together I crave her more than I've ever craved a woman before.

My shift at the station didn't finish until early Saturday morning and I was looking forward to going home, taking a shower, then heading over to see Ella. That is, until my phone rings just I was getting undressed and I see Ella's name on the screen.

"Hey, babe," I answer.

"Hey, did you just get home?"

"Yep, heading for the shower, then over to you."

"That's what I'm calling about. I just got a call from the hospital and I have to go into work."

"Shit, really?" I say, sitting down on the bed, feeling a little disheartened.

"Yes, I have a palliative patient who's being transferred home, so I need to go pick up some supplies and head over to get him organized," she says sounding more disappointed than I feel, and although it was a sound that I didn't like, I understood she loved her work.

"It's okay. These things can't exactly be planned, can they?" I say light-heartedly.

"Not really. I'm just sorry, we had plans and..." "It's fine, babe. It's your job."

"Okay. I'll text you when I can."

"You just concentrate on your job, okay?" "Okay. Talk later," she says, ending the call.

Dropping my phone onto the bed, I finish getting undressed, take a shower, and crawl into bed.

Chapter Fifteen

Ella

I knew as soon as I answered the incoming call from work that my plans for the day were over. After calling Jaxon, I could tell he felt just as bad as I did, but one of the down-sides of my job is being on call. Unfortunately, death waits for no one. Once I got into the hospital and read the file of the patient, my heart sinks a little, Jake Carter is a lovely man in his early sixties who's been fighting heart disease for at least the last ten years. When I say fighting it, he certainly has been. From changing his diet and lifestyle, to open heart surgery three years ago to repair a leaking heart valve, and now, after all the years of fighting to stay alive, his heart has finally given up the fight for him. After being admitted to a ward four days ago, he is now in end stage heart failure and the one thing he wants is to take his last breath on the farm that he and his wife built just after they got married, over forty years ago. A place where his children were born, where he's lived and worked, a place he loves, surrounded by his family.

After picking up my case which contains everything essential that I need to take with me, I do another check through it, refilling anything that's low or missing, then head down to the pharmacy in the hospital with the consulting Doctor's prescription for the palliative care medications that'll be needed, before loading up my car and driving out to the Carter farm.

When I pull up at the large ranch-style house, Ash is sitting on the top stair, getting up when I stop and greeting me when I exit the car.

"Hey," he says solemnly.

"Hi, Ash. How are you doing?" I ask, placing a comforting hand on his forearm.

"Under the circumstances?" He shrugs. I know how hard it is to put the situation into words, so I wasn't going to press him. Opening the back door of the car, I start to pull out my bag, which Ash takes from me, and we walk up the stairs and into the house. After walking down a long hallway and entering the end bedroom which is beautifully lit by sunlight filtering in through the floor to ceiling windows that take up a whole wall, I take in the breathtaking view over the Carter farmland. A large bed sits against the wall facing the windows and Karen Carter, Jake's wife, sits next to it, looking at her now frail and tired husband with such love that I feel a little guilty at taking that moment away from her when she looks up at me.

"Ella," she breathes. "I'm so glad you're here." She stands and walks around the bed to embrace me. Soothingly, I run my hands up and down her back as she holds onto me, hard.

"This is a lovely room," I say once she pulls back from me. "I thought he'd like to be able to look out over the farm."

"It's perfect," I say, giving her a reassuring smile before opening my bag, taking out the things that I need. Sitting down on the bed next to Jake, I visually take him in, checking his breathing pattern and his color while I reach down for his wrist so I can take his pulse, which is beating in a calm rhythm.

"Would you like some tea?" Karen asks, heading for the door.

"I would love some," I say, following her out and into a kitchen which has to be three times bigger than my own, with an equally bigger heavy wooden table surrounded by ten chairs. Taking a seat, I watch as she moves around the kitchen, bringing back a tray with a tea pot, sugar bowl, a small glass jug of milk, and two small China cups and saucers, before sitting down next to me.

"I've always liked my tea. Jake always said it was from my British ancestors," she says, filling the cups from the tea pot then handing me one. "I've made up the spare room across the hall from Jake for you. I wasn't sure of the whole process."

"I'm fine with whatever you need, Karen."

"I need my husband to be around for another twenty years, but I know that's not possible," she says with a small lift at the corner of her mouth.

"I know, but what is possible is for you to have him here, at home, where he wants to be, in surroundings that are controlled by your love."

"We've talked about it over the years. Jake always said, that as long as he was at the farm, with me by his side and pain free, he'd be half way to heaven," she says, looking down into her tea cup.

"Then, we will give him what he wants," I say, looking into her watery eyes.

"Thank you."

The next few days go by in a flurry of activity at the Carter place. From friends visiting and offering support with foil covered dishes in their hands, to family members coming to spend time with Jake, who was slowly declining into a peaceful sleep. Karen spends her time between preparing food and making sure people are fed, a coping mechanism that seems to help her get through the hours, to laying next to Jake, stroking his hair and his face as she speaks to him in hushed tones with loving words. I make a couple of very quick trips back home to feed Walter and give him some loving, and managed to exchange a few texts with Jaxon. Tonight, the Carter home is quiet and serene, so I take a mug of coffee out onto the porch, taking a seat on the top stair and pulling out my phone to read his last message.

JAXON

Carter? Any relation to Ash and Ethan?

ME

Yes, their father.

JAXON

Okay.

ME

How is work?

JAXON

Same. Can't wait to see you.

ME

Me too.

The sound of the screen door opening, causes me to jump a little. Turning, I see Ash, a bottle of beer dangling from his fingers as he sits down next to me on the stair.

"Someone special?" He nods at my phone before taking a chug of beer. "I think so," I say, pushing my phone into the pocket of my jacket. "The Aussie?"

"Jaxon," I say, making sure he knows he has a name. He snorts, draining off the rest of his beer. Moments pass in silence before he speaks again.

"Why him, Ella?"

A little taken aback by his question and what my answer might mean to him, I give myself a few minutes to think. I need to be tactful and mindful of the circumstances surrounding my being here, his state of mind and emotional fragility considering his father is laying in the house behind us.

"Not sure I can pinpoint one thing, Ash. I guess it feels right," I say and he lets out a sigh, looking out into the night.

"You know, I could make you feel right if you give me a chance," he says, looking at me with a look that makes me feel suddenly uncomfortable, a look that's a mixture of anger and possession, a look that makes my skin chill.

"This is not the time to discuss this," I say, standing and moving towards the front door until I am stopped by his tight grip on my wrist. "Then when will be Ella? I've been patient, waiting for you to notice me for years, and nothing. Then Aussie boy's here for what, a week, and you're spreading your legs for him?"

"Let me go and stand back," I say, looking him in the eyes.

Dropping his head, he does as I ask. "I'm sorry, I shouldn't have…"

"Forget it, Ash," I say, opening the door and walking back into the house, in need of putting some distance between us and satisfied when I hear the closing of his bedroom door.

Jake Carter passed away peacefully in the arms of his wife early the next morning.

Chapter Sixteen

Jaxon

I'm woken by the vibrating sound of my phone making its way across the bedside table. Grabbing it, I see Ella's name on the screen.

"Hey."

"Are you at home?" she asks hastily.

"Yep," is all I manage to get out before she continues.

"I'll be there in five," she says, ending the call abruptly and giving me a feeling of unease. Jumping out of bed, I pull on a pair of sweat pants and as soon as I come out into the lounge room there's a knock at the door. Opening it, I'm slightly stunned when Ella practically jumps at me, her arms wrapping around my neck, her legs wrapping around my waist.

"Hey," I say, stroking her hair and turning to kick the door closed, before carrying her to the couch and sitting with her still wrapped around me as she buries her face into the crook of my neck.

"Ella, look at me," I say gently, taking her face in my palms, bringing her face up to look at me.

"What's wrong?" "Nothing." "Bullshit. Did Ash..."

"No, nothing happened. I just really needed to feel you," she says, bringing her eyes up to meet mine, and I can see the honesty in them. I can see something else as well - is it fear? I feel my jaw start to tighten at the thought. *I swear, if that motherfucker did anything to her....*

"Talk to me," I say, letting my thumbs stroke tenderly over her cheeks.

"I'm fine. It was just a hard one. My emotions got the better of me."

"Isn't that a normal reaction?" I ask, slightly confused.

"Yes, it should be, but it hasn't been for me, for such a long time, until you," she says, staring at me with those beautiful, expressive eyes of hers that just make me melt with how much I can feel and see in them. The only thing I see in them right now is an honesty behind her words, which causes my body to relax a little as I smile at her.

"Well, I would say that's good news, then." Is all I say before pressing my mouth against hers. When her lips part, our tongues touch and tangle with each other's and the kiss grows deep with a hunger as Ella grinds herself against my now rock-hard erection. In a frenzy of hands moving to feel each other, we tug and pull at clothes which seem to go flying everywhere, until she's naked from the waist up, still wearing her skirt that's now pulled up around her hips. Pulling one of her nipples into my mouth, I flick it with my tongue, taking the pebbled bud between my teeth with a light tug which causes a deep moan to come from her.

With her mouth against my ear, she bites it with a whispered, "I need you in me, right now."

"Your wish is my command," I growl back. As she removes my painfully hard cock from my pants, I reach between her legs, sliding my fingers inside the soft material of her panties, pulling it to the side. Letting my fingers stroke between her soft folds, I feel the urgency of her desire as her wetness coats them.

"Condom," I mouth against the skin of her throat, then groan when she leans away from me, shoving her hand into her purse sitting on the coffee table where she'd dropped it and quickly pulling out a foil packet with a devilish grin. Within seconds she has it open, my cock sheathed, and is lifting herself to align her pussy with the head of my cock, before impaling herself onto it with such force I think I might blow my load before we even begin. With my fingers holding her panties to one side, I feel myself entering her where are bodies join together. As she starts to move up and down, it has to be one of the most erotic things I've ever felt, just feeling her wetness coating the shaft of my cock as it slides in and out. I take small bites at the soft skin of her shoulder, her throat, the side of her neck, until I'm back at her mouth as she fucks me hard, grinding herself against my balls. It's hot and frenzied, and all I can do is lose myself in her need. That need comes with my hands gripping her hips, pulling her down harder onto me as she throws back her head with a long, satisfied moan of pleasure which continues as I pull her down several more times, releasing my own pleasure into her greedy body before she collapses against me, panting, her hands stroking through my hair, her legs trembling as I wrap my arms tightly around her.

Once I get my breath back, I stand with her legs and arms still wrapped around me and make my way to the bedroom. Placing her on the bed, I pull off her skirt and underwear, and cover her with the sheet. Going into the bathroom, I dispose of the condom then slide in next to her, folding her up against my side where we both fall asleep, exhausted.

Waking, I reach out my arm, feeling the loss of her when I only find cold sheets and an empty bed. Sitting up, I scrub a hand over my face. Standing and grabbing my sweat pants, I head for the bathroom, then out to the lounge where I find Ella sitting on the couch wearing one of my t-shirts which swamps her, almost like a dress, with her legs curled up under her, typing away on an iPad.

"Morning," I say, causing her to look up and smile. "I thought you'd fucked me and chucked me, for a minute." I grin, going into the kitchen and putting on the coffee pot.

"Sorry, I had some paperwork to finish up and I didn't want to wake you."

"It's fine. You want some coffee?"

"Please." She smiles and goes back to typing.

By the time I sit next to her on the couch, handing her a mug, she's turned off the iPad and placed it on the coffee table.

"So, what happened?" I ask casually, taking a sip from my mug. "What do you mean?"

"At the Carter place."

"Nothing, besides the obvious. Why?"

"Because the woman who walked through that door this morning and fucked my brains out on my couch, was a very emotional one," I say, now looking at her.

"I don't know, I just needed to be with you," she says with a slight shake of her head.

"And nothing happened with Ash?" I eye her.

"No, nothing," she answers with frankness, so I let it go, but something just didn't feel right.

We share a late breakfast, followed by a shower, then she gets dressed and I walk her out to her car. Opening the door, she tosses her bag in, then turns to me.

"When are you on shift again?"

"Tonight, then I will be off for a couple of days. What about you?" I say, reaching out to an errant strand of her hair and tucking it behind her ear.

"I have the next three days off now."

"So, will I be seeing you?"

"I hope so."

"Tomorrow night?" I say with a hopeful grin.

"I'll be waiting."

Leaning down, I place a soft kiss on her lips before she gets into her car and drives away.

For the rest of that day, and through my shift at the station, I can't seem to shake off the weird feeling in my gut about Ella's behavior this morning. I mean, don't get me wrong, I love a confident woman who takes what she wants during sex, but there was just something completely different about her this morning. I'm not sure if it's because she'd had an emotional few days at the Carter farm and was just tired, or if something had happened with Ash. The thought of him touching her instantly causes my jaw to clench in anger, but the tension in my jaw is broken by the station alarm and the sound of running boots as Hatch, Liam and Ethan hurry out from the kitchen. Throwing down the cloth I was cleaning the truck with, I head for my locker, getting into my bunkers before running to the truck.

"House fire, Deacon Street," Hatch says as we strap in and exit the station with lights and sirens blaring. Luckily Deacon Street is close, but not close enough. By the time the truck pulls up to the curb, flames are bursting from every crack in the old house. Moving into gear, I make my way towards the front of the house, where the front door is completely gone. Taking my axe, I smash in a large, front window and duck as a roar of air and heat escape from their containment. Behind me, I can hear Ethan yell out to the crowd of people milling around on the other side of the street, watching as the house goes up like a tinder box.

"Does anyone know if someone lives here?" Ethan yells out through the loud noise of crackling and falling timber.

"Dotty Collins, but she's over here," someone else yells out.

When I hear the voice and look, I can see an elderly woman, wrapped in a blanket and clutching a tiny dog to her chest, her face blackened from soot. Grabbing the medical bag and the oxygen, I go over and pull a new mask from its packet, hook it up to the O2 tank, and slip it over her face.

"Do you have any pain?" I ask as I visually check her over, but she shakes her head.

"No, I picked up Daisy and ran as soon as I saw the smoke," she says, holding up her little pooch.

"Did you see where the smoke was coming from?"

"The kitchen," she says, shaking her head as her eyes fill with tears. "I must have left the damn stove on."

"It's okay. The only thing that matters is that you and Daisy, here, got out. You did good, Mrs. Collins," I say, trying to give the frail woman some reassurance.

"The medics are here now to take a look at you," I say, moving back for them to get to her, before going back to my team to help with the fire.

Considering the house was small and almost gone by the time we arrived, it still took a while to control so it didn't spread to any of the neighboring houses. By the time it was contained, the sun was coming up and Johnson, Mick, and Thompson had turned up to take over the clean up. After a shower, I notice several missed calls on the screen of my phone from Molly and a text from Ella. Pressing Molly's number, she answers on the first ring with a frantic, "Are you okay?"

"I'm fine."

"We heard it over the scanner."

"Yep, it's contained. Some of the guys are down there now on clean up duty."

"I'm not sure I'll ever get used to your profession," she exhales out.

"Not sure I'll ever get used to yours, either," I chuckle. "Were there any casualties?"

"No, the old lady who lived there got out before it went up." "That's good," she breathes out.

"Molly?"

"Yes?"

"Go to bed."

"Going now," she says before hanging up. Then I type out a quick message to Ella.

ME

Hey babe.

ELLA

I heard there was a fire. Everything okay?

ME

All good and under control, heading home
for some sleep.

ELLA

Glad to hear.

Chapter Seventeen

Ella

Seeing the text from Jaxon was a relief, letting me finally breathe easier. I'd heard about the fire on the local radio station that I had on to keep me company while I did some much-needed chores around the house. As soon as I heard about the fire, my stomach muscles bunched into a knot so tight I thought I was going to throw up my lunch. I knew Jaxon was on shift at the station and that he would be there. I also knew it was his job, a job he'd been doing for years and that he knew what he was doing, but my brain had different thoughts. So, with baited breath, I'd sat on the couch with my phone clutched against my chest, while I almost chewed my thumb nail off and waited. But after his text, I feel myself deflating like a balloon and my head start to hurt from the tension I'd been holding in this whole time. Going into the kitchen, I take a couple of pills from the Tylenol bottle and down them with a glass of water, then lean against the sink for a minute, trying to compose myself after the erratic thoughts and feelings that had been going through my mind. Thoughts of Jaxon being hurt, or worse, killed. Thoughts of him never walking through my front door again were more than a thought, because I was actually feeling the loss, which is crazy.

Maybe this is why I'd chosen to be on my own for so long. It was easier. No-one to worry about, no-one to feel for; it was simple and uncomplicated. The deeper my feelings for him were getting, the quicker I seemed to be losing control of those thoughts and emotions which had taken me so many years to control and lock into the steel box deep in the back of my mind where they couldn't cripple me again. Feeling my head start to throb more now, I head for my bedroom and lay on the bed. When Walter jumps up next to me, I run my hand over his soft fur and feel the rumble of his purr. I feel my body relax a little. Closing my eyes, I slow my breathing and concentrate on the rhythmic sound of his purring, eventually falling asleep.

Opening my eyes, suddenly awoken by a loud knocking at the door, I pull myself up from the bed with a groan at the interruption of my sleep. With my head now feeling a lot clearer and less painful, I make my way to the door and open it, expecting to see Jaxon. I'm surprised when I'm faced with a huge bouquet of flowers held in the hand of Ash.

"Ash?" I say, looking at him, bleary-eyed and a little confused. "Hey, these are for you," he smiles, pushing the flowers towards me. "They're for everything you did for my family."

"Thank you, but it's not necessary," I say, looking down at the beautiful mixture of fragrant colorful flowers.

"Mom insisted."

"That's really nice. I'll give her a call to thank her," I say, looking up at him standing with his hands pushed into the front of his jeans, appearing very awkward.

"Can I come in?" he finally asks.

"I don't think that's a good idea," I answer, shaking my head. "Sorry, I should have realized you'd have company," he says, taking a step back, his words coming out clipped and sharp.

"It's just a bad idea, Ash. After the other night, I think we said what we needed to say to each other, don't you?"

"The other night, I'd been drinking."

"Maybe, but it doesn't change anything. I'm sorry, Ash," I say, trying to gently reinforce some kind of boundary between us.

"So, now what? That's it?"

"Well, I was hoping we could still be friends."

"Fuck your friendship, it's worthless to me. You're worthless to me," he growls through clenched teeth, his face so close to mine I can feel his breath. His top lip is lifted in a snarl, his eyes looking directly into mine, and what I see in them sends a shiver of terror through my veins. I'm rooted to the spot where I'm standing, pinned by his angry stare which is broken when he abruptly turns to leave. The shock of his sudden movement causes me to jump back inside, closing and locking the door quickly. Leaning my back against it, I listen as he slams the gate closed, quickly followed by the sound of his truck starting and the sound of squealing tires as he takes off. Could this day get any worse?

"You're worthless to me." The words echo in my head as a pain sears through my chest and I am instantly thrown back in time, just by that simple word, worthless.

Sliding to the floor, with the flowers still clutched in my arms, I sit for several minutes contemplating Ash's words and his behavior. In all of the years I've known the Carter brothers, I never saw any evidence of Ash having any kind of romantic interest in me, and I'm pretty sure I never showed him any interest either. I know Leah often plays bed buddies with Cole, and occasionally we've shared a table at Finnegans with them, but never anything more, so his sudden behavior is strange and unexpected. Although Cole and Ash are brothers, they are the complete opposite of each other. Cole is always bright, friendly, and extremely funny, while Ash is always quiet, somber, and intense, which is why I know I've never given him an ounce of attention. I knew exactly what type of man he was, and it was definitely not mine.

Eventually, I pull myself up off the floor and take the flowers into the kitchen. Laying them on the bench, I go back down the hall to finish off the laundry I'd started earlier, in an attempt to forget they and Ash's visit ever happened at all.

When Jaxon arrives a few hours later, wraps his arms around me, and presses his lips against mine, I instantly feel lighter. "Hmm, you always smell so good," he moans as he buries his nose into my hair, inhaling deeply.

"And you always feel good," I moan back.

"Feel all you want," he breathes into the side of my neck. "Did you get some sleep?"

"Yeah, a few hours," he says, pulling his face from where it's buried to look at me.

"Was it bad? The fire?"

"The house was so old and run down, it went up pretty quick. Luckily, the old lady who lived there managed to get out on her own."

"That's good. I'm glad no-one got hurt," I say, walking into the kitchen with Jaxon following behind me.

"Yeah, me too. So, I was thinking you might want to go out for dinner to..." he starts to say, but stops abruptly. Turning, I see his eyes on the flowers.

"Nice."

"Karen Carter sent them, as a thank you."

"Thoughtful and well deserved, but they need some water," he says, motioning to the large bouquet which looks a little wilted. He's right. In my attempt to forget about the person who'd delivered them, I had, in turn, neglected them. His eyes lock onto the gift card attached, a card I hadn't even read. Scooping them off the bench, I start to undo the ribbon that's holding them together, over the sink.

"Can you get me that vase up there on the top shelf?" I ask, pointing up to the only one I own, sitting on the top shelf in the pantry.

"Sure." I watch as he effortlessly takes down the vase and hands it to me. After arranging the blooms, I clear away the paper and place the card in the basket of fruit on the counter. Looking up, I see him looking at me, his brows slightly furrowed. "Is everything alright?"

"Yes, fine. Why?" I say, giving him a reassuring smile. "You look a little off-color."

"I had a headache earlier, but I took a nap and I'm good now." "We don't have to go out anywhere if you don't feel up to it."

"If there's one thing I do feel up to, it's getting out of here and grabbing a burger at Kelly's diner. I am starving," I say, giving him a wide smile which he mirrors back at me.

"Now, that sounds like a great plan," he says, letting his keys swing around his index finger. Grabbing my jacket and purse, I follow him to the front door, pulling it closed behind me and leaving the memory of the day behind. If there is one thing this man deserves, it's my mind on him tonight and not on memories from the past.

One of the best things about a Kelly's burger is that the melted cheese, mixed with Kelly's magical and secret sauce, always manages to drip down your chin and coat your fingers. This is made even better when the sexy man sitting across from you takes a lot of pleasure in taking your cheese-soaked fingers into his mouth and slowly sucking every morsel off them. Needless to say, as soon as we'd eaten, neither one of us could wait to get back to my place, where Jaxon continued to show me just how much pleasure he gets from licking and sucking different parts of my body. All the way home, I could feel the burn of want and need bouncing between us. The cab of his truck was ready to combust with desire, leading me to believe that once we got behind closed doors, I would be lucky to have enough time to slip off my shoes, but there was nothing fast or hurried about it. Jaxon made love to me with a slow, languid passion. Every touch and taste taken with a groan of pleasure, until the endless teasing reignited the burning desire from earlier in the night, resulting in us coming together in an explosive combination of ecstasy, groaning, panted breaths, and sweat-covered bodies, which ended in pure satisfaction and contentment as I fell asleep in his arms.

"Come and meet your new daddy."

"Stepdad," I say under my breath as my Mom stands in front of me with her new husband, Henry; her arm hooked through his, her smile illuminated by the scarlet red lipstick lining her mouth. If it was up to her, Henry would have been Daddy number five, but he was number two. The other men she'd brought home didn't stick around long enough for her to shackle herself to them. Clare Thomas was slim, with bleached blonde hair and a set of boobs that entered a room before she did, and she knew how to use them to get what she wanted from the opposite sex. She was a selfish, greedy woman, who got worse after my real Dad was killed in a car accident after falling asleep at the wheel, exhausted from working three jobs in an attempt to keep his wife happy in the life he'd promised her when they got married. She was left with a small life insurance policy after his death, but it wasn't enough for her, so, she went out and did what she did best; flaunted her assets to the fish in the pond, then reeled them in. Henry, an accountant with a small amount of wealth, was the first idiot to have sex with her without a condom, and when my mom became pregnant with my younger brother, Henry did the right thing and married her. I didn't like him from the beginning, he was quiet and worked long hours, and was my mother's lap dog, but all that changed when she went into hospital to give

birth to their first child together. I remember being asleep in my bed and being woken by a movement on my mattress. Pulling my blanket up tighter under my chin, I felt a large body lay behind me and a large hand move over my waist and pull me into that body, his head moving closer to mine. "You're so pretty, Ella. Let me look after you. No-one will love you as much as I can," he whispered. I didn't move. He didn't do anything else to me that night, but fall asleep, his loud snoring and heaving body behind me as I curled myself into a tight ball, silent tears running down my cheeks and wetting the pillow under my head. No, he didn't do anything to me that night, but there were plenty more nights to come.

Chapter Eighteen

When I'm woken abruptly by what sounds like a wounded animal in pain, my eyes instantly open as Ella, still pressed against me, jumps and jerks in the circle of my arms.

"Ella," I say, turning to touch the side of her face. "Ella, wake up, baby," I say again, this time a little louder. Leaning up, I gently stroke the stray strands of hair away from her face which is covered in a light sheen of sweat, her brows furrowed and lips tight. Whatever dream she's having is causing her an agony I can't watch. "Wake up, sweetheart," I breathe against her moist skin. When she lets out an agonizing moan trailing the word, 'No,' I feel like I've been sucker- punched in the chest. Touching her shoulder, I give her a gentle shake and her eyes open, looking straight up at the ceiling. I watch silently as she blinks several times, her eyes wide, glassy-looking, and filled with fear as she frantically tries to fully wake up.

"Ella," I say gently and her eyes turn to mine. "What?"

"I think you were having a bad dream," I say, running the back of my fingers over her cheek.

"Really?"

"Yeah, a pretty bad one. Look, your covered in sweat. I'll get you some water," I say, pulling myself from the bed and wandering out of the bedroom and down to the kitchen. Filling a glass with chilled water from the jug in the fridge, I notice the card from the flowers in the fruit basket and my fingers begin to itch. I instantly feel guilty at how much I want to see what's written on that card. It goes against the grain for me to even contemplate invading her privacy, but you know what they say about curiosity and that cat, right? Picking up the card and looking at it for a moment, I'm tempted, but with a sigh I'm also a man of my principles. The only problem is, as I place the card back in the basket it slips from the envelope and there, in bold black letters, I see one word, ASH. Staring at the card, I take in a deep, calming breath while I rationalize the situation. Now, I can understand him wanting to give the nurse who looked after his family a bunch of flowers as a thank you. What I can't understand, is why Ella tried to hide both the gift and the card from me. Walking back into the bedroom, I hand her the glass of water which she takes and drinks down greedily until it's empty. Sliding back into bed next to her, she moves her head back against my chest, placing her hand over my heart, and I pull her in close. "I'm here if you want to talk," I say and she shakes her head.

"Just a dream. Sorry for waking you up."

"Anytime, baby," I say, kissing the top of her head. It doesn't take long for her body to relax as her breathing becomes long and deep, and my own body relaxes with the comfort of her warm body tucked into mine. But my brain has a different idea as it tries to put the pieces of Ella's puzzle together, until eventually, I fall asleep myself.

Over the next week, I find myself thinking way too much about Ella, which is usually my normal now, but this time the thoughts are more about her nightmare. When we woke up that morning and I had asked her about it, she shrugged it off, saying it was no big deal and I'm finding myself being torn about the fact that everyone has things in their life they'd prefer to keep private. I get that, but I can't ignore the weird change in her since she was at the Carter farm. It's pissing me off because, deep in my gut, I know it has something to do with Ash Carter, and the thought that something might have happened to upset her that night bugs me and throws my trust zone into a fragile area that has me wondering if and why Ella was lying to me?

After cleaning out the rig, I hit the small gym attached to the station to try and clear my mind, but after working up a sweat to almost exhaustion, I find she's still on my mind. Wiping my face, I lift my head when Jacob walks in and hands me a bottle of water, which I drink down in one hit as he takes a seat next to me on the bench. "Everything alright?"

"Yeah, why?" I pant out.

"No reason, apart from the fact you've been punishing the treadmill for the past hour. I don't think it's ever worked so hard."

"I'm sure you've given it a good run now and then."

"Not for a long time now. Between work and Ruby, I get all the workout I need at home," he says, grinning.

"TMI, mate."

"So, what's going on?"

"Not much. Just trying to clear my head."

"Problems?" he asks, raising a brow.

"I'm not sure," I tell him, because honestly, at this point, I really don't know myself.

"Can I help?"

"That depends."

"On?"

"What can you tell me about Ash Carter?" I say.

"That he looks like a prick."

"Well, I already know that," I chuckle.

"Not too much. I see him at Finnegans occasionally, usually if there's a live band playing. He comes in with his brother, Cole, and they always sit with Ella and her friend from the hospital...the blonde chic... what's her name?" he says, clicking his fingers.

"Leah."

"That's her. I think she and Cole have a 'friends with benefits' thing going on."

"What about Ella and Ash? Do they ever hook up?"

"Not that I know of. Honestly, I've never seen Ella show any interest in him, he's just kind of like Coles's sidekick, his wingman. In fact, I find it hard to believe that they're even brothers; Cole always seems to be laughing and joking, while Ash has this permanent 'resting bitch face' thing going on."

Nodding my head in agreement, I feel a little relieved that at least I'm not alone in my dislike of Ash Carter.

"So, you think Ash is trying to move in on Ella?" Jacob asks.

"I don't know what I'm thinking. What I do know is that she's been different since she spent those few days up there, nursing their father. It's just a gut feeling, you know?"

"Hey, I'm a big believer in that gut feeling. I'm also a big believer in not waiting around, procrastinating and turning yourself inside out, when you could just talk to Ella."

"You're right."

"I know I am. Plus I'm saving the station from having to buy a new treadmill." He chuckles before standing.

"Thanks, mate," I say with sincerity, grateful for his advice. "Anytime."

The talk with Jacob did wonders for my splintered thoughts. When I came to live in this town, it was to spend time with Molly and Caleb. It was also for a change, a new adventure, to meet new people and make new friends, which I seem to have done.

Honestly, I like it here and I like Ella, a lot, but getting into a messy situation which is turning my brain inside out based on some strange behavior and a gut feeling needs to stop. I need to step back a little. I'm guessing Ella has a past which she would rather forget about, and I get that, but that's not the problem. The problem is, have I walked into something currently going on between her and Ash? That's the question I will be asking Ella. I need to know where we stand before I fall hard for her. Fuck, who am I kidding? I've already bloody fallen for her like a stupid, love-struck teenager, complete with suspicious thoughts and possessive actions, which isn't me at all. That's something that needs to change, and the only person that can do that, is me.

This week was beyond busy, dealing with the aftermath of some fearsome storms that came out of nowhere to the South. I spent the whole week at the station, with little time to have any type of phone conversations with Ella, only managing to share a few brief texts here and there. By the end of the week, all I could do when I got home was shower, drop into my bed, and sleep for most of the day, only waking when I got a text from Ella asking if I'd be coming over tonight. I felt like a total asshole when I sent one back, letting her know that I was too exhausted to move out of my bed tonight, but would be over in the morning for breakfast. When she replies with a heart emoji, I didn't even have the energy to feel guilty. Well, not too much.

It's late in the afternoon when I wake again, change into swim shorts, and head out to the pool. Diving into the cool water without even thinking about it, I float on my back in the middle of the water and look up at the sun which is slowly setting, giving me a fleeting memory and a small pang of homesickness. Not for my apartment, because my home had always been where my mum was, but for the ocean and the vast, white sandy beaches where I could swim and walk for miles. Just for a moment, I swear I catch the scent of an ocean breeze and salty water. The rest of the night was spent with pizza and a beer in front of the TV, until I crash into bed again, waking up early the next morning.

I can smell breakfast cooking before Ella even opens her front door, and as soon as I see her sweet smiling face, my eyes wander down the length of her, casually dressed in leggings and an oversized sweatshirt which is falling off one shoulder, leaving it bare. All I want to do is feel her in my arms and take in her intoxicating smell, and as soon as she closes the door behind us, that's exactly what I do. I wrap my arms around her, pulling her into my body, and kiss those warm, succulent lips with a moan. It's several minutes before I can even contemplate letting her go, watching her as she walks into the kitchen and back to the stove, where something seems to be burning. Grabbing the pan off the heat, she drops it into the sink, turning on the water to cool it down.

"Looks like this fireman caused a fire," I chuckle. "Sorry."

"Don't be. It was just pancakes; it's easy to make some more," she says, throwing the burnt ones into the garbage and cleaning the pan, before pouring some more batter into it. Once she has expertly filled two plates with pancakes, she picks them up, motioning towards the small table and chairs in front of a large window in the kitchen. The table had been set for two, with a jug of orange juice, butter, and syrup sitting on a tray in the middle. Cutting off a large piece of pancake and stuffing it into my mouth, I close my eyes and let out a moan of sheer pleasure.

"Oh, wow. These are amazing."

"Thanks." She smiles, pouring syrup on her own.

"You're going to have to stop feeding me like this or I'm going to have trouble getting into my jeans."

"That's good, because I much prefer you out of them." She winks, giving me a sexy, cheeky grin. She looks so relaxed and happy, and I want to kick myself for maybe upsetting breakfast with what I need to say to her, but I know if I don't, I'm going to continue on the spiral of thoughts which have been driving me nuts.

"Listen, I need to ask you about something that's been on my mind a lot lately."

"Okay," she says slowly, giving me a puzzled look.

"Did you and Ash ever date?" I blurt out before shoving more pancake into my mouth and watching as she stiffens, placing her knife and fork on her plate before leaning on both elbows and moving forward, looking me straight in the eyes.

"Never."

Giving her a nod and a smile, I let out an inner breath of relief. Watching her closely for any kind of reaction to my question, I'm both relieved and a little stunned when she picks up her fork and starts eating her breakfast again and launching into a story about how Walter had woken her at the crack of dawn this morning by trapping himself inside the shower, unable to push the glass door open again. As she leans back in her chair, looking full and satisfied, once we'd finished, I pick up the dirty plates and take them over to the kitchen sink.

"Just leave them. I'll do them later."

"Nope. You cook - I clean, that's the deal," I say. Turning to look at her, I am momentarily in awe of this stunning woman, now with her eyes closed and face tilted up slightly, catching the morning sun coming through the large window.

"Ella?"

"Yes," She says, opening her eyes and looking at me. "Have I told you lately how beautiful you are?" "Not today." She smiles at me.

Wiping my hands on the towel, I walk over and hold out my hand for her to take. Feeling her small soft hand sliding into mine, I gently pull her up and slide my hands around her waist, leaning down to place a kiss on her mouth which still has the sweet taste of syrup coating her soft lips.

"Not only are you smart, sexy, and incredibly beautiful, I do believe I am falling for you."

"Really?" she whispers against my mouth.

"Yes. You taste so sweet, is there some syrup left?" "Plenty."

"Good," I say, picking up the half full jug of syrup and starting to move her towards the hall. "Because I have a plan for it." But before we reach her bedroom, where I'd planned to make a second breakfast of her delicious body, my phone beeps loudly in my pocket with a familiar tone which I recognize as the emergency call from the station. Groaning, I pull my phone from my back pocket and read the screen.

WORK

All staff not on shift need to immediately return to the station. This is an emergency call.

Groaning as I hand Ella the jug of syrup, I look at her. "I need to go."

"What is it?" she asks, looking slightly alarmed.

"Emergency staff call. That means there's a fire out of control some-where and they need assistance," I say, turning and quickly making my way to the front door with Ella following behind.

"Be safe," she says as I brush a quick kiss across her lips before running out to the truck and heading for the station.

Chapter Nineteen

Ella

"I'm falling for you."

Jaxon's words run through my mind, making my stomach flip flop into a thousand different positions, because I'd already fallen for him. It had happened so fast, I didn't even see it coming, and the feeling is both wonderful and terrifying at the same time as thoughts of my tainted past flood my mind. Buried secrets and mistakes, mistakes that could cause us both pain in the long term. I'm not sure if I'm prepared to do that to Jaxon, but how do I let him go after he's stirred so many emotions in me, emotions that make me feel alive again.

In the beginning, I was drawn to his playfulness, his charisma, his honesty, not to mention those sexy, rugged good looks he has going on, but the whole package also told me that he wasn't looking for anything serious. Well, that and the fact that he was here on a working visa, which also gave me the reassurance that whatever we did would be short lived. Instead, I got something out of this world; feelings which caught me off guard, feelings so unexpected that they're now leaving me torn between the pain and disappointment we might cause each other if it ends now, and a deeper and more devastating pain later, if we're both falling into this so quickly.

Flopping down on the couch, I reach for the drawer in the table beside it and pull out the small radio I keep for just in case the power goes out.

Switching it onto the local news channel, I patiently wait for any news about the emergency Jaxon was called out to. Thoughts, that if others were called in to assist, then it must have been something big, causing a knot to form in my belly.

Three mugs of coffee, and some pacing of the living room later, a voice on the radio finally announces that there's a house fire on the outer limits of the town which has been burning for the last few hours and that firefighters are on the scene trying to contain it. Apparently, the mechanic owner, who does most of his repairs from home, had some oil drums close to the house which had spurred the fire on.

Letting out a deep breath of relief that at least it sounds like the fire was under control and that there's been no announcement that anyone was hurt, I'm still not sure that the constant heavy feeling in my chest will be going anywhere until I hear from Jaxon himself. With that thought, I know that from the way I feel about him, I am screwed.

I'd tried my damned hardest not to keep looking at my phone. I went for a walk, which I had to cut short because I'd specifically left my phone in the house so I didn't look at it, but I just couldn't stand the thought of missing a text. I did some baking, then ate a sandwich for dinner, because frankly, after all the baking, I just couldn't be bothered to cook anything more. Then I took a shower, got comfortable on the couch with Walter, and watched a movie. As you can guess, after spending the whole day waiting for a text or call from Jaxon, as soon as I dozed off my phone beeped.

JAXON

Hey, sorry about tonight, but I am totally spent. Going to bed. Will call you tomorrow.

ME

Don't be sorry. Are you okay?

JAXON

All good here, just tired.

ME

So good to hear, get some sleep

JAXON

Night babe.

ME

Night.

Sitting up and grabbing the remote, I turn off the TV and the lamp, and take myself to bed, the stress of this whole day causing my brain to finally scream for some sleep. As I slip between the covers of my bed, my head sinks into the pillow and I finally feel relaxed as I drift off to sleep.

Chapter Twenty

Jaxon

Leaving Ella's, I drive straight to the station and run in, passing Thompson and Jacob on my way to get into my gear.

"What the fuck is going on?" I yell from the locker room.

"Most of the guys are off this weekend and there's a house fire over on Denton Road."

"Another one?" I say, coming out and jumping into the second rig with them.

"Yep," Jacob answers as he flips on the lights and sirens and we pull out of the station.

"So, why are we needed? Aren't there enough guys there already?" "This one is different. It's out at Travis Dale's place. He's a mechanic who works from home, which means a shed full of flammable shit. It seems to have started in the garage and spread fast, with the oil and gasoline drums catching fire. Now it's spreading over to the next property, and with these winds..." Jacob says, shaking his head and I know exactly what he means. Even though we've had some wet weather lately, things are dry enough for this to quickly get out of hand. Listening in on the radio, it sounds like the guys are having a hard time controlling the gasoline and oil fire as they try to smoother it with a deluge of water.

"We'll need foam," Thompson says as we get closer to the cloud of black smoke billowing up into the air. Turning up the winding dirt road, we tear up towards a two-story house, which thankfully looks untouched by the fire. Not far from it is a large three-door garage where I can faintly see the back end of a car peaking out through the thick black smoke funneling out through each doorway in three thick dark coils. Jumping out of the truck as soon as it comes to a stop, I pull on my respirator as Thompson pulls out three foam extinguishers. Picking one up each, we move towards the garage opening where Cooper is standing with the hose directed inside. A large stream of water from the hose is directed inside and a large stream of water is flooding back out.

"There's three drums down the back in the right-hand corner. I've tried drenching the fuckers, but nothing's happening," he yells. Giving him a nod in understanding, all three of us walk into the thick black smoke in search of the source.

The smoke is so thick, I can't see my hand in front of my eyes. This place is bigger on the inside than I expected, so I move towards the location Cooper said, trying to keep to the righthand side and taking cautious steps forward.

"It's back here!" I hear Jacob yell over my headset, then I see the small flames enveloped by smoke. Pulling the pin and squeezing the trigger, I make sweeping movements over the drums until my extinguisher runs empty. Luckily, Jacob's seems to calm the flames instantly, and thankfully the three tanks of foam get it under control. The place is still thick with smoke, but through it I spot a set of double doors next to the drums. Making my way to them, I lean back and kick them open and watch as a large amount of the black smoke is sucked outside, making it a little easier to at least see each other now. It looks like some of the flames from the oil drums have dropped down onto a pile of tires which have started to melt. We walk around the large area, checking for any more flames, smashing out another couple of windows to let the toxic smoke escape.

As the smoke starts to thin out more, I can see where the fire has escaped out of the drums and made its way up the back wall to the glass window above them, the intense heat causing the glass to crack and shatter, letting the flames escape and start on a path of destruction as it snakes its way through the long grass, igniting everything in its path.

From here, I can see a line of guys fighting what looks like a wall of flames moving through a field. Moving to the other side of the garage where I'd seen the parked car earlier, I see something on the floor. As I get closer, and the smoke clears, I see a distinct pair of legs sticking out from under the front of the car.

"We've got a body over here!" I shout into my helmet mic as I lean down and grab the booted feet and pull. The body slides easily from under the car, as it's lying on a wheeled board. Kneeling down, I pull off my gloves and press two fingers to the man's throat, feeling for a pulse. Nothing. Removing my helmet, I pull off my respirator and place it over his face as I start compressions on his chest. The air is so thick with the smell of burnt rubber and fumes, that it instantly gives me a slight chemical taste in my mouth as I push on the chest in front of me. Dropping their foam tanks, Jacob and Thompson move to either end of the board that the guy is lying on and bend down, each grabbing an end.

"Lift on three," Jacob says and as they lift in unison, I continue to try and do compressions on the chest of the lifeless body as they carry the board outside. Placing him down on the floor in front of the waiting medics, I let them take over. We watch with baited breath as they work on the guy and we're joined by the Captain.

Jacob hands me a bottle of water. Twisting the cap, I fill my mouth with the water, rolling it around and spitting out the remnants of the toxic taste in my mouth, before drinking down the rest.

"Is that Travis?" he asks, looking at Jacob with concern.

"Yeah." Is the only word he speaks as we watch the medics work tirelessly. Eventually, there's a cough and movement from the once lifeless body, and I hear breaths of air being expelled from the guys around me, as the medics quickly place the man into the back of the ambulance.

"I'm sorry to have to call you guys in, but we only had the two man crew on today."

"It's fine. What about the grass fire?" I ask, looking at the Captain.

"It took a while, but it's under control."

"Unlike these fires," Jacob says, looking at the Captain, his brow raised in question.

"I know, that's why there'll be an investigation."

"Does that include the one last week, as well?" I ask.

"Yes."

"Good, because either the residents of Durandale are getting bored with their homes and trying to pull an insurance scam by setting them on fire, or there's someone out there getting a kick from it," I say and notice that both Jacob and Thompson nod their heads in agreement.

"He's right. Get on it, Cap, before the next person isn't as lucky as Travis," Jacob says, pointing to the back of the leaving ambulance. "Now, do you need us or are we done?" he asks through slightly gritted teeth. When the Captain gives him a nod, he turns and starts to walk back to the rig, throwing "Let's go, guys," over his shoulder.

Although the trip back to the station is silent, I can tell by the sideways glance Jacob gives me, we're all thinking the same thing. If this is the work of an arsonist, then they usually escalate, starting off small and moving to something bigger. Which means more risk to not just the public, but to firefighters as well. Once back at the station, showered and dressed back in normal attire, we meet up at Jacob's truck.

"I really hope this is just a coincidence, guys," Thompson says.

"Seems too close for comfort. Let's see what they find from both sites, before we get our butts in a tangle. Now, I am going home to my wife - see you guys later," Jacob says, jumping into his pickup and closing the door.

"Catch you through the week," I say before pulling out my keys and heading to my own truck and straight for home.

I was hoping to drop into bed for some sleep, but when I see Molly sitting outside at the table, all hope of that just flies out of the window. Sighing, I walk over to where she is and sit in the chair across from her. Might as well get this over with sooner, rather than later. So, before she even asks, I tell her about the fire and our suspicions, which I know was a big mistake as soon I see the look on her face. Instant worry. And that makes me slump back into my chair in regret.

"Molly, you have to stop with the worry. It's not good for you, or the baby." "Don't tell me what's good for me. I'm a pediatrician, remember?" She says with a slight irritation.

"Look, you have a stressful job, you're married to a man who has a stressful job, and your pregnant. You have enough on your plate, without adding me to it."

"I'm sorry." She sighs.

"I don't want you to be sorry for caring about me. I just don't want anything to happen to you, or that bean you have growing in your belly."

"And I don't want anything to happen to my brother."

"We've been through this so many times. I was fighting fires when you were still in school, it didn't bother you then, yet for some reason it does now?" I say and as soon as I see the tears pooling in her eyes, I want to kick myself in the balls, because it hits me like a ton of bricks - she's scared of losing me as well as our parents, that's what's different now. Quickly standing, I move to her, leaning down and wrapping my arms around her shoulders.

"I'm sorry. I didn't think, but I get it," I say, kissing the top of her head. "You should know that you'll never get rid of me that easily. Besides, I plan on spoiling your kid rotten in my uncle duties. But I promise that I will do everything in my power to never leave you, okay?"

She gives me a nod, along with a sniffle, just as Caleb steps outside and hands me a beer, his eyes instantly darting to Molly's wet, red cheeks. "Molly?"

"It's okay, just these bloody crazy baby hormones," she tells him, reaching up and slipping her hand into his as he gazes at her, his eyes searching hers until he's satisfied with her explanation before pulling a chair up beside her.

"I heard about the fires being under investigation," Caleb says, looking at me as he takes a pull of beer from his bottle.

"Will you be taking it on?" I ask him.

"Not my department. Fingers crossed we don't have an arsonist in Durandale, though."

"I agree, anyone who doesn't think twice about watching someone else burn to death, has to be unstable. Anyone come to mind?" I ask with a raised brow.

"Not off the top of my head, but who knows? It could be a newcomer to town," he says with a pointed grin in my direction.

"Fuck off," I chuckle.

"If there's someone out there lighting these fires on purpose, we'll find them," he says confidently.

"Good."

After finishing off my beer, I make my exit back to my place and heat up some leftovers which I eat in front of the TV until my eyes start to droop. Heading to bed, I send Ella a quick text to let her know that I'm home, safe, and that I will be over in the morning so I can finish off that second breakfast I'd promised her this morning. With that delicious thought, I drift into a deep sleep.

Chapter Twenty-One

Ella

As soon as I hear Jaxon's old clunky truck pull up at the front curb, I almost run to the front door. Swinging it open and leaning on the door frame my arms folded in protection from the cool wind outside, I watch him open the gate and walk up the path towards me, his face wide with that beautiful sexy smile of his, his hair still damp from a recent shower. Placing his hands on my hips, he slowly guides me backwards into the house while his mouth devours mine. Kicking the door shut behind him, his lips are warm and his tongue is hot as it sweeps inside my mouth, tasting mine. With his hungry mouth, he takes what he wants from me, and I let him, until he finally breaks the kiss.

"Hey, beautiful." His words are low and deep, and my body reacts with a tremble of need.

"Hi."

"I am so hungry," he grumbles.

"Really?"

"Hmm," he moans, burying his face into the side of my neck and placing open-mouthed kisses against it.

"We had better get you fed then."

"Exactly what I was thinking," he says as he moves me back against the kitchen bench and lifts me onto it, the unexpected move making me yelp in surprise. Leaving me there and walking over to the pantry, he returns with the jug of syrup from yesterday, placing it on the bench next to me. His large hands move down my arms to the belt of my robe, untying it and slipping his fingers under the silk material to open it, revealing my naked body. I hear him inhale sharply as his eyes roam over my body and I see the hunger in his eyes when his hands move to my thighs and gently open them enough to move between them. I can feel the tips of his fingers glide up between my breasts until he reaches the material of the robe at my shoulders then pushes it off, letting it slide down into a pool of silk on the bench top. As I let my arms slide free of it, our eyes are linked, lost in each other's lust, only breaking when I watch him dip his middle finger into the jug of syrup and bring it back to one of my nipples, covering it with the sticky fluid before doing the same to my other now-taught bud. Moving his hand towards my mouth, he speaks in a low growl, "Open."

Feeling his middle finger glide across by bottom lip, he slides it into my open mouth, rubbing the sweet syrup over my tongue. Closing my lips around his finger, I let my tongue play with it for a moment, then suck hard as his finger slides back out with a light pop. When his head bows and his mouth latches onto my nipple, his tongue swirling and sucking at the peaked bud, licking it clean of syrup before doing the same to the other one, I let out a moan of complete pleasure at the sensation of his mouth on me. His warm lips and mouth sucking and licking which grows harder and more uncontrolled as his moans fill with an impatience which shows how hungry for my body he is, and I feel his hard cock pressing against the inside of my thigh. Placing open-mouthed kisses between my breasts and down my stomach, he presses his palm lightly against my belly, causing me to lay back on the bench.

Picking up the jug of syrup, he pours a thin stream onto my sex, then quickly moves his mouth between my legs, licking at the syrup as it runs down between my folds. His tongue is warm as he flicks at my swollen clit, sucking it into his mouth before letting his flattened tongue run up and down the lips of my pussy like a hungry animal, making sure he catches every bit of the sticky syrup as the heat of my sex causes it to warm and become runnier. With my hands grasping onto his head, trying to get more of the erotic and mind-blowing sensation his mouth is causing, I feel myself call out his name in a hoarse shout as my pussy clenches and spasms with pleasure at a very sticky, sweet orgasm.

"Now, that's what I call a satisfying breakfast," he says breathlessly, lifting his head from between my legs, his face glistening with syrup, and my own juices coating his lips and beard.

"I totally agree," I manage to pant out as I slowly start to come down from such an explosive climax. Sitting, I reach out and start to undo his belt. "My turn."

"No, babe, you don't need to," he starts, but I cut off his words by pulling him closer to me, letting my hand drop to cover his hard cock through his jeans. Placing my mouth on his, I instantly taste myself on his lips and make sure I lick at them with my tongue.

"Don't tell me that you're the only one who gets to experience the pleasure of syrup oral. That's just greedy and mean," I say with a playful pout. Slipping down his body until I am standing on the floor, I place my hands flat on his chest and slowly move him backwards until he reaches the chair at the kitchen table and flops into it. Sliding my fingers under the hem of his t-shirt, lifting it and pulling it up over his head so I can see his hard sculptured chest which I run my fingers over before turning to grab the jug of syrup from the kitchen bench and kneel in front of him. Running my hands over his strong thighs, I feel the hard muscles flex as I move between his legs and go back to opening his belt, followed by the button and zip on his jeans, letting his cock spring free. Taking it in my hand, I let my fingers feel the strength of it, with its silky softness and swollen veins. I let my tongue taste a small bead of moisture at the tip as Jaxon leans back into the chair with a moan, giving me better access to his thick length. Wrapping my lips around it, I suck it deep into my throat, letting my tongue brush against the silkiness of his skin and those thick veins now throbbing along his shaft. Keeping him in my mouth, I reach for the jug. Moving my mouth away as I let a small amount of the syrup dribble over the head, watching as it slides down his long thick cock, stopping just as it reaches his balls, making it look like a delicious sugary lollipop that I'm greedy to take back into my mouth and devour, making sure to lick and suck every inch until it's syrup free and I'm left with just the taste of him. Releasing his balls from the confines of his jeans, I cup them, stroke them, and place open-mouthed kisses against them until my tongue takes me on a path back along his cock, sucking it back into my mouth. Looking up at Jaxon, I see his head is thrown back, his face smooth and lost in his own pleasure until he must sense my eyes on him. As his eyes open and go straight to mine, followed by his hands on either side of my face, his thumbs stroke a path down my cheeks to where my lips are wrapped around his cock. It's then that I feel the tightness in his balls as he watches his shaft move in and out, sliding between my lips, and I take him in deeper and faster. With a growl, he throws back his head with a hissed curse as he fills my throat with hot salty fluid that keeps coming as his cock pulsates and throbs its release, and I swallow with a greedy hunger.

A few hours later, after taking a shower to wash the stickiness from our bodies, I revel in the comfort of being in Jaxon's strong arms. The comfort I get from being entangled in the warmth of his embrace feels like pure serenity. With his muscled body stretched out, and my cheek pressed against his chest, I watch the slow rise and fall of it and listen to his soft breaths of sleep which he fell into as soon as his head hit the pillow. Poor guy would have been exhausted from attending that house fire, even if he said they luckily didn't have to stay too long. It's not just the strength and endurance of the body which drains when fighting a fire, the strength and endurance of the mind takes a hit as well, so it's nice to see him relaxed and in a deep sleep.

Chapter Twenty-Two

Jaxon

Unfortunately, after spending the night at Ella's, I had to leave her before the sun came up in the morning; I needed to get back home and change for work. She insisted on getting up and making me breakfast, and I insisted that she stayed in bed to get another hour's sleep before she too had to get up for work. Kissing her goodbye took longer than I expected, due to the fact that she looked so sexy with her sleepy eyes, pouty lips, mussed-up bed hair, and just the pure warmth of her, but eventually I managed to pull myself away, locking the door on the way out. I got home just in time to grab a shower and get changed, then head into the station in the hope that Cooper was already cooking breakfast. Luckily enough, he was, and I was just in time to sit down with the guys and share it with them.

Thankfully, it was a pretty smooth week. In fact, it was so quiet, I found myself cleaning the rigs more times than what was needed, while some of the others watched TV or spent time in the gym. Ella texted me during the week to let me know there was a live band playing at Finnegans this weekend and Leah had asked her if she was going.

ELLA

What do you think?

ME

Sounds good.

ELLA

Great. I'll let Leah know we'll meet her there then.

ME

Perfect.

Still looking at my phone, all I can do is smile at the simplicity of the comfortable relationship we seemed to have fallen into. I'm not sure exactly what it is, but we just gel. It's like we're both separate pieces of a puzzle that fit together with perfection and ease. So strange to think that when I came here, I had every intention of relaxing, exploring, and enjoying life. I never thought that when I set my eyes on Ella that day in the hospital, I'd end up exploring a relationship with her, but fuck I'm so glad I did because I'm not sure I can give her up now. She's gotten under my skin and into my soul. Who would have thought the perfect woman for me was on the other side of the world?

By Friday night, I was having second thoughts about going anywhere but to bed, but when I picked Ella up from her house, I quickly woke up. She was dressed in a form-fitting, strappy black dress, the hem sitting just above her knees, showing off her long legs, which she wore with some sandals and a denim jacket, making her outfit look elegant and casual, her beautiful black silky hair cascading over her shoulders in waves. She was stunning and very fuckable right now, but I'd promised her a night out, so my twitchy dick will just have to be patient and wait.

Finding a park outside Finnegans was a feat in itself; it looked like everyone in town was here tonight. We made our way into the bar, where we weaved through the crowd to a blonde standing in the corner, furiously waving her hands in our direction. Thankfully, when we got to her, we found Leah had grabbed us a table which already had Cole sitting at, a beer in his hand.

"You remember Cole, right?" Leah says, motioning towards him. "Jaxon, right?" Cole asks, holding out his hand for me to shake, which I do because I'm not sure if I have a problem with this guy yet; I can't judge the poor guy on his brother's behavior. Placing my hand on the small of Ella's back, I guide her to sit, then go to the bar and order some drinks then take them back to the table, handing Ella a glass of wine before sitting and taking a swig of my beer as I drape my arm across the back of her chair.

"So, how have you been settling in, besides stealing my friend's attention away from me?" Leah smiles at me.

"I've been good, settled in perfectly. Durandale is a great place, although I can honestly say I'm not sorry for stealing your girl away from you." I smile back at her.

"Good job I get to see her all week at work then, I guess."

"Now, that's where you're ahead of me."

"So, Cole, how's your mom doing?" Ella asks him and I see his smile fade just a little before he answers.

"It's been hard and she sure hides it well. It helps that she has the farm to run, you know, it keeps her busy, but you know what they say about how time heals all wounds?"

"What about you?" Ella asks.

"What can I say? I miss the old grump, but we can't turn back time." He sighs and Ella gives him a small knowing smile.

We watch as the three band members take to the small stage and the lights dim slightly. They're good, mostly doing covers of groups like Pearl Jam and Alice in Chains, inserting what I guess are a few of their own songs here and there, and the crowd seems to be enjoying them. People moving to the music and singing to the cover songs, and as the night moves on and the drinks go down faster, people get louder. When the band finally finishes playing, the roars of disappointment almost blow the roof off of Finnegans, so the band sticks around and plays another few songs until the alcohol starts to cause the crowd to settle down and listen, or leave, having realized they'd reached their limits. I had a couple of beers, then stuck to drinking Soda water on account of having driven here, so when I head to the bar to get everyone else one last drink before we call it a night, I am very sober when I see Ash leaning against the bar, his eyes burning a hole through my head which I welcome and return, only breaking it to give the barman my order. I wonder where this slimy fucker had been hiding all night. I mean,

Finnegan's isn't that big of a place that it's easy to lose someone, but this is the first time I've set eyes on him all night. With a slight sense of victory when he turns his glare away from me first, I shake my head and grin to myself; this guy is definitely a whack job with an ego problem.

It seems I spoke too soon, because when the barman places the drinks on a tray in front of me, the whacko now seems to be standing next to me, one arm leaning on the bar.

"Looks like fun over on the love table," he sneers. Ignoring him, as I hand over some cash for the drinks.

"Ella's looking fine tonight," he says, then pauses for a moment before he continues. "She looks almost as good as she did that night out on my front porch."

When the barman hands me back my change, I inhale deeply and calmly before picking up the tray in an attempt to contain myself at his obvious baited jibe, although I couldn't control the swiftness of the turn of my head as I look at him. "Oh, sorry, didn't Ella tell you about the night she was there when my Dad passed away?" He grins.

"What Ella does in her job has nothing to do with me," I tell him with narrowed eyes.

"Yeah, she's very good at comforting people," he says, turning to lean his back and elbows against the bar, a smug look spreading across his face. I'm trying hard here, but this prick is starting to make my blood boil. Even though I know exactly what he's doing, he's trying to push my buttons, the fucker's succeeding. The reason I know this is because my teeth are grating against each other so hard, I'm sure I can feel the enamel turning to powder. Still holding the tray of drinks, I feel the flimsy metal starting to buckle, my grip so hard my knuckles are turning white.

"Fuck you," is all I manage to get out through gritted teeth as I turn to walk back to the table.

"Mmm, love her smell." And those words make me stop dead in my tracks, turning slowly to look at the fucker.

"You need to stop talking now, while you still have a mouth full of teeth," I growl.

"Hey, it's alright, I can wait. You're just a shiny new toy that she'll get bored with soon enough." He grins, holding his hands up in a placating gesture. Walking closer to him, I get right in his face because I want to make sure he hears every word I have to say.

"Listen, I don't care if you want to hang around in dark corners like a little creeper, or even cower in the corner like a dog waiting for scraps to be thrown your way, but I do care if you go anywhere near Ella," I hiss the words into his face.

"You can't stop me."

"Try me."

"Are you threatening me, Mr. Fireman?" He grins and I swear, it's taking everything I have not to push my fist down his throat.

"Yep, pretty sure I am." I nod, taking a step back from him, and after a few moments pass and he doesn't do anything, I turn around and continue walking back to the table, throwing a hissed curse back at him. "Just like I thought - pussy." Placing the tray of drinks down onto the table, Ella, Leah and Cole are deep in conversation, but when she hears me return, she looks up at me with a smile which instantly drops as her eyes zero in on something behind me. With the hair on my neck starting to rise, I know exactly who it is.

"What the fuck is your problem, mate?" I say, spinning around to face the vicious look on an angry-looking Ash.

"You, you're my problem. You think you can move into town and move in on our women, with your fancy accent and your big tough job," he yells into my face and I feel Ella grab onto my forearm. That just pisses Ash off more as his eyes move to where her hand is sitting then back up to mine. "Like I said, she's only using you," he spits out. "Ash," Ella says as she stands up and tries to move between us, but I gently move her behind me because this fucker has a screw loose and I don't know how much alcohol he's had tonight to go with it.

"And you," he says, pointing a finger towards Ella. "Why didn't you tell him about what happened the night my Dad died?"

"Because nothing happened, Ash. We talked, that's all," Ella says.

"Talked," Ash half-screams. "I told you how I felt and you threw it back in my face."

"No, you told me that you had feelings for me, feelings that you've never talked to me about before, and I tried to tell you that we're just friends."

"And I told you that your friendship is worthless, just like you," he sneers at her and I hear a slight gasp escape from her mouth.

"Okay, I think we're done here," I say, taking a step forward. "I think it's time you went home and sleep off the beer." Ash looks at me, then at Ella, and shakes his head.

"You know? If I would've known how easy it was for you to spread your legs, I would have asked you out sooner," he hisses out at Ella and all I see is red. I'm done sitting on my own anger, this fucker has pushed me to the limit. In a split second, I feel my hand clench into a tight fist, I feel the air breeze over my fist, and then I feel the impact of my knuckles connecting with his nose, accompanied by a loud crack as blood bursts from his nostrils as his head flies backwards and he stumbles back, losing his balance and landing flat on his back. I also hear what sounds like a cry of horror coming from behind me as I stand over Ash and he grips his nose with a moan.

"Stay the fuck away from her," I say with a finger pointed down at him.

Feeling a hand on my arm, I hear Ella say, "Jaxon." When I turn to look at her, I have a hard time deciphering the look on her face, she looks a little shocked, but she also looks furious as well.

"Sorry, Jaxon," Cole says, giving me a slap to the back. "I'll take care of him. You just take the girls home." Giving him a nod, I take Ella's hand in mine and lead her and Leah out to the truck. The trip home was silent and the air was thick with tension. After dropping Leah off and saying goodnight, I pull away from the curb and continue on to Ella's. Turning my head to get a quick glance at her, I see her hands scrunched together in her lap as she stares forward. When I finally pull up outside her house, I put the truck in park and turn to her.

"So, are you going to tell me what's going on?" I ask and see that she jumps slightly at my words.

"Nothing," she says, shaking her head.

"Then, why do you look so angry?"

"Do you really have to ask me that?" she says, turning to look at me, her brows arched.

"Yes, actually, I do," I say, leaning my forearm on the steering wheel and looking at her face-on.

"You got into a bar fight."

"No, I defended you."

"It was unnecessary."

"Unnecessary? The guy was being a dick, he asked for it. He's lucky that's all he got after the shit he was saying about you," I say in disgust, remembering his words.

"They were just words from a misguided drunk." She sighs.

"Really? So, what he said about you and him, they were just misguided words?" "Yes."

"So, why didn't you tell me about it?" I ask. Deep down, I know I shouldn't care about her conversation with him, but I do because she's been different since that night.

"Because there was nothing to say."

"Nothing to say, in general, or just to me?" I ask.

"Now you're being ridiculous."

"Am I? Because from where I'm sitting, it looks like you're actually trying to protect the prick."

"Yes, he might be a prick, but you didn't have to get into a fight with him," she hisses.

"It was one punch, which he deserved."

"Violence is violence, no matter how you word it."

"Why are you so pissed at me? He's the one you should be mad at," I say, throwing up my hands now, getting exasperated.

"Because you threw the first punch," she says, reaching for the door handle, swinging the door open and getting out, before slamming it shut. "Go home, Jaxon. I'm tired," Is all she says before I watch her walk up the path to her front door, open it, step in, and close the door behind her without even a glance back at me.

I sit in the truck for several minutes, looking at her front door as I mull over my actions at the bar tonight. Did I over react? I don't think so. I mean, the bastard was obviously pushing my buttons, and I could see on his face how much pleasure he got from trying to allude that there was something going on between him and Ella, he was definitely baiting me. So, is that where I went wrong? Was he trying to get me to lose my temper in front of Ella? And if so, why?

"Oh, you dickhead," I say to myself, smacking my palm against my forehead when I realize that I'd done exactly what Ash had wanted me to do. I was the one who lost my shit in front of Ella and hit him, and now he can play the victim while causing waves between Ella and I.

Pulling a cold beer from the fridge when I get home, I flip the lid into the sink and take a large pull from the bottle, then flop down on the couch because even though I figured out Ash's plan, I'm still pissed off that Ella basically sent me to the dog house over it, and I still think he deserved it.

Chapter Twenty-Three

Ella

Standing in the shower, I let the hot water run over my face and mix with the tears which had burst through my control as soon as I had shut the door behind me. My hands tremble slightly as I try to wash them away. I am so mad at myself for losing control of everything, my feelings, my life. I should have known from the beginning that the kind of life I want is not the one I am ever going to have. I should have turned Jaxon down that first time and never looked back, but instead I went and fell in love with him. Sliding down onto the shower floor, I let the water cascade over my body, hoping it will take everything away and wash it down the drain. As I ask myself what have I done, I realize that this breaking point had been coming for the last few weeks. Even within the comfort of being with Jaxon, I could feel myself slowly starting to drift into my old habits of self-deprecation, letting insecurities creep into my brain, and no matter how hard I'd tried to let my past stay in the past, it seems to be getting harder to fight it. I'm not sure I can do this again, not after all these years.

After sitting on the floor of the shower until the water ran cold, I finally pull myself up, dry myself off, and slip into bed. Feeling weak and so completely depleted of everything in my mind and body, I quickly fall into a deep sleep, so deep that the next time I wake it's to the sound of my phone ringing. Blindly letting my hand feel for it on the night stand and bringing it to my face, I see Leah's name on the screen as I swipe to answer it.

"Hello," I manage to croak out, my throat feeling the effects of the endless amount of crying I'd done in the shower.

"Wow, you sound terrible," Leah says. "Thanks."

"I just wanted to call to see if you were alright, but your voice tells me everything."

"I just woke up."

"Ahh, I see. Sorry if I woke you."

"It's okay. What time is it, anyway?" I say, trying to open my swollen eyes wide enough to see the time on the bedside clock.

"Ten-thirty."

"Holy shit," I gasp, sitting up in bed, now more awake. "So, are you alright?" she asks, sounding concerned.

"Yeah, I'm fine."

"I was worried about what happened last night. You didn't look too happy when I left you."

"It was just an uncomfortable situation."

"I guess it wasn't a nice way to finish off a great night, but that's Ash for you."

"I just think Jaxon fighting with Ash was unnecessary, that's all."

"Are you kidding? Ash was being a total ass last night. I saw him a few times hiding in the corner, looking over at us, and as soon as Jaxon went to the bar, he slithered up to him like a snake. I couldn't hear what they were saying, but knowing Ash, it wouldn't have been anything nice."

"I know."

"Well, as long as you're okay?"

"I am. Thanks, Leah."

"You're welcome. I'll catch up with you tomorrow, then. Meet me for lunch?"

"Sure, sounds good," I say before ending the call and pulling myself out of bed. After going to the bathroom, I then head out to find Walter to give him his breakfast.

Sitting at the kitchen table with a much-needed mug of coffee, I look at the contacts list on my phone. My finger hovers over Jaxon's number for a few moments, trying to build up the courage to call him, but the nervous fluttering in the pit of my stomach grows into a tight ball of anxiety and I just can't bring myself to press the call button. Placing the phone back onto the table, I sip my coffee and gaze out of the window in an attempt to try to clear my head and get myself back to where I was, but the thought of not ever being with Jaxon again makes me feel sick. I'm torn because on one hand he has somehow become a comfortable anchor for me and I love being with him, he makes me feel safe, but on the other hand he has unknowingly unleashed my past, a past which had taken so much from me that when I moved here I was an empty shell, I had nothing more to give, I had been groomed my whole life to think and feel worthless. It wasn't until I decided that I needed a career, some way of supporting myself instead of sleeping in my car and living off my dwindling bank account, that I moved in with Leah, put myself through school and got my nursing degree. But not only did I get my degree, just mixing with the other students and the daily hustle and bustle of studying had ultimately been my unforeseen savior, instilling me with a once lost confidence and strength which grew bigger every day. Once I'd bought this house and made it my own, I felt so accomplished in the fact that I'd done it all myself, thoughts of my past drifted further and further to the back of my mind. That was until Jaxon came into my life.

It sounds cliché, but it's not him, it's me. The only thing he brought into my life was sunshine. He made me open up my heart to him, trust him, love him. I let down my guard, but for some reason, instead of taking strength from his comfort it's made me feel weak and vulnerable once again. I'm not sure if it's just me, or this whole situation with Ash which has caused this crack to form in my world. One thing I do know is, seeing how easily I've slipped back into my insecurities and how the feeling of having no worth again came so easily, it shows me that I might not be ready for Jaxon Cane. The last thing I want is to pull him into my world of uncertainty. He deserves so much more, and more is something I can't give him right now, so I need to let him go.

When my phone vibrates its way across the table, breaking me from my thoughts, I look down to see Jaxon's name flash across the screen. By the time I procrastinate over whether to answer it or not, it stops and is followed by a text.

JAXON

Hey, just wanted to check you're ok.

When I read his words, my heart melts just a little from his kindness after I was an ass last night. Leaving the phone on the table, I wash out my mug and go to change before coming back to answer him.

ME

I'm fine, but I owe you an apology. I overreacted, I'm sorry. I watch as the text is delivered, then the little grey dots start to move as he types a reply.

JAXON

No worries, but we need to talk. Lunch?

As I read his text, the tight ball of anxiety tightens even more in the pit of my stomach, because my heart wants to say yes, but my head is telling me that this thing between us needs to come to an end as painlessly as possible, and this is where it starts.

ME

Sorry, can't. Have plans with Leah.

JAXON

Ok, let me know when you're free.

ME

Ok.

I never thought sending a text to someone would hurt so much.

Chapter Twenty-Four

Jaxon

I lay in bed most of the night, going over what happened at Finnegans I'm pissed that Ash got to me, and I'm pissed that Ella got to me as well. I don't think I did anything that any other person wouldn't have done in the same circumstances. Yes, I did have a 'come to Jesus' moment last night when it hit me that I'd given that prick exactly what he'd set out to achieve, but I'm also annoyed that Ella blew me off and wasn't interested in discussing things either. The only thing I can do at this point is give her some space and time to think, and hope that she does.

When I woke this morning, the first thing I did was look at my phone to see if Ella had sent me a text or called, but she hadn't. Still resigned to giving her some time and space, I really tried to ignore my phone. I went for a morning swim, then a shower, put a load of washing in the machine, had some breakfast, and after picking up my phone and checking the screen for the twentieth time this morning, I relented and sent her a message, just to see if she was okay and if we could have lunch and talk. Even though I don't want to talk about it, I do feel the need to clear the air. I'm not sure what it was about last night's events that affected her like it did, but I do need to know and understand. So, when she texted me back, telling me she had plans with Leah, I instantly know that I'm still in the dog house, because she never makes plans for the weekend as it's the only time we get to spend together. Dropping my phone on the table, I flop down on the couch, running my hands down my face, completely perplexed by this whole situation which seems to be getting more out of control by the minute.

Sitting here on the couch, I'm inwardly fuming at not only what happened, but because I miss her. I should be waking up next to her, in her bed, with her stupid cat trying to squeeze in between us. We should be sharing breakfast and then the day together, not this. After flipping through the TV channels and finding nothing, I decide I can't sit around here all day, stewing. I turn off the TV, grab my phone and keys, and head out to the pick-up, but once inside, all I can smell is her perfume filling the cab, and now my nostrils, and that just pisses me off more.

I'm not exactly sure where I'm going, but as I drive with the windows down and the warm breeze blowing around me, I don't really care. Over the next few hours, I just drive, only stopping for some lunch at a roadhouse along the way. By the time I pull up to the curb out the front of Molly and Caleb's, the sun is starting to set, and as I get out of my truck and stretch, I realize how much that drive cleared my head. Walking through the side gate, I see Molly in the pool.

"Hey," I say with a lift of my chin.

"Hey. It's a little early for you on a Sunday night, isn't it? You don't normally get home from Ella's until way after midnight," she says, swimming up to the side of the pool as I sit on the edge of a sun lounge.

"I wasn't at Ella's, I went for a drive," I say, scrubbing a hand over my face. "Oh. Is everything alright?" she asks, sounding a little cautious.

"No idea," I say, shaking my head and looking at her.

"What happened?"

"I'm still trying to work that one out myself," I say, watching as Molly moves to the stairs and walks out of the pool, picking up a towel and wrapping it around herself as she sits down next to me.

Taking in a deep breath I say, "We went to Finnegans to see the live band. One minute, we're having a great time, the next, I'm in a fight with Ash Carter. And now, Ella is pissed off at me."

"You got into a bar fight," she gasps, her hand going to her throat. "It wasn't like that. He said some things about Ella, and one thing led to another."

"Jaxon," she scolds.

"Don't do that, Molly. I'm not a kid."

"Sorry,"

"And it wasn't like a full-on fist fight, with broken furniture and shit. It was one punch, and the prick deserved it."

"He must have, because you don't rattle easily."

"I know. Doesn't change the fact that Ella's not talking to me, though."

"Maybe she's not mad at you, but at the fighting. Maybe it scared her and she reacted."

"See, that's the problem, right there. She won't open up to me. I mean, I've told her everything about us growing up, and Mum and Dad, but when I ask her the same questions, she just clams up and changes the subject. I mean, we enjoy being with each other, but it doesn't mean shit if there's no trust in the relationship."

"Maybe you just need to give her a little time."

"Yeah."

"You want to come and have some dinner with us?" she says, nodding towards the house.

"Nah. I'm beat and I have an early shift in the morning, so I'll get something to eat, watch a movie, and get an early night," I say, standing.

"Okay," she says. I'm turning to walk away when she says, "I'm sure it'll be fine, Jaxon." At this point, I'm hoping she's right, because if I'm feeling like this after not seeing Ella for just one day, I think I'm severely fucked.

And fucked just about sums up my whole week. We had around three days of solid rain, which for some reason means that every driver on the road thinks it's a good idea to speed along in their cars that have almost bald tires, or drive through flooded areas. I swear, when it rains hard, every dickhead decides to come out and play, which left me soaking wet for most of the time I was at work. To top off my awesome week, every time I texted Ella, I was lucky if I got more than two words back. So, let's just say, when Cooper and a couple of the guys ask me if I wanted to join them at McNair's bar for a few drinks when our shift was over on Friday night, I jumped at the chance. After all, I'd spent most of the week being wet on the outside, so, I think I can handle being soaked on the inside by drowning myself in a few beers.

"So, you off to see the girlfriend tonight?" Cooper says with a shit-eating grin on his face.

"No mate, I'm in the dog house at the moment." "What do you mean?" he asks, looking puzzled.

"You know? Kicked to the curb? Sleeping on the couch?" "Ahh, lover's tiff, hey?"

"Something like that," I say, taking a mouthful of my beer. "So, what did you do?"

"Why does every one presume I did something wrong?" "Because we men usually do," he chuckles.

"I punched out Ash Carter for being an arsehole and talking shit about her. Now, she's mad at me."

"That's what you get for being chivalrous," he agrees, holding out his bottle so I can clink mine against it.

"Exactly," I say, finally feeling pleased that someone agrees with me.

As the night went on, with many more drinks, so did the drunken verbal vomit that spewed from of our mouths. That night, Cooper and I bonded over lost loves and the strange behavior of the female sex. We pondered, theorized, dissected, and conquered in our own alcohol-soaked brains, and eventually, when it was closing time, we ended the night with a lot of manly hugs, bromance style, and a drivel of promises that would be forgotten by the morning. Then the barman called us an uber, with instructions to make sure we got home.

Cranking open one heavy eyelid, I glance at the door to the bathroom with a groan. You see, my bladder is telling my brain that I really need to get up out of bed before it explodes from the pressure from the stupid amount of liquor I drank last night, but my brain is saying just go ahead and wet the bed and let me go back to sleep. Just as my eyelids begin to slowly close, my bladder and the small amount of brain cells I have working at the moment, kick into gear and I slowly, and I mean at a snail's pace, pull myself up into a sitting position with the help of my bedside table, letting my legs slide off the bed with a loud thump. That instantly causes my brain to pulsate with pain. Grabbing onto my head with a groan, I try to make it stop as I cautiously and very slowly stand and make my way to the bathroom to take care of business.

It was a tough process, but I did manage to get myself undressed and into the shower. Once the water hit my face, it felt so good that all I could do was place my palms flat against the tiles and stand there, letting the hot water soak over me. In fact, that's all I did until the hot water started to turn cold and I reluctantly turned it off and wrapped a towel around my waist. I swear, I could hear every step I took pound in my head like a sledge hammer as I walked to the kitchen. I grabbed a bottle of water from the fridge and downed a couple of pain killers, before turning back to the bedroom and back into bed.

The next time I woke, I could actually blink without pain, and my head was feeling slightly better than earlier. Fuck knows what we drank last night, but I don't think I've ever felt like the living dead after a booze-filled night in my life. At least this time when I get up out of bed, pull on a pair of shorts, and go into the bathroom to brush the cotton out of my mouth, I feel more human.

Later that afternoon, after several bottles of water, a few mugs of hot coffee, and more pain killers, I felt normal enough to see if Caleb was home and able to give me a lift down to Finnegan's to pick up my truck, which thankfully he was. On the way there, he had so much fun taking the piss out of my sorry drunken state, turning up the music in the car to a screeching level while he laughed and took pleasure at my agony, throughout the short, but painful trip. When we turned into the parking lot outside Finnegans, I was so relieved to see my truck and get out of Caleb's vehicle of torture, I couldn't get out quickly enough, almost breaking my neck in the process. As he drove off, I could hear him laughing louder than the music. Once in the truck, I sat for a few moments, contemplating whether to go back home or drive to Ella's. We needed to talk and I really needed to see her; this radio silence was slowly starting to drive me nuts. I know I'd said I would give her some thinking time, but fuck that, I need to know what she's thinking. I need to know if she's missing me just as much as I'm missing her. I need to know if what we have is real. So, putting the truck in drive, I pull out onto the road and head to her house.

Knocking at her door, I take a step back and wait for her to answer.

Although I can hear the soft sounds of music coming from inside, and then the soft steps of her feet over the wood floor, it still feels like it takes an eternity for the door to click open. Then I'm looking into the slightly stunned, but beautiful, face of the woman who has the power to crush me today, and that thought hurts.

"Jaxon?" she asks, her voice light, but cautious.

"Hey," I say, pushing my hands into the front pockets of my jeans, feeling slightly awkward over turning up like this.

"What are you doing here?" she asks without an ounce of malice. "I think we need to talk, don't you?"

I watch as she leans against the door frame, dressed in a simple t-shirt and pair of shorts that show off her smooth, long legs as she bites her bottom lip, now looking more awkward than I feel. For just a moment, I get a pang of regret for coming here and making her feel so uncomfortable.

"You want to come in?" she says, stepping back and opening the door for me to enter. Closing it behind me, I follow her to the kitchen, taking a seat at the kitchen island. "You want a drink?" She motions towards the fridge.

"Just water, thanks."

"How have you been?" she asks, handing me a bottle of ice-cold water which I open and take a mouthful of.

"I don't know. Maybe you need to tell me."

"Jaxon," she breathes out my name and it sounds so delicate and so weary. Closing her eyes and dropping her head, she pauses before lifting it back up to look at me.

"Look, I know what I did upset you, and I'm sorry for that, because that is the last thing that I intended to do. When I got home that night, it took me a while, but I realized that I gave him exactly what he wanted."

"What do you mean?"

"It takes a lot to push me over the edge, but that fucker pushed hard, because he knew that when I cracked it would make me look like an asshole with a problem and him look like a victim, and that's what he wanted."

"I don't understand what he'd gain from that. What could he get from it?"

"You."

"What?" she gasps. "But why?"

"Because he has feelings for you."

"But I don't understand. Over the years, I've barely spoken to him besides hello and goodbye, and I have never given him a reason to ever think I was interested in him. In fact, it would be the opposite. I was only cordial with him because he was always tagging along with Cole and Leah," she says, looking and sounding confused at the thought of Ash having any interest in her.

By the look of the tiny creases of a frown visible between her brows, she's actually a little worried.

"Sometimes, it doesn't take much to wake up a weirdo like him. Maybe it was your support and compassion when you were looking after his Dad, or it could have just been the simple fact that he saw you with me." I shrug.

"Maybe I did something and I can't remember," she says, rubbing a hand over her forehead. When I let out a sigh, she looks at me. "What?"

"Nothing. I've just had these thoughts running around in my head for days and just realized that they're stupid."

"What thoughts?"

"That you and he had something going on before I came into the picture, and you'd gone out with me to somehow make him jealous," I say with a shake of my head, now feeling like a total idiot after seeing her response to his unwanted attentions.

"What the hell, Jaxon," she gasps. "I know, I know."

"I would never do anything like that," she says, shaking her head, now looking even angrier than she had when I first walked into the house.

"Yeah, well, you kind of left me thinking all kinds of stupid shit. And when you wouldn't talk to me, my brain went a little overboard."

"You're right. I should have handled it better than I did. I just needed some time."

"And?" I ask, impatiently waiting for something, anything, to come from her mouth.

"I was angry that night. I hate violence and confrontation; it takes me back to somewhere I never want to go again."

"Look, I know you have things in your past, we all do. I've opened up to you, but you, you just froze me out of yours. A big part of a relationship is trust and communication, but I can't help you if you won't talk to me," I say, staring straight into her big blue eyes that are filled with anguish and fear.

"It's not you that I don't trust, Jaxon, it's me," she whispers.

"I don't understand."

"I can't trust myself to be what you want."

"I want you, Ella, just the way you are," I say, moving in closer to her.

"Believe me, Jaxon, you don't. I'm broken, damaged from a past that's taken me years to put behind me and I thought I had, until I met you," she says, lifting her head to look at me with so much pain in her eyes that I feel it slam into my chest. "Meeting you was the best thing that's happened in my life for so long, and it was also the worst. When we're together, it's so wonderful and magical, I feel like my heart is bursting apart. But I also feel like I'm losing myself in you, going back to old habits that keep reminding me that the shadows from my past are still there, in the background, just waiting to come out, and I don't want to do that to you."

"But isn't that my choice?"

"I know it sounds bad, but it's not you, it's me."

"Please, don't insult my intelligence with that old cliché. We're two grown adults who can sit down and work this out," I say, trying to keep my voice as calm as I possibly can considering how on edge I'm feeling right now.

"I just don't "

"What? You don't want to try? Is that what you're saying? So, everything we've shared over the past few months, the connection between us, you're not even willing to try and save it?" I ask.

"It's not that."

"Then, what is it? Because that's exactly what it looks like to me. I'm here to fight for us Ella, are you?" My words come out in a harsh whisper as I try to contain my anger and frustration that she'd give up on what we have. But when she looks at me with watery eyes and a defeated expression, I get my answer. Silently, I turn and walk out her front door, climb into my truck, and drive home.

Chapter Twenty-Five

As soon as the door slams, I let myself slide to the kitchen floor, the tears I'd been holding onto bursting out like a dam bursting its walls, the pain in my chest vibrating up my throat and releasing in the form of sobs of anguish and pain, at the feeling of loss from letting him walk out the front door. I'm not sure how long I stay on the floor. Minutes? Hours? My eyes are depleted of tears and my body is aching from the endless sobbing that had taken over my body, having finally left me completely exhausted. Pulling myself up, I walk over to the couch and lay down, pulling the knitted blanket that hangs across the back over me. I knew this was going to be hard, I just didn't realize how painful it would be. Seeing the hurt in his eyes felt like a steel rod being pushed through my chest, because the last thing I wanted to do was hurt him.

Over the past eight years, I had constructed a bubble around myself for protection. A bubble that had become impenetrable and safe. When Jaxon came along, I had stepped outside of it without being scared. With him, I felt safe and comfortable. So much so, that when I started to slip back into my old habits, I didn't even notice. It was just little things at first, like making sure I woke before him so I could have break-fast ready when he got up, panicking over having the right ingredients to cook a meal for him on the weekend, apologizing for things when there was no need, but when I woke up one morning and looked in the mirror at myself and all I saw was bags under my eyes, hair like a bird's nest and looking ragged, I felt guilty that he would wake up to something that looked like me. My sleep pattern became erratic as I tossed and turned all night, wondering if I was acting like Jaxon would expect, if I was happy enough, pretty enough. And when my dreams started filling with voices that I had long stored away, I started listening to them.

"You're worthless."

"You're nothing without me."

"No-one will ever love you, except me. I will always love you." "You can't do anything right, everything you ever do will crumble."

Those words had filtered into my dreams every night since the fight at Finnegans. It was like I was on a carousel and couldn't get off. I didn't want to close my eyes because of the nightmares and as a result, I was so exhausted I was constantly dozing and being assaulted by the vicious voices from my past. I knew I had to stop it; I couldn't do this anymore. I needed it to stop. The more I thought about what had triggered it, I realized it was when I had fallen in love, when I'd let my guard down and let him in. It was a reminder from my past, telling me to stop kidding myself into thinking I can have love and happiness when I can't because it's owned by my past. I feel as though I'm at war with my own brain. One side is trapped and bound to the past, the other side is telling me to talk to Jaxon, tell him how I feel, my thoughts and fears, but I'm afraid that once he knows my truths, it will spoil anything we have.

On Monday, I called in sick to work, letting them know that I wouldn't be in for a few days. I needed to pull it together. I had a responsibility to my patients, to be in the right frame of mind when I treated them, and right now I was feeling anything but. My head is throbbing from the constant crying and over-thinking, and my body aches from spending so much time curled up on the couch, only getting up to feed Walter when he nuzzles against my face with a comforting purr.

Until this morning, when I was awoken by a stream of sunlight coming in the front window, zeroing in on my face and causing it to warm gently. As it seeps into my skin, it feels as though it's entering every vein and tiny blood vessel in my body, moving along like liquid heat until it's brought a warmth into me which feels calm and serene. For the first time in the last couple of days, my mind feels tranquil, my thoughts collected and quieter. Pulling myself up from the couch, I walk down the hall to my bedroom, strip off my sweat pants and t-shirt, and step into a hot shower where I wash off the last few days of pity, and self-punishment, watching as they disappear down the drain with the soap bubbles as the water runs cold. Cooking myself a plate of bacon and eggs, along with a huge mug of coffee, I sit at the kitchen table and start to feel more human with every forkful. I was going to make a batch of pancakes, until I saw the jug of syrup in the pantry and quickly changed my mind, not wanting to go there just yet.

Chapter Twenty-Six

Jaxon

When I left Ella's, I drove around for a while in an attempt to clear my head. This didn't work, so I grabbed a pizza and a six pack of beer and went back home to lounge in front of my TV and see if eating and drinking would help. It didn't. I ended up lying awake in bed for most of the night, replaying our conversation over and over again, trying to see if I'd missed something. I just couldn't believe that she'd give up that easily. Had everything we'd shared meant nothing? I couldn't believe what the look in her eyes and her body language told me, that whatever was holding her back was also causing her as much pain as I was feeling. So, what do I do now? Do I give her some time and not give up, or do I let it go? The thought of letting her go causes a sharp pain, right in the middle of my chest. I don't want to even think about never seeing her again, never touching her, tasting her lips against mine, hearing her laugh, seeing her smile, or sharing another moment with her. Although she seems to have given up on us, I'm not sure if I can.

Something besides the fight with Ash upset her and got her running for the hills, but until she lets me in on the secret that's causing her so much pain, my hands are tied. All I can do is step back and wait. Even if my need to protect her is strong, I can't protect her from herself. Eventually, I must have talked myself to sleep, because when my alarm blares into my ear it's six am, and I still have the same thoughts of Ella swimming around in my head. After a shower and a strong coffee, I feel slightly more awake, which is a good thing because I have another forty-eight-hour shift ahead of me and I intend on not spending it thinking about Ella. *"Yep, good luck with that, mate,"* I think to myself as I head over to station thirteen.

The week was pretty busy, something I was thankful for as it took my mind away from thoughts of Ella. Well, at least when I was awake it did. Once I lay down for some sleep between calls, she's all that comes into my mind; her smiling face, a vision of pure perfection no doubt about it, inside and out. So, with a picture of her in my mind, I allow myself to languish in the warmth of her, because it always sends me to sleep.

Somewhere during the week, while Cooper and I were working out in the station gym, we talked, which I found weirdly easy to do with him. I think it's because he listens without interrupting or commenting, only giving you advice if you ask for it, but he makes a great sounding board, for which I'm grateful because it was exactly what I needed.

When I got back to the guest house early Friday morning, I went straight into the main house where I could see Molly moving around the kitchen, dropping my backpack at the door, causing her to look up and smile.

"Good morning," she beams. "Want some breakfast? There's plenty here," she says, pointing down at a pan full of fluffy-looking scrambled eggs.

"I would love some," I say and watch as she pours out two glasses of juice and fills two plates with eggs and toast. Picking up the plates, she motions for me to grab the juice and follow her to the kitchen table. I did, noticing the table was already set for two.

"Am I eating eggs meant for Caleb?" I ask as I sit down across from her.

"Something like that." She shrugs. "Molly." I scowl.

"He got called into work before the eggs were cooked, hence the fact that there's enough food for two. Now, eat," she commands gently.

"How is that bun cooking?" I say, pointing towards her still-flat stomach. "Much better now I'm in the second trimester." She smiles. "So, how was your week?"

"Pretty good. Nothing too out of the ordinary."

"How's Ella?" she says and the question makes me pause, my fork full of eggs halfway to my mouth as I look at her.

"Can't answer that, I'm afraid," I say and continue eating, concentrating on my plate as I wait, and Molly doesn't disappoint me.

"Why is that?" she asks.

"I guess you could say she dumped me."

"What?" she gasps, dropping her fork onto her plate with a heavy clang. "What happened?"

"I'm not sure exactly," I say. As I lift my glass to take a drink of juice, my eyes look into hers and I can almost see the little cogs going around and trying to click into place, reflected in them. "So, what are you sure about?" she asks, eyeing me with curiosity. Sitting back in my chair, I run my hands through my hair, letting out sigh. "It has something to do with her past. Everything was fine until all this shit happened with Ash and she started completely ghosting me. Before you say it, I gave her some time and space before I went to see her to talk, but..."

"But what?"

"She was different, almost scared, about what was between us. She talked about losing herself and how she wasn't good enough."

"I'm so sorry, Jaxon."

"So am I, because I went there to fight for us and she just gave up."

After a few moments of silence, Molly spoke. "I don't know what to say. I mean, if I knew anything about her past that would give you any clues, I would tell you, but I've never known her to be anything else but a friendly, caring person."

"Yeah, well, there's not much I can do. If she doesn't want to trust me enough to talk to me, I can't actually force her to date me." I grin a little, wanting to lighten the mood in the room. Molly gives me a little smile, then stands, picking up our plates and walking into the kitchen. I follow with the glasses, relieved that she seems to be content with what's happening in my crazy life, with no intention of giving me any of her sisterly advice right now. Placing the glasses into the dishwasher, Molly hands me the plates and when I close the door, she wraps her arms around my waist.

I pull her in close, kissing the top of her head. "I'm always here for you," she says.

"I know."

Once in the guest house, I close all the blinds, strip off, and take a nice long shower before slipping into bed, thankfully clean, tired, and now with a full belly. As soon as my head hit the pillow, I was out like a light. Waking several hours later and sitting outside by the pool, I feel more human than I had during the whole week, but still thoughts of Ella are flooding through my mind. Who am I kidding? They won't be leaving me for a long time, if ever. She's not a forgettable woman, and to be honest, I don't want to forget her. I just want her to move a little bit to the side, just enough for me to function in my daily life without the pain.

Later, I was standing in the kitchen, warming up a bowl of pasta in the microwave, when I heard a loud banging at the door. On opening it, I find Cooper standing there, dressed in what I can only say is the cleanest pair of jeans and button-down dress shirt I've ever seen him in.

"Cooper, what are you doing here?" I ask, puzzled at the sight of him standing on the doorstep.

"We are here to take you out, so go get dressed and spruce yourself up."

"We?"

"Yes, WE. Isn't that right, boys?" he yells out behind him, and before I can blink, Thompson, Mick, Ethan, Johnson, and Caleb were all pushing past me and spreading themselves around my couch and kitchen bench.

"What the hell is going on?"

"We thought it would be good to have a guy's night out. You're one of the guys, so go get dressed. We have about an hour's drive ahead of us."

"Caleb?" I ask, looking at him questioningly as he stands, leaning against the bench.

"Come on, you heard the guy," he says, and what could I do? It wasn't as though I had any plans for the night. And it couldn't be that bad of a plan if Caleb was going, because Molly would never let him go anywhere undignified. It also helps that he's a cop. So, with a shake of my head, I go and change into a clean pair of jeans and white button-down shirt, fix my hair, and with a spray of deodorant, I'm done.

Out at the curb, we jump into Cooper's dual-cab Ford Ranger, everyone jostling for space as we try to fit our large frames into the cab.

Once all the movement and cursing has stopped, I ask, "So, where are we going?"

"Jug's place," Cooper says and all the guys hoot out loudly. "What the hell is Jug's place?"

"Jug's...you know...boobies," Thompson says, cupping his hands to his upper chest and jiggling them around.

"Really? A strip club? Come on, the last time I stayed out drinking with Cooper, I had a headache for three days."

"Then, get ready for an ache in a different head after tonight." Cooper chuckles as he starts the motor and pulls away from the curb with a loud screech of the tires, leaving me wondering if this is going to be a huge mistake.

All six of us squashed up in the cab of a Ford that usually seats six normal-sized humans for just over an hour, was uncomfortable yet funny and invigorating. We drove to the next town over, Belville, then out along some pothole-ridden road into the darkness of nowhere, until finally in the distance I could see flickering lights that, as we pull up and park, end up belonging to two large neon jugs moving in a pouring motion, sitting on what I can only describe as a huge windowless barn, without the big doors, just a little door with a huge bouncer guarding it. After getting out of the truck, and with the sound of painful groans filling the air as we all try to stretch out the kinks, I can hear the steady, thumping beat of music coming from inside.

"Let's go," Cooper says, slapping a hand on my shoulder.

We enter the building after the bouncer scans us over with a metal detecting wand, along with a seriously bad-ass stare. Once inside the small area, we stand in front of a desk until another door opens and a scantily-dressed blonde, with boobs hanging out of a tiny scrap of material, greets us.

"Good evening, gentleman. Your cover charge and entrance fee tonight comes to one hundred dollars each," she says, pulling out a handful of what look like small colored cards which she stamps and hands to us once we've paid, shoving Liam behind us as he'd grumbled and complained about the price. The pretty blonde moves around the desk and places her hand on the handle of the door, opening it to a blast of loud music and flickering lights.

"Have a wonderful evening, and welcome to Jug's," she sings before closing the door behind us. This time, we are met by a petite redhead dressed in what I would call a napkin with strings.

"This way, gentlemen," she mouths, motioning for us to follow her through the club which is pretty surreal compared to the barn-like thing we'd just walked into. This place is like a modern nightclub inside a fake barn. If it wasn't for the fact that I was seeing this with my own eyes, I would never have believed it. I was expecting an old- style, wooden saloon, with hay on the floor and spittoons in the corner. Once we're seated at a table in front of a stage, the waitress takes our orders, returning quickly with our drinks.

"So, Molly is okay with your coming to a place like this?" I ask Caleb with a raised brow.

"Yep, your sister is pretty cool." He smiles proudly, taking a drink of his beer as I shake my head in disbelief. Looking around, I notice that, besides the bouncer on the door, everyone who works here is female, even the bartender. The waitresses who're walking around, are all dressed provocatively, while keeping all their sexy bits covered, much to the annoyance of the male customers who keep trying to get their atten-tion. The place is abuzz with excitement, the atmosphere abundant in male testosterone and alcohol, but as I sit here with all the other guys in the room and wait for the show to begin, a flash of Ella's face snaps into my mind, accompanied by a sudden feeling of emptiness which sits in the bottom of my stomach, and followed by a sudden feeling that I shouldn't be here. At the same time, I'm slapping myself in the back of the head, because I have no reason for feeling like I am doing anything besides enjoying a night out with the boys. Finishing off my beer, I signal to the waitress for another round for the table, and by the time I'd finished off another beer and was on my third, I seem to have washed that momentary guilty feeling right out me and was ready to have some fun tonight.

When the lights dim in the room and the spotlight hits the stage, focusing on a pair off long legs in thigh high stockings and heels, the crowd goes wild with wolf whistles and cheers. As the legs walk closer to the front of the stage, the spotlight moves up over a curvy body covered by a sparkly sequined silver bodysuit which stops at a very large pair of breasts bursting from the lowcut front. For a moment, the room is so silent with anticipation you could have heard a pin drop. Suddenly, the stage lights up, showing a very comical- looking, over-painted face and a blonde hairdo I can only explain as an upside-down ice cream cone. When the pouty red-painted lips open and yell into the microphone, the voice is deeper than my own.

"Good evening, gentlemen, and welcome to Drag Night at Jug's. Now, sit back, relax, and enjoy the show." At that, the crowd goes wild, with more wolf whistles, cheering, and clapping; the room erupting with excitement. Turning, I look at Caleb, who's trying hard to contain his laughter behind twitching lips.

"You bastard. No wonder Molly was alright with you coming out tonight," I laugh. "You knew, didn't you?"

"Are you disappointed?" he asks, a huge smile spreading across his face.

"Not at all. This is just what I needed."

Chapter Twenty-Seven

Ella

After taking a couple of days off work, I get in early the next morning and take a look at my schedule, checking if I have any palliative patients going home or staying on the ward. When I find that I haven't, I head down to the ER where I've been rostered on for at least the next few days, which is good. Not only does Leah work there, but the pace is usually fast, and just what I need to keep my mind busy and focused on something other than regretting letting Jaxon walk away. I've spent the last few days feeling confused and anguished at the loss of the comfort and happiness I felt when we were together, and I keep doubting myself. I feel like I've made a panicked decision based on my own insecurities, and at the thought of losing myself again; I'd judged him based on the actions of others, when all I wanted to do is protect him from me. Now, after a few days of more rational thinking, I've realized that I took the easy way out, because it's always been easier to hide and bury my head in the sand and just stay in my little self-created bubble of safety, protected from anything and anyone that exists on the outside of it.

This is why I'm so glad to be back at work today. I can be somewhere where the day is based on concentrating on others, where there's a disciplined and precise order, where I have no room in my mind for anything other than doing my job. Thankfully for me, it's a busy day, and by the time I get home, take a shower, get a bite to eat, and slip into bed, I fall asleep easily and quickly. Over the next few days, I slowly start to feel stronger in myself, I find that my thoughts are becoming clearer. So clear, that when Leah turns up on my doorstep on Friday night with a bottle of wine, I have a smile on my lips for the first time in a week.

Sitting on either side of the couch now, with a glass of wine in hand, I take a sip then look at Leah. "Thank you," I say, lifting my glass to her.

"For?"

"The wine...the company."

"You looked like you needed it. In all the years I've known you, I'm not sure I've ever seen you look so broken," she says with a concern I feel like I don't deserve from her. We've been friends for a long time, and I trust her deeply, yet I've never told her anything about the secrets I've held onto for so long. I've done a lot of thinking lately, so much soul searching, but when I think about my patients, my house, I realized that the day I landed in Durandale was the day of my rebirth; the only person keeping my past alive is me. So, it's time to put it to rest, for good, because it doesn't define who I am, I do, and I need to start by trusting the people who trust me. After taking another mouthful of wine and a deep breath, I start at the beginning. Over the next hour, I let Leah into my past. She's quiet while she listens, although her face shows many emotions as my story unfolds, until her eyes become watery and she wipes away tears which break free and fall down her cheeks when I stop taking. The room is silent for several minutes as she takes in what I've told her, and I take in that, at last, I have shared my story with someone.

"Thank you," she finally says. "Thank you for finding the strength to share that with me. I'm not sure what to say, there are no words I can give you that can take away anything that you went through. I am so sorry, Ella."

"Thank you for letting me unload on you. I feel a little selfish now, because you look so shattered, but I feel so much lighter."

"Good, I'm glad."

"No judgment then?" I say with a wince of awkwardness. "Fuck no. Why the hell would you think that?"

"I don't know. I guess I always felt as though I let it happen."

"What the fuck, Ella? You were a kid, powerless, you didn't let anything happen. These people were supposed to protect you," she says, a mixture of shock and anger on her face.

"I know, but maybe I could have stopped it."

"And you did. You moved to Durandale, put yourself through nursing school, renovated this place by yourself...Hell, you work in palliative care, one of the toughest areas to take on in this profession. You took control, Ella, that's how you stopped it." Hearing the strength and truth behind her words hits me hard, because for the first time in my life, I feel believed and verified. I almost feel...bigger.

"You have to see that you've already taken back that power," Leah says, breaking me from my thoughts.

"I thought so too, until this mess with Jaxon."

"I don't think it's a mess. I think you've been protecting yourself for so long that you've forgotten how to not do it. When Jaxon came into your life and you momentarily let down your guard, you panicked with the feeling of losing control. So, getting it back came out of pure instinct."

"So, it's always going to be a problem then?"

"Only if you let it."

"So, what do I do?"

"Take it back, Ella. You need to realize that you're the only one who controls what you're feeling," she says, picking up the wine bottle and filling my glass.

"I'm not sure if it's that simple."

"Nothing is simple in life, but you've already proven to yourself that you can weather a storm."

"So, I guess I should look for my umbrella, huh?" I say, giving her a smile.

"Something like that. Look, I think you need to talk to Jaxon, explain why you reacted the way you did and give him the chance to not only listen, but to speak as well. I guess it all comes down to if he's worth the fight," she says with a lift of an eyebrow, causing me to chuckle.

"That's exactly what Jaxon said that day I let him walk away."

"Then you need to fight. I know you can; you know you can. Let the people who care for you in and take back your life, otherwise you might as well never have left Wisconsin all those years ago."

That night, after Leah had gone home, I lay in my bed staring up at the ceiling, my hand lazily stroking the fur of Walter's back as he lay next to me and Leah's words running through my mind. Everything she said makes sense to me now, if only it would have on the day Jaxon had turned up on my doorstep to talk. If only I would have listened...if only...

Over the weekend, I felt so much stronger as I started to clear the cobwebs of memories and thoughts from my head, thanks to Leah. I felt happier having made the decision that I needed to talk to Jaxon, he was too important to me to just let him go. I needed to show him that I was ready to fight, and hope that he still was.

At work this week, I found I had a smile on my face and a bounce to my step. It felt like, with every day, my emotional strength was growing, while shredding the restraints of the past. Feeling empowered, I took out my phone and texted Jaxon.

ME

We need to talk. Dinner Saturday?

Pressing send, I watched for the little grey dots to bounce to let me know that he's received and read the message, but there was nothing. Pushing the phone back into my bag and closing my locker, I vow to be patient; he deserves it. Walking down towards the ER department, I notice there seems to be a flurry of movement, crash carts being set up, dressing packs being pulled out, and then I see Leah.

"What's going on?"

"Getting prepped for incoming. Larry's Paints is on fire, so we have some casualties on the way."

"Do they know how many?"

"Could be at least five, not counting the firemen who went in." As soon as she said the word firemen, my stomach dropped and rolled with unease. I knew Jaxon would be in there, and the thought of him getting hurt caused a pain in my chest which penetrated deep into my heart as I silently hoped we still had time. Feeling Leah's hand on my arm, I look at her. "He'll be fine. Come on, we have a lot to do."

Chapter Twenty-Eight

Jaxon

The night at Jugs was one of the best nights I've ever had, and one that I don't think I will ever forget. I laughed so much at the comedians on stage, my stomach hurt, we were still laughing when Cooper dropped Caleb and I off at home. We rolled out of the place at closing time, thankful that Cooper had the sense to stick to drinking water all night. After a shower, I got into bed, still smiling, but now with Ella's face in my mind. It seems to be my sleeping pattern now, and I wonder if she's doing the same as I close my eyes and fall asleep. That great mood between the guys at the station carried on throughout the week, with the help of not much happening. But you know that old saying about the calm before the storm? Well, it came with a vengeance early Friday morning when the alarm in the station went off, waking everyone at 3 am. Everyone scrambled quickly as we pulled on our gear, jumped into the rig, taking off with lights and sirens blaring as we got a brief on what we were heading to. A fire at a paint supply warehouse just outside of town, and by the look of concern on the faces around me in the cab of the rig, I'm thinking this isn't going to be an easy job.

As we approach the scene, I can see what looks like an eight thousand square foot warehouse engulfed in flames and smoke. This place is huge, with black smoke billowing from the open delivery doors and a window. The black toxic smoke is escaping from wherever it can, with several spiraling tornados of orange flames entwined with the thick black smoke and reaching for the sky. The acrid smell of paint and chemicals soaking into the air surrounds us as soon as we jump out of the rig and start pulling out the equipment needed. Cap started yelling out orders.

"Thompson, Cooper, Liam, I need you on the ladder and up on the roof. Cut us some holes in that metal and get some hoses in there. Cane, Mick, Ethan, as soon as we get some water dousing from the roof, I need you in there. We have three people still inside."

Watching the guys run up the extended ladder to the roof, I start checking air tanks and getting suited up, then we head to the large opening of the delivery doors and look into an abyss of blackness. I feel it as the adrenalin starts to course through my body, causing every muscle to tense and bunch together. Gripping an axe and waiting for the signal to enter the building, only causes more tension in my body which is ready for what lies ahead. As soon as the Cap gives the signal, we move forward into the black chasm and are instantly engulfed in smoke. Pushing past the smoke wall, we are met with walls of angry orange and red flames licking up the tall pallet rack shelving to the stacked containers of paint, running over the top and trying to swallow everything in its path. Cautiously walking further into the space, scanning as much of the area as I can, I slowly move deeper into the warehouse, aiming for the back and hoping that there's some kind of office area down there where someone would have gone for cover. When you're trapped inside a building that's filled with heat, flames, and smoke making it hard to see and breathe, you tend to look for somewhere enclosed for protection. The only problem with that is it's a temporary reprieve which ultimately turns into an oven which becomes inescapable. As we move further down, we finally hit the back wall and Ethan starts swinging his axe at the metal wall trying to give us an escape route in case we find the people trapped in here. It will save us from taking them back out the front doors, the way we entered, because looking behind I see some of the pallet shelves are starting to fold and melt under the intense heat of the flames. Letting my hands slide along the back wall, I let them guide me to where it seems to end, and I move in the opposite direction, following Mick until we finally find what we're looking for, a room with a door. Mick kicks it open with one swing of his boot, letting the smoke pour from it. Thankfully, the room appears to be small and there, in the back, three bodies are huddled together under a table, all holding some type of material over their mouths and noses. Motioning for them to come out, they quickly move out from under the table. The first guy I grab hold of is coughing profusely. Taking off my mask, I place it onto his face and yell for him to breathe as we guide them out of the room and move towards Ethan, who's made a hole in the metal wall, but not one big enough to get through. Sitting the three men on the floor, Liam hands his mask to them to share, then all three of us start swinging our axes at the wall, concentrating on the hole already there. The first few swings were easy, until the toxic smoke started to seep into my lungs, causing me to cough and rendering me unable to swing for a moment. Stopping to cough and try to clear my airway before I start swinging again, Liam has to stop to do the same thing. As I swing the axe at the wall with determination, the hole starts to get bigger, until Ethan leans his shoulder against it and starts to ram at it; an action all three of us take up until a large piece of metal finally splits and drops enough for us to push a way out. Helping the workers up, we push our way out of that fucking tin can, falling on the grass outside with a gasp of not fully pure fresh air, but something a lot better than what's inside. I hear Mack say something into his radio as Liam and I lay flat on our backs, trying to breathe in the air between coughing spasms.

By the time we're able to stand and walk, and help the workers along the outside of the warehouse to the front, there are many different flashing lights from the rigs that have come to assist from Swift City FD and Belville FD, along with police and ambulances. The place looks like a disco on speed. Once we get the workers into an ambulance and on their way to the hospital, Ethan, Liam and I are hooked up to some oxygen while getting our vitals checked. Sitting at the back of the ambulance, we watch as the tough exterior of the warehouse, which seemed to be containing a lot of the flames, with them only escaping from the areas that had been pierced for the hoses, buckles and pops in and out with the changes in the temperature inside. It's pretty mesmerizing and fascinating to watch, if you didn't include the danger involved and toxic smoke in the air, it would be relaxing. At least the smoke coming out of the front of the building appears to be becoming greyer in color, a good sign that the fire is running out of fuel and slowing down.

"Okay, hop on up into the back," the EMT says, slipping the blood pressure cuff from my arm.

"What?" Liam and I speak in unison as we both stand.

"You two are going in to the hospital to get medically checked out. That stuff in there is toxic and you both inhaled a good portion of it." "We're fine," Liam says, folding his arms over his chest in defiance.

"No, you're not. Your vitals are all over the place and you both have crackles in your lungs. Now, get in the back, or do I need to call your Captain?" he warns with a raised brow and a look that says, 'Try me.'

"Fine," I breathe out and get into the back of the ambulance with Liam behind me.

The situation is made ever-more embarrassing when we're met by two wheelchairs at the hospital and pushed into the ER. I feel the shame of heat burning at my face, something that Liam shares with me as I look at him, and all he can do is look down at his feet as we're wheeled into a cubical with two beds and the curtains drawn. An older woman enters from behind the curtain, wheeling in a trolley.

"Okay, boys, time to get undressed from the waist up and get on a bed. Separately, that is, not in the same one." She grins and starts to organize her trolley as we stand and start to remove the heavy layers, starting with our coats. When she looks up from her trolley, she clearly lets her eyes roam over our shirtless torsos, her hand flattening against her chest.

"Well, be still my heart. I have my very own live sexy fireman calendar sitting right in front of me; it must be my lucky day." She smiles, causing me to smile even more at her compliment.

"Well, thank you. Looks like we got the prettiest nurse tonight, as well," Liam says, causing a blush to color her cheeks.

"It looks like it's a win-win situation then. Now, lay back on the bed and I'll get you hooked up to get some vitals, oxygen, and take some blood," she says, slipping a blood pressure cuff onto my arm and clipping a pulse oximeter onto a finger, followed by a mask that has oxygen starting to flow through it, before moving to Liam to do the same. After she had drawn blood, she left with a, "The Doctor will be with you soon, so just relax," over her shoulder. Even though I feel like a total fraud, lying here on a hospital bed, hooked up to these machines, the clean smell and the coolness of the sheet against my naked back feels so good that I relax into its comfort, taking in slow deep breaths through the mask and enjoying the pureness of it after breathing in all that chemical-laced smoke earlier. This feels better than a cold beer right now; so good that I close my eyes and fall asleep.

I felt her presence in the room without even opening my eyes. I'm not sure how long she'd been in the room, but I feel the warmth and scent of her as she stands next to the hospital bed, the heat of her eyes as they roam over my face, and I let myself bask in it for a few moments. I open my eyes to stare straight into hers which show a combination of concern, fear, and tenderness, all fused together, causing her eyes to look bigger as I look into them.

"Ella?" I croak out from beneath the mask, the constant flow of oxygen had caused my mouth and throat to become dry. Ella notices and reaches for the glass of water on the bedside table, removes the mask from my face, and brings the straw to my lips.

"Take a sip," she instructs. The liquid flows over my tongue and down my throat, taking away the parched feeling almost immediately, and once I've drained the glass, she places it back onto the table.

"Thanks."

"How are you feeling?"

"We're fine, this is all just precautionary," I say, motioning my hand over the fact that I'm lying in a hospital bed, hooked up to machines and oxygen.

"You both took in a lot of smoke filled with chemicals," she says, pushing her hands into the front pockets of her scrub shirt.

"Just one of the hazards of the job, I guess. We've been seen and everything is fine. Dr. Warner nicely convinced us to stay overnight for observation and will discharge us in the morning," I say, looking over to a sleeping Liam. "So, no need to worry."

"But I do."

"Well, thanks for your concern, but I can assure you we're both okay," I say, trying to ease her concerns, wanting her to leave and stay, all at the same time. It was just too hard to be this close to her without touching her.

"Please, don't be like that," she almost whispers, turning her head away from me.

Taking in her rigid, defensive stance, I'm a little unsure of what she wants from me, given the circumstances that caused this tension between us.

"I sent you a text message," she says, breaking the silence and turning to look at me.

"My phone is back at the station; what was the message?" "I just asked if we could talk." She shrugs.

"I see."

"I know I made things uncomfortable between us, caused this crack." She waves a hand between us. "But I would really like us to talk."

"Okay."

"Okay." She nods, relaxing her stance. "I'll leave you to get some rest," she says as she turns and walks to the door, then stops. "I'm really glad you're okay," she says, without even looking back at me before walking out of the room.

We were discharged early the next morning, with a clean bill of health and a dire need to get back to the station, which for me was foiled when I am greeted by a very angry-looking Molly as I walk out of the hospital room. As soon as she sees I'm unscathed, her anger quickly dissipates and she throws her arms around my neck.

"Why didn't you call me?" she growls.

"Because I called Caleb instead, letting him know I was fine, and with strict instructions not to wake you."

"What am I going to do with you, Jaxon Cane?" she sighs, letting her arms slide away from my neck and taking a step back, her eyes doing her usual wander over me, just to make sure I'm visibly alright.

"Stop worrying about me, would be an awesome start." I grin at her.

"Impossible," she huffs and threads her arm through mine. "Come on, I'm your ride back to the station so you can pick up your truck."

Thankful that it's Friday and I'm officially off shift now, I drop off my gear and drive straight home for a long hot shower, a change of clothes, and something to eat. Taking my plate of eggs and toast to the kitchen table, I swipe the screen on my phone to see the text from Ella. Reading her invitation for dinner tonight, I type out a reply and press send, too tired at this stage to even think about tonight. After finishing my eggs and washing up the plate, I get into bed, feeling my body relax instantly. I had been kidding myself thinking that the hospital bed was comfortable last night. It was for about ten minutes, then it turned into a block of concrete. Not to mention the constant buzz of machines and having my vitals checked every two hours. Yes, I can honestly say the chemicals had obviously messed with me last night because this bed, right here, was so much better.

Chapter Twenty-Nine

Ella

Seeing Jaxon lying in that hospital bed last night was unnerving. When Leah said that Jaxon and Liam had been brought in from inhaling toxic fumes, I'd felt my heart pound so hard in my chest I thought it was going to rip through my skin. I'd wanted to get into that hospital room so badly that I waited outside for almost an hour while doctors and nurses went in and out, only going in once everyone had finished what they were doing. I stood at the door for a while, just looking at him, eyes closed, mask covering his mouth and nose. I'd let my eyes look him over for any injuries, but there were none visible from what I could see. He had his lower half covered by a sheet and when I looked at his bare chest, I breathed a sigh of relief when I saw the strong muscles gently rising and falling; he was breathing and without difficulty. As soon as I moved closer to the bed, it was as though he could feel my presence and his eyes opened and stared straight into mine.

The tension in the air between us was uncomfortable and awkward, but the warmth in his eyes as he looked at me cut through it, putting me a little at ease, even though the tone of his words reminds me how hurt he'd looked the last time we spoke.

The only person I have to blame for that is myself. I deserved the questioning look he gives me, followed by one of reassurance, letting me know that he's alright, but it's the almost dismissive one telling me that I have no need to worry or be here that causes an ache in my chest, an ache that I need to fix, for both of us. Seeing him lying there in the hospital bed, the worry, the fear of something happening to him, sealed the fact that I need to lay myself bare to him and hope that he'll be able to forgive my crazy thoughts and actions over the past couple of weeks. Even more importantly, that when I let him into my past, he won't look at me in a different way.

Once I got home, I took a shower and got changed. Pulling a casserole out of the freezer, I slipped into the oven before making a simple green salad to go with it, then poured myself a glass of wine and tidied an already clean house, just to keep my mind busy from constantly checking the time, while I anxiously waited for six pm.

Draining the last of the wine from my second glass, I almost choked on the liquid when there was a knock at the door. Placing my now-empty glass of courage on the coffee table, I run my sweaty palms down the sides of my leggings, take a deep breath, and open the door to Jaxon, standing there dressed in jeans and a t-shirt, one hand pushed into his front pocket, the other holding a bottle of wine.

"Hi." He smiles.

"Hi, come in," I say, moving aside. Walking in, he holds up the bottle of wine.

"I hope this is okay?"

"Wine is always okay," I say with a grin. Taking the bottle from him I walk into the kitchen and slide it into the fridge. "I have cold beer in the fridge, if you want one."

"I'm good. I'll wait and have some wine with dinner," he says, taking a seat at the kitchen bench. "Something smells good."

"Just a beef casserole. You ready to eat?"

"Always," he chuckles. Handing him the plates and silverware for the table, I take the dish from the oven, place it on the table, then grab the salad and some fresh dinner rolls, while Jaxon grabs two wine glasses from the cupboard and opens the fridge.

"There's a chilled bottle already open in there," I say, scooping up some of the meaty goodness and placing it onto both plates. "How are you feeling?" I ask as I pass him the salad bowl.

"Good. We both felt fine, but the Cap wanted to be sure."

"You can never be too careful with chemicals. You can feel fine at first and show symptoms later."

"Yeah, I know. This is amazing," he says scooping up a forkful of meat and placing it into his mouth with an appreciative moan.

"Thank you. So, what happened up at Larry's? Do they know what started the fire yet?"

"Not yet, the investigators will be in there as soon as it's safe." "In all the years I've lived here, I have never seen so many fires. Do you think the fires are related in some way?"

"Seems a little too coincidental to me. I guess we'll just have to wait and see."

After we finished our meal, Jaxon helped with the dishes, then we took our glasses of wine into the lounge and sat on the couch. Now relaxed and full, and with a couple glasses of wine in my stomach, I was feeling a little more confident and braver about having the talk with Jaxon that I've been procrastinating over all week. Taking a sip of the wine and a deep breath, I pull my legs up, tucking them beneath me, and look towards Jaxon, who's leaning back at the other end of the couch.

"I need to start by apologizing for the way I've been acting. I know I've been confusing and irrational, and that's something that you didn't deserve," I say.

"Alright. So, what do I deserve?" he asks, his eyes searching mine for an explanation.

"You deserve the truth," I say, letting out a deep breath. "Where do I start?" I ask.

"How about from the beginning."

Nodding my head, I look down into my wine glass for a moment before I begin.

"I was nine when my father died. We were really close and I missed him so much. For a while there, I felt like he had left me alone, with no-one, even though I had my mother. As soon as he was gone, it was as though she was happier, and I couldn't understand why because I was so unhappy. Anyway, she started going out with different men. She'd bring a new one home on Saturday and by Friday he'd be gone, but a new one would quickly take his place. Then, one day, she walked in with Henry, her new husband," I say, glancing over at Jaxon as he tips back the rest of the wine from his glass and fills it again.

"I didn't like him from the start, not only because he made it clear he was replacing my father, but because he had a permanent fake smile plastered across his mouth. He was crude and would grab my mother's ass in front of me. Sometimes, I would feel him watching me."

Reaching for my own glass of wine, I take a large mouthful, swallowing it down hard before I continue.

"My mother became pregnant not too long after they were married. She had a hard time with her pregnancy. She never told me what was wrong, but as an adult I'm pretty sure she had gestational diabetes and high blood pressure. She became pretty sick about two weeks before her due date and was put into hospital, leaving me at home with Henry." I look up at him again when I feel him move, sitting up and leaning his elbows on his knees, his eyes on mine and a distinct crease line forming across his forehead.

"Ella?" he whispers.

"It's okay. I need to tell you. I need you to understand that the problem has never been you, Jaxon," I say and he gives me a reluctant nod of understanding.

"It started with little things; a slight touch of his hand on my shoulder as I walked past, a light stroke of my hair, his eyes staring at me so deeply it felt like he was trying to crawl under my skin. Then he started to buy me things, presents for being such a good girl and looking after him while mother was in hospital. When he wasn't at work, he would spend all of his time with me. We would talk for hours and he would listen to me, and I started to like him more every day. He gave me what I wanted, he gave me what my mother never gave me, he gave me the attention that I craved and I didn't feel so alone any more. I felt wanted, needed, and loved."

Those thoughts make me shiver; the skin of my arms prickling with unease as I rub my hands over them. The shame that I'd felt for years, for feeling that way about a monster who knew exactly what he was doing, came rushing back. It took me years to realize that I had nothing to feel any shame for. I was a child who only wanted to be cherished and loved by a parent, even one who used his kindness and attention to hide his need for control and power over a child. I am so deep inside of my thoughts that I jump when I feel Jaxon's hand touch my forearm. Staring up into his eyes, I find they are full of understanding and support to keep going, to keep expelling the hatred and poison that I'd kept locked up inside for all of these years. The pads of his fingers make gentle swirls against the skin of my arm, the warmth of his touch is comforting and reminds me just how safe I feel with him, so I continue.

"He started taking things further just before my mother gave birth to my brother. He would tell me that he was the only one who loved me, and how he thought I was so pretty and couldn't understand why my mother saw me as ugly and naughty, and that he was the only one who would love me. That's when he started coming into my room at night and..."

My words trail off as I remember the fear. I don't want to relive those endless minutes where I would pull my sheet up over my head and cry into my pillow as I begged and cried for him to stop. At first, he would visit my room every night, but that quickly turned into numerous times a day, so many times that I didn't cry any more, my body became silent and still as I waited for his painful assaults to be over, letting my mind drift into a warm, comforting, safe place where I could hide.

"By the time my mother came home with the new baby, she was too busy and always too tired to do anything, so his visits increased and were more secretive, more hurried, and rougher. I guess by that point, he was taking out the frustrations he had with her on me. They argued constantly, she used to kick him out of the house at least once a week. I remember one time when she kicked him out when I was about fifteen, I could hear them arguing, then I heard noises and the sound of furniture moving around. When the front door slammed, I ran into the kitchen and found her sitting on the floor with her back pressed against the cupboard, her face in her hands. When she looked at me, she had blood running from a split on her lip. I snuggled up to her and made the mistake of telling her that he'd been hurting me, too. I should have known better, because the next day she explained to me how wrong it was to make up such disgusting lies, just before he walked back in through the front door holding a bunch of flowers and she threw her arms around his neck."

"Jesus," I hear him curse under his breath. Looking at him, I can see the strain on his jaw as the muscle along it ticks. I should stop, but now that I'm at this point, I just want to get it all out so he knows everything.

"He stayed and the abuse got rougher, more punishing, he even took me to the local doctor to put me on birth control after the time he didn't use a condom. I could see that it wasn't the thought of explaining how I'd gotten pregnant; it was more the thought that another baby in the house would take more attention away from him." The sharp movement of Jaxon standing jolts me from my thoughts and I look at him, now pacing back and forth in front of the couch, rubbing a hand at the back of his neck.

"Please tell me this fucker is dead, Ella, because..." he growls out and I put my hand up to stop him.

"He is, died about four years ago," I say and watch as he closes his eyes briefly with a shake of his head, inhaling slowly and deeply before sitting back down on the couch.

"By the time I'd hit eighteen, I was done, I couldn't take it anymore. Every time I tried to talk to my mother about it, all I got was a backhand across the face and cursed at for being a slut or something else disgusting. So, one night, I packed some clothes into a backpack, grabbed the housekeeping money from the coffee jar she kept in the kitchen cupboard, emptied his wallet, and left," I say, looking down at my hands and letting silent moments surround us, purposely giving him time to absorb my words.

"And you came here, to Durandale?" he asks gently.

"No, not straight away. I made it to Lexington, Kentucky, pawned the jewelry I'd stolen, and was able to stay at a cheap motel for a while until the money ran out. Then I lived on the streets for a while. I met up with a girl around the same age as me, Callie, and she took me to where she and her brother, Ryan, shared a one-bedroom apartment. They were nice and I didn't know anyone. I certainly didn't know what I was doing. I had no life experience. I took people on face value...big mistake."

"What happened?"

"You know, drawn in by kindness, a couch to sleep on until I got onto my feet, type of thing."

"Until?" he asked cautiously.

"Until Ryan took an interest in me which wasn't reciprocated. He was nice, tentative, and charming at first, but that quickly turned possessive and manipulative. He told me things an unsecure teenager wants to hear, I was beautiful but weak and I needed him. He bored himself so deeply inside my head that I couldn't find myself. I became subservient to him, pre-empting his thoughts and actions, making sure everything was done exactly how and when he wanted it done, having his breakfast waiting for him when he woke, laying naked and in position at night before he went to sleep, and once again I found myself sucked back into a world like the one I'd run from. So many nights I lay awake wondering why this was my life, only to ultimately accept my unresistant weakness. He was a younger, carbon copy of my stepfather, only more physically abusive, until one night when he was done with me, he whispered something against my ear that changed everything."

"What was that?" he asks, his voice tense.

"He said, 'Your worthless, I'm the only one that will ever want you.' That night, I lay there and realized that I'd been called worthless, ugly, and rotten, and been unwanted and used for so long that I believed it, and it was time to stop believing that and start believing in myself. So, I came up with a plan that night to keep up the facade with Ryan; I'd done it most of my life with no reward, now it was time to use it. Over the next week, I pounded the pavement from dawn to dusk until I finally convinced a local nursing home to take me on as a personal care assistant. That day was the beginning of my life. I loved it there and took every shift they offered. I worked my ass off until I had enough money saved that I could disappear from Lexington, Ryan, and everything from my past."

"So, what made you come to Durandale?"

"Honestly, I looked on the map for the furthest place I could find, and Durandale was on the other side of the country. I got lucky. I had a great reference from the nursing home back in Kentucky and got a job in the same field pretty quickly. That's where I met Leah. She worked there too and had a spare room at her place."

"So, you studied nursing together?"

"Yeah. I put myself through nursing school and saved every penny I got until this house came up for sale at a pretty good price. It was weathered, rundown, and in desperate need of some tender loving care, a lot like me, and the rest is history."

"That's why this house is so warm and comfortable, you put everything you never had into this home," Jaxon says, and he's right. "I did, it became my own little world, kind of like a tiny house in a snow globe. I felt safe, protected."

"And then, I guess I came along and put a crack in it," he breathed out the words, sounding regretful.

"That's not a bad thing Jaxon; meeting you was a good thing. I just wasn't used to stepping outside of my snow globe. It seemed I'd exchanged one prison for another, only this one was of my own making, and when that small crack started to fracture into something bigger, I felt like I was being sucked out of it way too fast and I panicked. This bubble is the only safety I've ever known," I say, lifting my hands out towards the walls of the house. "I'm so sorry, Jaxon."

"You have no need to be sorry," he says fiercely, looking straight at me.

"But I do, because in my heart I trust you, but I listened to my head."

"No, what you did was go into protection mode, which is what any normal person would have done; you were scared and it was a natural reaction. I mean, this thing between you and I, it came out of nowhere and was so explosive. Then, at the same time, you were dealing with a crack in your snow globe world, your job, and Ash being a dick, you had me pushing you to let me in…I'm the one who's sorry Ella, so fucking sorry," he says, scrubbing his hands through his hair in frustration. Standing and moving over to the window, he stares out, taking a few moments to compose himself, and I let him because I've just dumped a fire bomb on him. As the spreading fire moves and ignites, I watch his face change from one emotion to another, until I finally break the silence.

"Jaxon." As soon as I say his name, he turns his head to look at me, and as his eyes search mine, I hope he can see the regret and hope that I am feeling in them. When he gives me a half-smile and makes his way over to the couch, sitting down beside me and taking my hands between his, his fingers stroking and caressing mine, I feel hope grow. I watch as my small hands are engulfed by his large, rough ones; so strong, yet his touch is so gentle.

"Please, Ella, look at me." His voice is low and calm as I look from where our hands are to his face. "I'm sorry for pushing you into a corner where the only thing you could do was relive such horrific memories. Thank you for sharing them with me. I wish I could take them all away from you, but I can't. What I can do is help you make new memories, if you let me," he says with an earnest sincerity so strong it stuns me for a moment because his reaction to what I've told him is not what I expected.

"You want to make memories, with me?" I almost stutter out the words. "I would have thought that was pretty evident by now. Unless I've been doing it wrong." He grins.

"You haven't. I just thought…" My words are cut off by the soft brush of his knuckles over my cheek.

"Shh, don't even go there, baby. I know what you're thinking and I'm telling you now that I'm more than willing to take on all your baggage. Fuck, I'll even carry it for you." He grins and his words make me chuckle, even though my eyes are swelling with unshed tears. "Don't cry," he says, leaning in and planting a soft kiss on the tip of my nose before pulling back and wiping the tears that are now falling slowly down my cheeks with his thumbs.

"I hope these are happy tears." "They certainly are," I say, wrapping my arms around his neck and sliding onto his lap, molding myself into his warm body, needing to be as close as I possibly can, and hoping that he can feel the burst of emotions that have just caused my heart to explode over him. We sit like this for a long time, just feeling each other, no need for words, everything being said with an embrace.

Chapter Thirty

Jaxon

When I hear Ella's breathing deepen and feel her body slacken in my arms, I stand and carry her into the bedroom, place her on her bed, then slip in next to her and pull her into my arms. Still fully clothed because I don't want to wake her, and because I don't want the temptation of having my arms around her naked body, well, not tonight anyway, I just want to sleep next to her and know that she is finally back in my arms. I could see she was totally wiped out from sharing her story with me tonight. The total mental exhaustion of what she'd been through, not just from her past, but what she's had to deal with over the past few weeks, has me shaking my head and looking down at her beautiful sleeping face in awe of her strength. What a fucking life she'd had to endure; finding the courage and bravery to escape from it, not once, but twice; moving to a strange town, with strange people, all alone; and still being able to build a career and a home for herself. Fucking amazing. I knew she was hiding something, but I wasn't prepared for what she told me and I really had to keep my emotions in check because at every one of her words I experienced more emotions in one hit than I'd experienced in my whole life. Sadness at her loneliness, disgust at her treatment, anger at a torturous life no child should ever experience, fury and murderous thoughts against her torturers, protectiveness for both the child she was and the woman she is, and a sudden feeling of uncontainable love flooding through my heart as I promised to never let anyone ever hurt her again. With that warmth running through my body, and the warmth of her snuggled against my chest and wrapped in my arms, I drift off to sleep. Woken by the annoying, yet familiar, chime of my phone, it informs me that the text is from the station. Blindly reaching out, I let my fingers search for my phone on the bedside table. Scooping it up and prising my eyes open to the I glare of the text which reads.

STATION: Early morning meeting at 7am. I groan and toss it back on the table.

"Please tell me you don't have to go into work," a sleepy voice beside me murmurs.

"No, just an early morning staff meeting tomorrow," I say, closing my eyes and pulling Ella in closer to me.

"Good, I have plans." "You do?"

"Yes, a shower and breakfast." "Hmmm, pancakes?"

"Not this morning, I ran out of syrup."

"Hmm, wonder how that happened?" I grin, remembering exactly how it had happened.

"I still have my clothes on." Ella yawns, looking down at herself. "I can fix that, if you like." "I bet you can," she chuckles. "Did you get a good sleep?"

"I slept like a log; it's amazing what a good confession can do."

"How are you feeling? You know, about last night?" "Relieved," she says, leaning up on one elbow to look at me, letting her fingers stroke through my hair. "And after a shower, I'll feel even better," she says, sliding away, jumping off the bed and going into the bathroom, leaving me feeling suddenly cold and rather lonely. As soon as I hear the shower start to run, I get out of bed, stripping my clothes off as I make my way into the bathroom where I'm hit by the sight of a naked goddess standing under the stream of water. All I can do is watch for a few moments before I open the glass door and join her. "Room for me?" I ask, placing my hands at her hips and turning her to look at me.

"Always."

Pressing her naked body against mine, I revel in how soft and warm she feels under the water. Running my hands down her back to her luscious ass and palming the cheeks, I pull her in even closer as my mouth devours hers. Her nipples, taught and hard, press against my chest as my hard cock presses against her stomach. Running my hands up to her face and splaying them on either side, I deepen the kiss, dipping my tongue inside, taking small nips and bites of her bottom lip. I can taste her even through the river of water running between our lips. I run my hands slowly down her sides, and up over her ribs, until I have her beautiful soft breasts cupped in my palms, letting my thumbs slide over those beautiful pink nipples. Breaking the kiss, I let my head lean down to take them into my mouth, one at a time, swirling my tongue around the tight buds as I watch Ella's head tilt back with a moan of pleasure. Moving her to face the tiled wall of the shower, I take her hands in mine and place them against the wall, then let my palms slide down her back to her hips, moving them back against my own. Using my legs, I gently move her legs wider apart and let my shaft slide between her ass cheeks which are slippery from the water. Placing a palm gently against her throat, I guide her head back to give me access to the side of her neck, where I place open- mouthed kisses against her skin and the shell of her ear as my other hand cups her sex, letting my fingers run through her folds to the hard nub of her clit which pulses against my fingers as I tease and rub it before sliding a finger into her heated depth, causing her to whimper at my touch. With my fingers deep inside of her and my thumb pressed against her clit, I can feel the heat of her arousal coating my fingers, making them slip in and out of her. When I remove them, I hear her moan in protest at the loss, until I rub the head of my cock against her slickness before pushing into her in one stroke; taking a moment to just stay there, letting her adjust, feeling her pussy stretch and contract along my length. When she starts to move against me in an effort to relieve her climbing arousal, I take her hard and deep, keeping a steady pace with long, hard, deep thrusts, letting my fingers move against her clit, opening her folds wider to allow me to sink in up to my balls. When Ella's body starts to push back even harder onto me, and I hear her moan my name, I move faster inside of her.

"Harder," she moans.

"Like this," I hiss out, our bodies moving together at a savage pace as we each climb towards release. I swear, I see glistening sparks flash into my eyes at the same time as Ella moans out my name on one long breath, and I join her with a loud growl of pleasure as I release my seed deep inside her body and ride the waves of her orgasm as it contracts and quivers around my cock. Still inside her, I wrap my arm around her waist for support as her legs tremble with the force of her orgasm, pressing soft kisses to her shoulder as our breathing moves from heated pants to slow, calmer breaths. Feeling Ella's stance strengthen, I release my hold and she turns in my arms, reaching her hands up and placing them on my cheeks, bringing my mouth down to hers with a soft kiss.

"I love you," she breathes against my mouth, causing my mouth twitch into a grin.

"Good, because I am so in love you, and I promise to always protect you with everything I have. And you have to promise that we'll always talk to each other, no secrets, ever, okay?" When she smiles and nods her head, I press one more kiss to her lips before grabbing the shower gel, soaping up the sponge, and enjoying even more of her body.

We spend the rest of the day just enjoying each other, both in and out of the bed. It felt like we were discovering each other all over again, and were back to comfortable and relaxed. I love seeing Ella this way. She even opened up about the guilt she'd felt for years over leaving her little brother behind, and how she'd attempted to contact him, until it was made clear that he didn't want anything to do with her. It seemed that her mother's lies about her running off in the middle of the night to live in sin with a local boy, had been imprinted into his head ever since he was a baby. But she still had hope that sometime in the future he might seek her out and they could reconnect. Later that night, we ordered take out and ate Chinese in bed while she questioned me endlessly about Australia. I talked until it got late, too late for me to go home, and honestly, I didn't want to. I knew I had to get up early for my shift at the station in the morning, but I didn't want to leave the serene comfort of Ella being in my arms, the warmth of her body next to mine, being able to look at her as I fell asleep and knowing that her beautiful face would be the first thing I saw when I woke in the morning. Nope, wild horses couldn't drag me away from this woman tonight, was my last thought until the alarm on my phone woke me up at 4.30am, then I had no choice. When Ella stirs next to me, I quickly silence it and whisper for her to go back to sleep, squashing her protests of getting up to make me breakfast with a soft kiss to her lips.

"It's no trouble," she insists.

"And it's no trouble for me to grab something on the way. Just go back to sleep. I'll call you later." And with one last kiss, I begrudgingly pull myself away from her and out of bed, grabbing my jeans and shirt and getting dressed in the hallway. I grab my keys and close the front door quietly behind me as I head for home to change, then into the station.

All the guys are in attendance, even those not on shift, and I join them around the large dining table as Cap chooses to stand at the head of the table. The tense look on his face makes me feel uneasy.

"Thank you for coming in this morning. There's been a development in the investigations into the recent fires and you all deserve to know everything as it happens. Investigators have found evidence of accelerant at both the paint supplies and Travis Dale's place."

"What about the house fire?" Cooper asks.

"Unfortunately, the cause of that fire was determined to be accidental. It seems the ignition point came from the stove that had been left on, causing a towel to catch light."

"Great. Just what Durandalee needs - a fire bug," Ethan groans.

"So, what do we know?" Liam asks.

"Well, we do know it's not a professional; the ignition points were too messy."

"Great, that's all we need - a wannabe arsonist who's an idiot," Jacobe grumbles.

"Look, as soon as I know, you'll know. The FD investigators and the local police are on it, so let's hope they find this person before anything else goes up in flames. So, just be vigilant out there. Keep your eyes open and be careful," Cap says, looking just as stressed as we're all feeling about this unwanted news. There's nothing worse than someone who gets off on fire.

Chapter Thirty-One

After the weekend spent baring my soul to Jaxon, I feel so much lighter, like a huge weight's been lifted from my shoulders, and I'm relieved that I'm now finding it easier to talk to him about almost anything. I realize that I had worried myself half to death over what his reaction might be, when all I needed to do was share my truth with him. The thing that made it hard that week, was wanting to be close to him. That was impossible due to both of our work schedules, so we had to make the best of texting and late-night phone calls when I was home and he was supposed to be taking a rest break. I'm not sure I can explain the excitement I felt as the weekend grew closer, or the fluttering in my belly when he turned up on Friday night, coming straight from the station after his shift finished. Most of the weekend was spent in bed, just enjoying each other. We did manage to cook some food and eat now and then, much to the joy of Walter who kept wandering into the bedroom, giving us both a look of annoyance until I got up and fed him.

It was a magical weekend, spent together with no more barriers in place. We ate, laughed, talked, and discussed the recent scary information that Durandale had a fire bug in the community.

Even though Jaxon played it down, reassuring me that they would be caught, I still noticed the concern in his eyes. This became more evident when we were over at Molly and Caleb's for dinner on Sunday night. I was helping Molly in the kitchen, while Jaxon and Caleb sat outside on the patio with a beer, deep in conversation.

"Looks like they're trying to solve the problems of the world out there," Molly said, nodding to them outside.

"More like a fire problem."

"How crazy is it? Fingers crossed they catch whoever is responsible."

"And quickly," I agree.

"So, how are things between you two?" Molly asks with a subtle grin.

"Really good." I smile.

"I'm glad you worked things out."

"It helps that he's a very understanding and patient person."

"He is," she says, looking over to her brother with a glow of pride.

"So, how is the pregnancy going?" I ask.

"Doing good now. The first trimester was a little crazy, but things have settled down, thankfully," she says and I watch as her hand drops to run over the small, but noticeable, bump under her sundress. Looking at her warm smile, I instantly kick myself for not being a good friend over the past month.

Placing my hand on her forearm, I say, "I'm sorry I haven't been around for you, lately. I've just been dealing with some things from my past that came to the surface unintentionally; I needed to deal with them and let them go."

"Oh, Ella, you don't have to apologize, we all have to take time out to heal ourselves. As long as you've found your peace and you're happy, that's all that matters."

"I have, and I am," I say with tenderness as I glance over at Jaxon.

"You know, both you and Jaxon have enough sparkle in your eyes to start a fire by yourselves," she chuckles, and the warmth of the smile she gives me makes me feel a part of something, a family, for the first time in my life. After dinner, Jaxon drove me back home, bringing his work uniform and backpack with him so he could spend the night, which I fully agreed with, the more time I get to have him in my bed the better. When his alarm went off in the morning and he jumped into the shower, I got up and made him some breakfast. Not because I felt obliged to, but because I wanted to. I wanted to enjoy watching the sun come up while sharing a mug of coffee with him before he left. He's looking tired, but that's what happens when he insists that he'd swap being tired for the whole week, just to be buried inside me for the whole night.

After Jaxon left, I jumped in the shower myself, taking the time to wash and condition my hair and languish in the wonderful ache of my well-used muscles; enjoying the reminder of last night. Wrapping a towel around my body, I start to dry my hair with the blow-dryer, thankful that I have plenty of time before having to head into work myself. I had just finished, and was putting the dryer away, when I heard a knock at the front door. Walking towards it, with thoughts that Jaxon must have forgotten something, I had no hesitation in opening the door in my towel with a smile. "What did you forget?" I ask.

When I see who's standing in front of me, my smile instantly drops and my body freezes. Pulling my towel tighter around me and folding my arms across my chest, I manage to swallow the icy lump in my throat to talk.

"Ash, what are you doing here?"

"Waiting for him to leave," he says, pushing his way into me, causing me to step back and grip onto the wall in order to keep myself from landing on the floor. I'm stunned as I watch him slam the door behind him and flip the lock, and I start to take small backward steps away from him.

"You need to leave, now," I tell him with as much strength in my voice as I can muster, considering the dark look he has on his face as he looks me up and down in disgust.

"Look at you," he seethes, stepping closer and running a finger over my collar bone. "Freshly showered. At least you washed him off you, I guess."

"What is wrong with you?" I say, flinching at his touch and taking another step back.

"Wrong with me? Nothing. It's you, and your games," he snarls, leaning his face closer to mine.

"Games?" I stutter.

"Please, don't give me that innocent look. It doesn't work anymore,

Ella. You fooled me once, not again," he says, shaking his finger at me with a maniacal grin.

"Ash, please, I don't know what you're talking about."

"You know exactly what I'm talking about. The subtle flirts, the doe- eyed looks, I saw them all, only I was trying to be a gentleman and take things slow. Then that fucking fireman walks into town and you're are all over him like a rash, and made me feel like a fucking idiot."

"No, it wasn't like that. I thought we were friends. If I'd known how you felt"

"What?" he spits out, cutting off my words. "What? What would you have done differently?"

"I don't know. We could have talked about it," I say, rubbing a hand across my forehead.

"Yeah? Well, too late. I'm done. I've tried to take him out of the picture, but he's a slippery bastard, resilient. You could almost say he's fireproof."

His words hit me like a punch, and I am momentarily stunned, just long enough to read between the lines. When it hits me, I let out a gasp in shock at what he's just said.

"You started those fires?" I ask, taken aback by his confession.

"Not that it did any good. The fucker's still alive, isn't he?" he snorts, looking at me.

What I see in his eyes, scares me. They're dark, almost black, crazed and deranged, with anger which causes me to rethink my approach with him right now. Taking in a deep, calming breath in order to get rid of the quiver in my voice, I say, "Why don't I make us some coffee and we'll sit and talk; we can work this out." I watch as he starts to pace back and forth in front of me, rubbing his hand across the back of his neck, his face distorted in concentration, until he finally stops his pacing right in front of me.

"It will take more than fucking coffee to fix this," he growls into my face.

"I know, but it's a start," I blurt out.

"Shut up."

"We can work this out, see where things went wrong."

"Shut. The. Fuck. Up," he breathes out, punctuating his words slowly as he lifts his hand and wraps it around my throat. "I know what went wrong. You did, when you went to him, instead of me."

"I know we can fix this," I manage to pant out as the grip of his palm on my throat starts to tighten.

"So, do I. I couldn't get rid of him, but I can get rid of you."

"Ash, please?"

"Ash, please?" He mimics my plea with a mocking laugh, his hand squeezing harder. I try to swallow to make room for some air to get into my lungs. His eyes staring straight into mine, he grins at my struggle to breathe, and panic starts to rise in my chest with a chill. I can hear my rapid heartbeat pounding in my ears as I start to see tiny stars before my eyes. I'm going to die. After everything I've been through, after everything I've found, he's going to take it all away from me. I'm not sure if it's the terror, or the lack of oxygen getting to my brain, but for some reason I hear the word that once made me feel weak, but is now going to give me strength...Worthless.

Pulling on every ounce of strength I have left in my body, I lift my hands and grab onto the hand wrapped around my throat, letting my nails sink into his flesh as deeply as I can. As he flinches from the pain, it causes his grip to loosen just enough for me to take in a deep breath, filling my deprived lungs with air. When I feel my towel drop to the floor, I pull back my leg and bring it up with everything I have, kneeing him hard, right between the legs. The strike causes his hands to immediately go to his groin, releasing his grip on my throat. It wasn't enough to put him down to the ground, but it was enough for me to break away and run down the hall to my bathroom, the only room in the house with a lock on the door. I flick the lock and lean against the door, gasping in air as my eyes frantically look around for something to use as a weapon. Pulling open the drawers, I search for something, anything, and when I pull out a small pair of scissors, I feel disappointment and relief at the same time; they are small, but they're something. Grabbing a pair of sleeping shorts and t-shirt off the top of the dirty hamper, I quickly pull them on and press my ear against the door, trying to listen for where he is. I can hear some movement out at the front of the house, I just can't tell what room he's in. Pressing my ear harder against the door, all I can hear is silence. Then I hear what sounds like cupboards being opened and closed, a silence, followed by the heavy sound of his boots on the wooden floor boards coming down the hallway and into the bedroom. Pulling away from the door, I expect him to try and break it open, instead I hear a dragging sound and something bumping against the door, followed by more silence. What is he doing out there? Maybe he's calmed down and come to his senses? Looking around the bathroom and up at the tiny window, I let out a defeated sigh at the knowledge that there's no way I can fit through it. Leaning against the bathroom cabinet, I try to think of something or some way to get out of here, or at least get someone's attention on the outside.

My thoughts are in overdrive, running on fear and adrenalin, when I suddenly smell something weird. Quietly getting onto my knees, I look under the door and see his feet. He must be sitting on my bed, waiting for me to come out, but what is that smell? Inhaling the air deeply, I quickly realize what the smell is. Smoke.

Standing, I palm the small pair of scissors, and pace the small room. If I can smell smoke, then there must be fire, which only leaves me with two choices. Either I stay in here and burn, or I take my chances with him and the scissors. Taking in a deep breath and gripping the scissors, I walk to the door and flip the lock, but when I turn the handle, the door doesn't move. Leaning my body against it, I push, but it won't budge. He must have put something against it.

"Might as well make yourself comfortable in there," I hear Ash taunt. "What are you doing, Ash?"

"Just sitting here; watching, waiting." "For what?"

"First, I'm going to watch your precious house burn down around us, then I'm going to watch you burn with it." He laughs.

Sliding down onto the bathroom floor, I feel defeated, but only for a moment.

Chapter Thirty-Two

Jaxon

Shoving my backpack into my locker, I smile to myself as I inhale the combination of body wash and Ella's scent left from her body being wrapped around mine this morning. I have to admit that when my alarm went off after only a couple of hours sleep, I didn't want to move. Not because I was tired, but because I wanted to stay right where I was, with her delicious warm body held tightly in my arms. My chest swells with the knowledge that she is mine.

My thoughts are interrupted by the bang of the locker next to me, causing me to lift my head and see Jacob standing there. "Hey mate, I didn't expect to see you anytime this week."

"And I didn't expect to be here anytime this week, either," he says, looking slightly annoyed.

"Isn't Ruby due anytime now?"

"Yes, that's why I'm here. Apparently, I'm driving her crazy and smothering her."

"By?"

"She says that I'm constantly watching her and following her around the house like a lap dog." "And are you?" I chuckle. "Maybe," he sighs, then throws up his hands. "Okay, I am, I can't help myself. Every little sound she makes, makes me think it's time."

"It's normal. It's scary, this is your first baby."

"And the last, if it's going to be this stressful."

"I can't believe she kicked you out of the house and sent you to work," I laugh.

"Laugh it up, buddy, because if this phone rings," he says, holding up his phone to me. "You will be working with one man short, because I will be out of here."

"And I wouldn't expect anything different," I say, slapping my hand on his shoulder.

After filling up on one of Cooper's stomach-bursting breakfasts, Jacob and I head down to the trucks with the intention of doing an equipment check, but before we get there the fire alarm sounds, blaring through the station.

"I haven't even digested my breakfast," Jacob groans as we make our way to the lockers and get suited up.

Within seconds, the engine rumbles to life and we're pulling out of the station and speeding down the road.

"What do we have?" Jacob asks Cooper.

"House fire, Dawson Street." As soon as he says the street name, my stomach tightens.

"What number?" I ask.

"337."

"That's Ella's house!" I bark out. "What the fuck?" Jacob spits out.

"Move this fucking truck faster, Cooper!" I yell, knowing that he already has it at top speed, but all my senses have moved into an irrational process as my heart starts to pound out of my chest.

"Jaxon!" Jacob yells, causing me to look at him. "Pull it together, man. I need you to have your head in the game, okay?" I give him a nod, although the only place my head is at the moment is getting to Ella.

Pulling my phone from the inside of my coat, I press Ella's number and listen as it rings out and her voicemail picks up. Cursing, I toss the phone onto the seat beside me. With my hand already gripping the door handle as we turn down Dawson Street, I can see some people scattered along the road, looking in the direction of her house. Before the truck comes to a stop, I shove the door open and jump down onto the road, followed by Jacob. As Cooper brings the engine to a full stop, Jacob has the back open and tosses me an axe as he starts to roll out the hose. As I head towards the house, the screeching sound of tires causes me to turn and I see a police car pulling up to the curb, with Caleb jumping out and running towards me.

"A neighbor called it in. She heard smashing glass and a woman yelling before she saw the smoke. Ella's inside Jaxon." His words ring in my ears as I run towards the front door. I can hear someone behind me yelling for me to stop, but as adrenalin courses through my body all I can hear and see is Ella. With two kicks at the front door, it splinters at the hinges, making it easy for me to push through into clouds of smoke coming from the kitchen. Looking into it, all I see is a wall of red and orange flames as they engulf the whole room. Hearing boots close behind me, I move down the hallway just as Jacob pulls the hose into the house, unleashing a torrent of water into the kitchen.

"Ella!" I yell, moving down the hall, pushing doors open as I go, searching every room, until I reach the bedroom. Stepping in, I see a chair wedged up against the bathroom door. Quickly kicking it away, I burst through the door and find Ella curled up on the shower floor with a towel pressed against her face.

"Ella," I say, opening the glass door just as she jerks her head up to look at me. Reaching down, I pull her up to her feet, letting my eyes scan over her briefly before pulling her into my arms, breathing out a relieved breath.

"Are you hurt?"

"No. It was Ash, Jaxon. He's the firebug," she pants out.

"Come on, I need to get you out of here." Pulling off my coat, I wrap it around her shoulders and lift her up into my arms, pressing her face against my shoulder. "Keep your eyes closed and don't look, okay?" When she closes her eyes and buries herself deeper into my chest, I start to move out of the bedroom and down the hall. The house is filling with smoke, but I notice that Jacob has the flames almost out in the kitchen. Taking the front stairs two at a time, I don't stop my legs moving until I have her standing at the front of the truck. Holding her at arm's length, I let my eyes roam over her, looking for any noticeable injuries, relieved to see nothing evident. That is, until I see the round, dark purple marks on her neck that look like bruises made by fingers. Running my fingers gently over them, I begin seething inside that he'd put his fucking hands on her.

"I'm okay," she stutters out. When my eyes move from her neck up to her eyes, I see the fear in them and pull her into my arms.

"It's okay, I've got you, baby," I breathe into the top of her head as I run my hands up and down her back, letting her know that I'm here, trying to stop the trembling in her body as her fingers grip onto my shirt which I feel dampening from her tears. We just stand here, oblivious to the sounds and movement around us, until a booming voice comes around the truck.

"Look who I found," Cooper says, holding Walter up to Ella as she reaches out to grab the cat, pulling him to her chest and kissing the top of his head.

"I am so glad to see you," she croons to him with a smile.

Looking up, I see another police car arrive as officers take off in different directions and Caleb walks over to us.

"Are you alright?" he asks Ella with concern, which changes to relief when she nods her head. "Come on, I'll get you out of here, take you back to my place, Molly's there," he says, wrapping an arm around her shoulders as she looks to me.

"Go. Molly will take care of you. As soon as I get done here, I'll be there," I say, pressing my lips against her forehead, thankful for Caleb, right now. I watch as he escorts her to a police car, placing her and Walter into the back seat. Looking at the house through the smoke, it looks like Jacob has the fire, that was thankfully contained to the kitchen, out. I start to help him with the hose as he pulls it from the house, then I see two police officers running to the back of the house. Looking questioningly at Jacob, he shrugs his shoulders, but that question is answered when a tall figure runs out from the side of Ella's house. Ash. Dropping the hose, I take off across the neighbor's yard after him. Taking a dive and grabbing him around the knees, he drops to the ground and we roll until I have him under me, his arms pinned across his chest.

"I'm going to kill you, you motherfucker." I spit the words into his face, anger and rage coursing through every vein in my body at the thought of what could have happened today.

"Then do it," he pants out, his top lip curling into a crazed grin, and I totally lose it. Pulling back my arm, I swing and connect with his jaw which cracks as blood dribbles from his mouth. When I pull my arm back again, I feel a strong hand grip my bicep.

"Jaxon, he's not worth it," I hear Jacob say, and when I look down into the dark eyes of this monster, this person who'd put so many people's lives at risk just to get what he wanted, I remember his game plan and realize that this is exactly what he wants. If I go to prison over him, then neither of us will have Ella. Well, he's not going to get that. When a police officer places cuffs on Ash, I stand and watch as they pull him to his feet and lead him away.

"Thanks, mate," I turn and say to Jacob.

"Any time, mate" He grins.

When we get back to the house, the guys are putting everything back onto the fire truck and I make my way inside. There wasn't too much damage as it had been mainly contained in the kitchen which is now a blackened, burnt out shell. Thank fuck it was the only thing lost today. Once I've secured the front door and jumped into the truck, I instantly feel everyone's eyes on me.

"You good, Cane?" Cooper asks.

"Yeah, mate, let's go," I say, tapping my hand against the back of his seat. As soon as we get back to the station, Liam pulls up in his SUV and walks straight up to me.

"I'll take the rest of your shift tonight. You go, take care of your lady," he says, slapping a hand on my shoulder before heading into the station. I am momentarily overwhelmed at the camaraderie and friendship I have with these guys and touched by his gesture. Quickly stepping out of my turnouts, I jump into the shower, change, and head for home.

Walking into Molly's kitchen, I find them both sitting at the table. Ella's hair is wet from a shower, and she looks like she's wearing one of Molly's sweatsuits, and holding a glass of wine which she places down and stands as I make my way to her, taking her into my arms.

"Are you alright?" I ask again, just to hear her voice, and for my own sanity.

"I am now you're here," she says.

Placing a kiss to her mouth, I feel an instant relief when the warmth of her lips touches mine. Stepping back, I sit her down at the table and pull a chair in close to her, taking both her hands in mine.

"The house is salvageable, it's just the kitchen," I tell her and she breathes out in relief.

"What about Ash?"

"He's in custody. He was still at the house when I grabbed him." "You grabbed him?" she says, startled, her eyes wide with shock. "Of course, I bloody did. He's lucky he's still walking." "Jaxon." She breathes out.

"He's okay, nothing an ice pack to his face won't fix...and a very long jail sentence," I say with a grin.

"I just can't believe that he did that, it's crazy."

"It's amazing how far a man will go for love," I say, looking deep into her beautiful eyes which soften with my words.

"So, it seems."

Later that night, laying in bed with Walter curled up asleep at the bottom and Ella safely in my arms, I finally feel myself relax, knowing just how lucky I am that I didn't lose her today.

"Are you okay?" she asks, running her hand down my chest.

"I am now. For a moment there, when your address came over the radio, I thought my world had come to an end. Just the thought of losing you...I just can't, Ella," I breathe out the last few words painfully.

"You will never lose me. Remember, you were the one who found me."

"And I am never letting you go," I say, pulling her in closer, I turn to look at her. She's absolutely amazing, strong and so beautiful, and she's here with me, safe, and she's all mine. Letting the back of my fingers caress along her cheek, I lean in, letting my lips touch hers and whisper, "I love you."

"And I love you," she whispers back, her soft breath tickling my lips.

"But there's one thing I want you to remember," I say. "What's that?"

"Don't ever think you're not worthy, because you are worth everything to me," I say before letting my mouth show her just how much.

The End

Epilogue

Jaxon

3 years later Manly Beach, Sydney Australia

Nothing beats laying back on the soft white sand, with the afternoon sun warming my body on Manly Beach, with my eyes closed behind sunglasses, the sounds of crashing waves, kids laughing while they play, the squeaky noise the sand makes from feet walking on it, and the amazing smell of sunscreen mingled with the fresh smell of the ocean breeze. It's only been a year since I was last here, but it feels like much longer. If there's one thing I really miss about Sydney, it's the beaches, and I'm so glad I decided to keep my apartment instead of selling it. This way, both Molly and I can use it when we come back for a vacation, and I can rent it out through Airbnb between visits.

This is the third time I've been back since moving to the US. The first was to renew my visa, which thanks to having the Durandale Fire Department behind me went smoothly, and the second time was to bring Ella for our honeymoon. After the fire, Ella stayed with me in the guest house while we repaired the damage done to her house.

Once it was finished, I moved in with her and Walter. Ash Cooper is serving out a very long prison sentence after being charged with three counts of arson and attempted murder. Jacob and Ruby became the proud parents of a handsome baby boy. And life for me in Durandale got a whole lot better on the night Ella and I were sitting out on her front porch, enjoying the full moon, and I shocked her by getting down on one knee and proposing, and she shocked me by saying yes.

"This place is so beautiful," I hear Ella say. "It is," I say, sitting up next to her.

"Do you miss it?" she asks.

"What? Living here? Sometimes, but home is where the heart is and my heart will always be with you. Besides, I like Durandale and we can come back here whenever we want."

"Uncle Jax!" A small voice yells out excitedly and I look up to see a pair of beautiful blue eyes peeking out from under the brim of a hat that is bigger than the body of my two-and-a-half-year-old niece, Grace. Flopping down onto my lap with a sand encrusted, wet bottom, is instantly forgiven when those baby blues, blonde curls, and toothy grin smile at me. "Play," she says, smacking her sandy hands against my chest.

"Okay, squirt," I say, tickling her tummy before lifting her up to stand. "Go to mummy, I'm coming," I say and watch as she runs back to where Molly and Caleb are paddling at the water's edge.

"She has you wrapped around her little finger." Ella smiles. "What can I say? I'm a sucker."

"You'll be an even bigger one next year when you have two wanting you to play." Looking at her, I'm slightly confused, then I look towards Molly and back to Ella.

"Molly's pregnant?" I ask.

"Not that I know of," she says with a grin, and it takes me only a second to process what she's saying.

"You're pregnant?" I say, wide-eyed, and she nods with the most illuminating smile across her face, and all I can do is pull her into my arms, tilt her head back, and kiss her wonderful mouth in appreciation of what this beautiful woman has given me...everything.

OTHER BOOKS BY J.GRAYLAND

Enjoy a captivating and powerful romance. Grab your copy today.

Freedom Twisted Freedom Forever Free

Freedom series Box set

Stay Connected

Twitter:

https://twitter.com/ladyarcher1

Instagram:

@j.grayland_author_blog

Facebook:

https://www.facebook.com/profile.php?id=100017500892338

Goodreads:

https://www.goodreads.com/author/show/16842698.J_Gray

Email:authorjgrayland@hotmail.com

All Author: https://allauthor.com/author/jgrayland/

BOOKBUB: https://www.bookbub.com/authors/j-grayland